Over the Middle is the 2nd Book in my Sports Romance series. Each book can be read on their own and feature a different couple. If you'd like to read Book 1, make sure to pick up Blitzed: A Secret Baby Romance.

* * *

O. M. G.

That's the only thing on my mind when I'm assigned to help superstar tight end, Duncan Hart, rehab his elbow. With a body that looks like a sculpted masterpiece, his chiseled features melt the hearts of women everywhere, including mine.

There's just one problem. Duncan's an a**hole, with an ego the size of our football stadium. He lives for the roar of the crowd. He thrives on it. And he wants to *let* me experience the **Hart Attack** — yes, he has a name for it. But that's not going to happen. At least, that's what I keep telling myself...

All's fair in love and war, and I have two choices — take him down, or let him score.

**Over the Middle is a full-length romance with an HEA, no cheating, and no cliffhanger! Includes bonus novel Relentless for a limited time.

Table of Contents

Chapter 1
Duncan

"Have a seat, Duncan," Coach Bainridge says as I come in, my arm still in a sling. I'm feeling pretty good, though, and I'm looking forward to ditching the damn thing as soon as I leave the athletic complex. Three weeks of wearing the damn thing around is grating on my nerves. "How's the arm?"

"The elbow's fine. Only reason I'm wearing the sling is so that the Academic Director doesn't shit himself too early. You know he saw dollar signs evaporating into the air during the Green and White game."

Coach Bainridge winces at the memory, and I'm glad about that. It was his fault that I'd even been out on the field during the meaningless glorified scrimmage that does nothing more than give the boosters a hard-on and a reason to pull out their credit cards. My side, the Green team, made up of offensive upperclassmen and defensive lowerclassmen, was comfortably ahead in the mock fourth quarter when Coach left me in for the second to last series, and I got pinwheeled by some backup junior, named Derek Young, who was trying to

4

make a hit on the biggest star the Western University Bulldogs had. One flip over the jackass's shoulder pads, and I landed on my left elbow, with resulting chips in the elbow that required surgery a week later. It's now four weeks after the game, and I'm ready to get back to work.

"Duncan, you know that the AD cares more about your status as a healthy member of the student body than anything else."

Oh, now that's rich. I know the shit the AD pulls for the glory of Western. "We both know that's bullshit. I'm an athlete-student, not a student-athlete that the conference likes to promote. The football team brings this university millions of dollars in profit each season. And you know that if your biggest offensive threat goes down for the year, those millions evaporate like piss in the summer sun."

Yeah, I'm arrogant. But it's deserved. Last year, I led the conference in receptions, yards after catch, and receiving touchdowns. Fuck, I even threw for one during a trick play during our opening game against Navy. I was first-team All-Conference and second-team All-American as a junior, and now, as a senior, I am the best player on a team that has a chance to win the conference championship, if things go right.

And Bainridge knows it. He's been coaching at Western for a decade now, and his contract's up soon. He needs me more than I need him. Still, he tries. "Duncan, watch your language. You may be an important part of this team, but you're not above the rules."

"Rules?" I ask, leaning back and laughing hard again. "In case you haven't noticed, Coach, me and rules get along about as good as you and your ex-wife. How's that going, by the way?"

Bainridge's glower is funny, but he's wrong about something. I do have rules. In fact, I have four rules for football. I'm not the guy who came up with them, but I've never been someone who thinks I need to be overly worried about borrowing from others. Anyway, my four rules are quite simple.

Hit.

Stick.

Crack heads.

Talk shit.

On the football field, I hit *hard*. I may be a tight end, but I handle defensive tackles and ends thirty to sixty pounds heavier than my two forty without a problem.

I *stick* too, whether it's catching anything thrown within my reach or sticking a route. When I was in high school, I played defensive end, and I stuck plenty of helpless idiots there too. Now that I'm in college, I run my routes perfectly, I block my assignments perfectly, and I am perfect.

Crack heads. Yeah, that's right. I'm going to bust your balls, take your heart, and stomp on that motherfucker more than once before the end of the game. If you're on defense, you're my bitch, and I mean prison style too. I'm not going to go easy on you, regardless of whether you're the best in the country or some guy who's fighting for a spot on the team.

And of course, I talk shit. I'm going to tell you how good I am and exactly what I'm going to do to you while I do it. It makes it all the better when I whip your ass, take your heart and your girl, and maybe your sister too, if she's hot enough.

Coach Bainridge doesn't seem to agree with my

assessment, however, and his face turns a little pink as he listens to my question. It's a low blow. I mean, it wasn't his fault his ex-wife ran off with a younger guy. "You little shit. You're lucky that you're even still on this team after the stunts you've pulled. I could throw you off the team, you know."

"And if you do, I declare for the supplemental draft that's coming up soon, get selected, and cash in early while you get your contract bought out. I'll be in the pros while you're stuck doing what? Analysis on some second-rate cable network? That's really supposed to scare me?"

Coach smirks, and for the first time in our entire conversation, I'm somewhat disturbed. I'm the one who's supposed to be in charge of this conversation, not him. Then why does he look like he's under control? "I don't think so, Duncan."

"What's that supposed to mean? In case you don't remember, I'm not one of your scholarship losers. I'm fully paid up. My dad paid all of my way through this school. I can walk, and it doesn't hurt me. You can't hurt me."

Coach leans forward, putting his forearms on the desk, and shakes his head. "Oh, but Duncan, I can. You say you can declare for the supp draft, and that's true. But try getting drafted if it comes out that you're a ball hog and a bad teammate who causes drama for any team that drafts him. The teams can find out about your party habits. The League nearly crucified the last little shit who tried to ride out the gravy train while having your sort of past. What's he doing now? Oh yeah, that's right, drug rehab in an in-treatment facility about an hour south of Santa Barbara with no contract and about ten million dollars' worth of lawsuits sitting in his lap when he gets out."

7

Shit. "You can't. I'll sue you for defamation of character."

Coach laughs again, like I've just told the funniest joke in the world. "Sue me? Duncan, first, you'd have to prove that I did actually reveal any information, and there are so many sources out there. The reality is that for three years now, I've been covering for you, not revealing anything about you."

Like that matters. "Yeah, just like every other coach around college ball. You guys get a player with my talent, and you bend over backward to make sure we stay eligible and putting cash in your pockets. How much is that Nike endorsement contract the team signed last year worth to you? Half a million a year?"

"That contract is written with the knowledge that players like you come in and fade out. There are some who have a good year, then shit happens," Coach counters, still smiling a little smile that disturbs me. Maybe Bainridge knows something more than I do. "By the way, I know you had that agency do an evaluation of your potential draft position over the summer, and I know the results. Coming off the chips in your elbow, and as a tight end, regardless if you have good speed and hands for that position and can play slot, you were looking at nothing higher than a third-round pick in April's draft, weren't you?"

Damn, Coach knows more about me than I thought. Talking with an agent like that is technically against the rules, although I never signed any contract with them, so there's nothing that can be proven. "Something like that."

Bainridge nods and continues. "But if you put up good numbers this year, you've got a chance at a first- or second-round pick, which doubles or even triples the money you get on that rookie contract. I know you don't give a fuck about the money—you care about the fame and your reputation. Being some third-round scrub pick is nothing. Being a first- or second-rounder though, you come with expectations and a greater potential of fame. You think you're the first egotistical prick I've had to deal with in twenty years of being a head coach?"

Of course I don't. It was one of the reasons I picked Western. I knew that Bainridge ran a program that produced League-level players nearly every year. He'd just had a dry spell, and there were whispers that maybe he'd lost his touch as a recruiter, that he was getting too old to keep up with the modern game. Not that I cared. I cared that Western got a minimum of nine games a year nationally televised. "You covered for the other guys."

"Of course I did. You're right. But I also demanded at least a modicum of professionalism from each of them. Which meant that I overlooked their poofty, underwater basket-weaving major schedules, the girlfriends that got stacked two and three deep at times, the parties, the drunken frat antics, all of it . . . *IF* they showed up and did their jobs for the team and produced on the field. Now, I will admit you've been a tougher nut to crack than most of the others. I could hold their scholarships over their heads. But I know what drives you, Duncan. I take away your ability to get fame, and you're stuck. So that's what I'm holding over you. You either get with the program, or some of the front offices in the League get anonymous but easily verified reports about your antics during the past four years."

9

Fucking asshole. But he has me over a rock. "What do you want?"

"I talked with Coach Taylor. He says you've been avoiding coming down for a rehab."

"Of course. That meathead can't tell me what to do." When I say meathead about Coach Dave Taylor, that is exactly what I mean too. The guy has a neck larger than his head and seems to think that the cure for everything is squats and deadlifts. If he got an AIDS diagnosis, he'd probably go do some power cleans to cure it.

Bainridge doesn't agree with my opinion. Nothing new there. "Actually, he can. In fact, he's got a PhD in kinesiology and rehabs more athletes in a year than some strength coaches and trainers rehab in a lifetime. So here's the deal. For your own damn good, I'm ordering you to go down to the weight room tomorrow as soon as your last class is finished. When is that?"

"Two," I grumble, knowing if I lied, Bainridge would just look it up anyway. He gets that information from the registrar's office every semester. "So three?"

"Two thirty," Bainridge counters. "Coach Taylor has an offseason lift with the volleyball team scheduled to start at three, and I won't let some prima donna player of mine screw with his schedule. So you get your ass down there by two thirty, and you talk with him. I don't care if he wants you to sleep in the weight room and do wind sprints before breakfast. You do them, and you do them exactly according to protocol. If he says walk, you walk. If he says run so hard you puke, you'd better bring a bucket."

"Why the fuck are you doing this?" I ask, and I know

10

I'm pouting. Still, this sucks, and I can't do a fucking thing about it. "You just want to see how hard you can push me for a year? Getting your rocks off or something?"

"Actually, whether you believe it or not, I'm doing this because I think you actually do have the talent to be a good pro-ball player. In fact, you're one of the most talented players I've seen on this team in the twenty years I've had at Western. But . . . you're lazy and undisciplined. You take those habits to the pros, and you're going to be broken in half. So I'm going to make you learn discipline and how to work hard and be a man instead of an overgrown boy. That it will just happen to benefit this football team is what is known as a win-win. Understand me?"

I nod, and I'm not happy, but at least it's not as bad as I thought. He has what my father calls leverage, and most people with that amount of leverage don't exactly give it up this easily. Still, I can't be sure that this was all that Coach wants. "Okay, I'll be there. Now, is there anything else you want?"

Coach shakes his head and points at the door. "You should probably get going, Duncan. After all, you still have a doctor's appointment this afternoon to make sure you're medically cleared to start your rehab tomorrow."

I get up and resist the urge to kick the chair across the room. Instead, I grab my backpack and go to the door, pausing before I open it. "You know, Coach, I'm going to take this shit and shove it down your damn throat some day."

"Good. That means you'll be scoring touchdowns while doing it, too. Now get out."

I leave the Coach's office, and I'm determined not to act like anything is wrong as I head out. I'm Duncan Hart, and

11

there's no way that I can be made to look like a punk ass bitch. I'm going to play it cool.

Unfortunately for me, I'm playing it so cool—especially when I see a couple of girl's volleyball players heading down the hall toward the gym they use for practice, with their tight, thick volleyball asses snug inside those ridiculously hot short shorts they wear—that I'm not really looking where I'm going.

"Hey, Linda," I say to the one I know. "Whatcha doing tonight?"

"Don't even try it, Touchdown," Linda replies with a little mix of hatred thrown in. Okay, so I'd slept with her twin sister. That didn't mean I had to be hated, did it? Besides, I noticed Linda checking me out even afterward, especially when I was wearing my football pants, which are nearly as tight as her shorts. She wants the Hart Attack. Her sister loved it, and I know they talk.

"Come on, you know I'm not that—"

I'm not looking where I'm going. My eyes are fixed on Linda's ass, and I collide with someone, knocking them to the ground and causing me to stumble into the wall. "Holy shit! Look where you're going next time."

I see long blonde hair, maybe a girl's, as I grab my backpack, but before I can do anything else, the alarm on my phone rings, and I need to haul ass. My doctor's appointment is in twenty minutes, and since I can't technically be without my sling, that means I can't ride my motorcycle. Thankfully, the campus bus is convenient enough, and I catch the bus right as it starts to pull away, taking it the ten-minute ride to University Hospital.

12

I'm glad that Western University has one of the better orthopedic departments in this half of the United States. I couldn't imagine what it would be like to have dealt with any sort of injury at some cow college in the middle of nowhere.

"Mr. Hart? Let's get you to X-ray," the nurse, a cute little thing who's already eying me as we walk down the hall, says as she leads me to the scanning room. I check out her name tag, and I have to do a double take. I've seen her before, but this is the first time I've seen her name tag. Really? Someone actually named their daughter Nancy Drew? You've gotta be fucking kidding me. "You're feeling no pain, right?"

"None that the doctor can help me with," I say, giving her a smirk. Nurse Nancy might just be what I need to relieve some stress. "You might be able to, though."

"Oh?" she purrs, leaning in. She's got a tight little body—that's evident even through her uniform—and she's showing me just a little bit of cleavage with her scrub top. "Find me after the exam. Maybe we can see what I can do for you."

"For sure." I smirk. "Think I can get the speedy service? You know, I'm having so many aches and pains in my hip area."

"Swelling?"

"Lots of it. *Huge* amounts of swelling."

The nurse is breathing heavier. She's already DTF, and I take her hand and give her a little kiss on the knuckles. "After my appointment, where will you be?"

"Department desk," she half-moans. Her brown eyes are half-lidded and she's biting her lip. "I can take a meal break

13

then."

"And we can get some privacy?"

She nods, and I kiss her knuckles again. "Good. Now, let's get the scans done."

The exam room is really high-tech, with the X-ray not being some old school sit there and take photos machine, but instead, they are able to give you a live scan of the area. I can even watch my elbow move on the video monitor above my head. The X-ray tech records for a minute, then tells me I can go see the doc.

"Mr. Hart?" Dr. Lefort says. "How're you doing?"

"Ready to get out of this sling and back to the real world," I answer, flexing my arm. "You keep me in this thing much longer, and my bike's going to forget who I am."

Lefort laughs, an interesting side effect of my mouth sometimes. I either piss you off, or you think I'm funny. Some people think both at the same time, but Lefort is amused. "Well, let's take a look at the video. Hold on here . . . okay."

He replays the video, nodding and humming to himself in places. "And you're not feeling any pain?"

"None."

"Let me see the incision. You know, I still don't understand why you didn't let me do the surgery arthroscopically. The scar would have eventually been no more than the size of a thumbtack hole."

I look at the two-inch line on the inside of my arm and grin. It's perfectly aligned with the tattoo I want to get, a half-sleeve that'll go from my shoulder to my elbow. "Chicks dig scars, doc. You know that, right?"

Lefort laughs again and has me flex my arm a few more

14

times. "Okay. You're cleared to start rehab. I assume you'll be working with Coach Taylor?"

"Unfortunately," I grumble. "Coach Bainridge ordered me to."

"Don't knock it. Dave's a good man. Helped me with my rehab when I tore up my hip going hiking last summer. And doctors make the worst patients, because we know that we already know it all."

I smirk at his joke and roll my arm. "Think I can ride my bike?"

"Give it a few days," Lefort replies, scribbling on his clipboard. "Not because you don't have the strength, but just to reacquaint yourself with using the arm. At least wait until this weekend. All right then. I'll forward this to both Coach Taylor and Coach Bainridge. Good luck, Duncan. I'm looking forward to seeing what you can do this fall."

"Thanks, Doc. Take it easy."

Chapter 2
Carrie

"Good afternoon, Coach Taylor."

"Carrie Mittel! How're you doing today?" Coach Taylor says, and I smile. Even though he's forty-five, with a bald head and a handlebar mustache that looks like he should be a biker or something, he's one of the nicest guys I've known . . . when he's outside the weight room. I took two classes with him in the past, a freshman Introduction to Kinesiology course, and then in the first semester of my sophomore year, I took Human Body Mechanics. In class, at least in the lecture portion, he's smart and personable and really funny a lot of the time.

But get him in the weight room for labs, or especially when the bars come out for the squats for team workouts, and 'Coach' Taylor disappears. Instead, out comes 'DT' Dave Taylor, former USA's Strongest Man in the under 220 lb.

weight class, and one-time owner of the world record in the squat for that same weight class. That man is a berserker and a borderline psychopath, I think, but in a good way. Age and wear and tear have maybe slowed him down some, but Coach Dave Taylor knows his stuff.

So do I though, which is why he invited me to intern with the training staff starting last semester. It started with a lot of grunt work, and that meant for the first six months, my job was to carry weights, pick up after people and mop the weight room and training room, but most of all, to watch. I watched and learned as Coach or one of the other assistants put groups and individuals through their paces. Once the semester was over, he 'graduated' me to doing tape jobs as well, and I've been doing those for the spring semester. Maybe soon, I'll actually be allowed to work with people in rehab and movements too.

"I'm doing okay. What's on the schedule for me today?" I ask, hanging my bag on the hook that is designated for me. "Anything cool?"

"Maybe, but to start, just normal stuff. Women's basketball's going to be coming by soon for their pre-workout wraps and tape jobs. Think you can handle that? I've got volleyball at three, but I'm handling them myself today."

I grab my clipboard and write it down. He insists that we all carry clipboards and that we write down our work. Tracking is big with him. "Sure. Anyone got anything new?"

"Nothing I know of. Check the computer before you get to work," Coach says. "I might have something for you, but I'll let you know a bit later. I don't want to jump the gun. How are your own workouts coming along?"

17

"I'm putting in my time—you know that." It's actually one of the areas that I struggle with the most. I got interested in training during my senior year of high school, when a shoulder injury in softball cut my playing days short. Not that I was good enough for a school like WU anyway, but the rehab was really interesting. Being a long-time athlete, my natural frame combined with my athlete's eating habits meant that my so-called 'freshman fifteen pounds' was more like the 'freshman fifteen kilos,' and I still don't feel good wearing overly tight or sexy clothes, even if I've gotten some of the bad weight off. At five eight and one seventy, I'm still nobody's fashion model, unless you are using Ashley Graham as your template. And if I ever get compared to her, I'm in good company.

"You know, Carrie," Coach says, bringing me out of my reverie, "I keep telling you, drop the worries about your waist, get some protein cycling going, and hit the workouts hard, and it'll come in time. You'll have to pick up the bat again if only to keep these athletes away."

I smile and brush my blonde hair behind my ear. I'm proud of myself as-is, and I *have* gotten attention from cute guys. I like to think I'm a good size for my frame. "I know, Coach. I'm sure you're right, but sometimes, matching up what I know from class and what I end up doing in my own life . . . it's not easy."

He nods, then chuckles. "Sounds like me. You should have seen the rehab I put myself through after my last torn quad. There's no way I'd tell one of the kids who come in here to do that. I'd lose my job. Still, if you need guidance, my door's open."

"Thanks, but first, I'll take care of the basketball team.

18

You know how they are with their ankles and knees."

"Good. If I need you, I'll give you a holler."

The training room is actually right next to the weight room, which is in the basement of the main athletic building at Western University. The Madison Pavilion houses the coaches' offices, the main indoor arena where basketball and volleyball games are played, and in the basement are the weight room, the training room, and the wrestling practice room. Next door is the smaller secondary arena where volleyball, girl's basketball, and other smaller sports do their practices, plus the regular student weight room.

Of course, across the street from Madison Pavilion is Allen Field, where the football team plays, which dominates the skyline of WU and makes the Pavilion look small. It's not that surprising. I guess it takes a lot of space to make seating for eighty thousand people.

There is no way I could see it where I am right now anyway, being underground in the basement. I get to the tape room, where I see Alicia Torres, one of the basketball girls, already waiting. "Hey, Carrie. How's it going?"

"Good, Alicia. Aren't you a bit early?"

Alicia is a point guard for the basketball team, and despite her diminutive size—she's only five six and a hundred fifteen—she's fierce and has no fear, but because of that, she has a lot of bumps and sprains on a pretty regular basis. One of her weakest areas is her left ankle, and I take out the pre-wrap and tape to start getting her ready. "Well, you know how it is. Now that we're almost in summer semester, I've got more free time on my hands. Derek and I . . . well, let's just say we're traveling different paths."

19

"Oh, that's too bad," I reply. Derek is . . . I guess *was* . . . Alicia's boyfriend, a senior who's graduating in a few weeks. "What happened?"

"He took the offer for the job in Berlin, and he felt that the distance was just too far. It's not too bad, though. I mean, he and I weren't too serious. But that means I've got some extra minutes in my schedule, and I figured I'd get down here, get taped, and get some extra warmups in."

I take off Alicia's sock and prop her foot against my thigh, aligning the joint just the way I want it. "And your ankle's doing okay?"

"Yeah. In fact, you do a better job with it than anyone except Coach T. Don't let the other folks hear that, though. You know how bitches be hatin'."

I laugh. Alicia always has a way of phrasing things that seems to put a smile on my face. "Thanks. I hope you just keep doing your warmups and rehab that I gave you, and you won't need the tape at all."

"Nope. Them other bitches will need it, though, when I break their ankles with my crossover," Alicia continues, laughing. "This year, I'm planning—"

I look up as her words fade out, and she's smirking, shaking her head as she looks through the window that allows people in the training room to see the weight room and vice versa, a holdover from when this was a coaches' office before some renovations about five years ago. "What?"

"Looks like Touchdown is here. Surprise, surprise. That man-slut is never in here unless it's a mandatory team workout. What's his deal today?"

I turn around and see the same guy who knocked me

20

down yesterday coming in and heading to Coach Taylor's office. Of course, I recognize him. He's Duncan Hart, the star of the football team and one of the hottest guys on campus. Six four, two forty, with a body that looks more like it was designed by science and sculpted instead of grown. He's the sort of guy who can look at you and make you feel like you're a fly in a spider's web. After that, it's only a matter of time.

Not that he's ever noticed me. I'm a year behind him, and I doubt I'm his type. I'm pretty much invisible, now that I think about it. Only Coach Taylor, a few of my classmates, and the athletes I work with know me, and even then, only partially. I'm too busy busting my ass and making grades to worry about a social life.

"Don't know," I say to Alicia, turning back and looping the pre-wrap around her ankle. That's the easy part, and I yank the spongy wrap to cut it quickly. "Hey, you're a rising senior like Duncan, right?"

"Yep. But I've got two years of eligibility left, since I redshirted my freshman year. I'm going to use it to get started on my Master's while still under scholarship. Why, what's up?"

"Why is he called Touchdown? Linda from the volleyball team called him that yesterday, right before he nearly ran me over in the hallway upstairs. He didn't even help me up."

Alicia chuckles and nods. "That's Touchdown. A lot of us girls around campus that know him call him Touchdown for two reasons. One, of course, is the connection to football. When you're the man who creates more points than anyone else, you get nicknames like that."

"I should probably know who he is, but the football

21

team's the pickiest with student trainers, and I haven't gone to any games in what little free time I have. Studying, you know?" I say honestly. Maintaining a full-ride academic scholarship is hard, and spots in the training community are few and far between. I don't want to graduate only to face a job market where the best I can do is compete for clients at the local Globo-Gym. Most of them are housewives, and who would choose me to train them over some hot guy who can *really* motivate you?

"Well, the other reason is a bit of a joke, too. There's debate on the exact details of the particular number, but he's got a reputation around campus with the girls. I once jokingly called him Eighty-Three, since that's his jersey number. I bet that guy sees more ass than a proctologist."

"Ew." I laugh at Alicia's disgusting joke. "Still, Touchdown? That's just . . . I mean, I'm not sure I've had eighty-three orgasms in my life," I joke back as I wrap another strip of tape around her ankle. I quickly finish the job and give her foot a squeeze. "How does that feel?"

She circles her foot to the inside and then the outside, then smiles. "Good. You seriously know how I like it—not too tight, not too loose. Thanks."

"No worries. Make sure you do your warmups," I say, helping her on with her sock. Alicia thanks me and gets her shoe on, walking out of the training room while I put my stuff away. Just as I put the tape back in its bin, I hear a knock at the door, and I turn around to see Chelsea Brown, one of the other student trainers and another rising senior, at the door. "Hey, Chels, what's up?"

"Coach Taylor wants to see you in the office. He sent

me to take care of the rest. Who's been by?"

"Just Alicia—got her ankle done."

"Okay. Thanks. Anything I should be aware of?"

I check my clipboard and shake my head. "No, just ankle tapes. Thanks, Chels."

I go through the weight room, noticing a couple of hot guys from the baseball team getting in some work with the midsection routine that Coach Taylor likes to call 'Puke City,' and I admire their builds before one of them gives me a wink. Really? Was he just winking to make me blush, or was he checking me out?

"Hey, Carrie?" Coach Taylor calls from his office, startling me. "You forget something?"

Yeah, my brain, which is not where it should be. I shake my head and go into his office. "Sorry, Coach. Just had a brain fart. Chelsea said you wanted to see me?"

He nods and indicates Duncan, who's sitting in one of the other chairs, his legs stretched out in front of him and his hands behind his head. This close, he's even sexier than I'd seen from a distance, with coal black hair and gray eyes that can only be described as smoky. There are flecks of something in his eyes that glitter and shine, like gold or diamonds hidden in the midst of all that smoke. "This is Duncan Hart, from the football team. Duncan, have you met Carrie before?"

"Hi, Carrie Mittel," I say, offering my hand, but Duncan just sits there with his little cocky smile, his hands not moving as he just undresses me with his eyes. I suspect he does that with every woman he sees between the ages of eighteen and forty, but I could be wrong. It could be fifty from how Alicia described him. I drop my hand and turn to Coach.

"What do you need, Coach Taylor?"

"Duncan here is coming off elbow surgery. Nothing too major, just a debridement and some partial fractures of his ulna. I remember that in the course you took with me, you did a paper on elbow rehabilitation, didn't you?"

I nod, seeing where this is going. "Yes, Coach, on rehabilitation protocols after Tommy John surgery."

"Good paper. While Duncan's rehab won't be anywhere near as extensive, I'm assigning him to you. Monday, Wednesday, and Friday, four thirty start. Duncan, Carrie may be only a rising junior, but she's one of the best I've got. You give her any of your shit, and I'll be the one breaking a barbell off in your ass. Got it?"

Duncan's cocky little smile slips slightly, and he scowls before nodding his head. "Whatever. So, Carly—"

"Carrie. My name's Carrie," I correct him. I hate getting my name screwed up. It pisses me off. "Unless you want me to start calling you Dunc."

"No, thanks," Duncan says, getting to his feet. I'm not short for a woman, but he towers over me. I'm tempted to back down, but instead, I stand my ground, looking up at his sexy gray eyes and trying not to let the flush that I feel in my chest creep up my neck. "So I guess I'll see you tomorrow."

"Four thirty. Be ready to work," I reply, not moving when Duncan steps to move past me. He stops, and I raise an eyebrow. "What?"

"Can you let me out?" he huffs, and I step to the side. Duncan doesn't make contact when he leaves, but only by the slimmest of margins.

I wait for him to go out, then turn back to Coach

24

Taylor, who's giving me an amused look. "How was that?"

"Good start," Coach says. "Stick around a bit. How are you on your elbow rehab knowledge?"

"Bit rusty since this last semester didn't touch on them, but I'll brush up this evening. Do you want me to script the exercises too?"

Coach shakes his head and nods at the chair Duncan just left. "Have a seat. Carrie, I assigned Duncan to you for two reasons. First, the rehab protocol is actually pretty simple. The reason Duncan was sent down here by Coach B from the football team is because he wants Duncan to learn a little bit about hard work and sacrifice before he declares for the draft next winter. So I get to write something that'll put him through his paces. The main thing he needs is a babysitter, and since you're still pretty green, I thought he'd be a good case for you to start with, since there isn't anything training-wise that'll be too difficult."

"But . . ." I say, noticing his expression, "you have something else you want to tell me."

"Yeah," Coach Taylor says. "I chose you because you can be tough when you want to be. That's what Duncan needs. He'd try to intimidate any of the male students I could assign to him, and to put it frankly, the female students . . ."

"He'd seduce," I finish, and Coach Taylor raises an eyebrow. "Alicia Torres was getting her ankle wrapped when Duncan came in. She filled me in on *Touchdown*."

Coach Taylor nods, then laughs. "We get one like him around here every few years. He's not the first football player to be called Touchdown. In any case, he's probably going to make a pass at you. Watch yourself, okay? You're a good kid. I don't want to see you getting yourself all emotionally busted up for a guy like Duncan Hart."

"Don't worry, Coach. I won't," I say. "Did you know he nearly ran me over in the hallway yesterday afternoon and didn't even stop to help me up? You can tell by his face that he didn't recognize me either. You think I'm going to let someone like that get to my emotions?"

"Still, be careful. All right, I'll get you the protocol for him by the time you leave this evening. Thanks."

I go back to work, finishing up my taping duties with Chelsea before she goes on to monitor tennis practice, since the tennis team doesn't practice near the Pavilion. When I'm done, I go get my backpack and change clothes, grabbing my own workout clipboard from the rack and starting my routine. If I'm going to get Duncan's respect, I need to show him that I can hang in here and that I know what I'm doing.

And of course, I'll have to not back down from him. Which is hard, because even as I do my kettlebell swings, I'm still seeing those gray eyes flecked with reddish gold and diamonds and that face framed by coal black hair.

Chapter 3
Duncan

I get a rising junior as my rehab specialist? Even worse, my specialist is a *chick*? Is this some sort of joke, or is Coach Taylor just fucking with me?

Thoughts run through my head as I get back to my apartment, fuming as I sling my backpack against the couch. I have a two-bedroom spread in the Vista Towers, not the best set of condos around, but good and close to campus. Best of all, I could bring just about any woman here and it won't be a problem. College chicks are impressed by the hardwood floors and handcrafted furniture, while any professional woman thinks that I'm *doing well for my age*, like they expected their college stud to be living in some frat house or something like that.

Not that I have a problem with frats. Some of the guys that I can possibly call friends are in frats. I say possibly because, to me, well, a guy in my position can't be sure if they're just being my friend because they know I'll be big time someday. Still, at least frats are up front with their aims, so they aren't quite as insufferable as the others.

"Speaking of insufferable," I mutter, thinking back to Coach Taylor and that assistant . . . Carrie. Yeah, that's it, Carrie Mittel. All bitchy attitude and arrogance. Oh, she did a paper on Tommy John surgery. Big fucking deal. I've caused two Tommy John surgeries so far in my football career, laying bitches out.

Still, she has a cute face. I'll give her that. And despite hiding her body underneath a t-shirt that looked like it should have been set aside for someone my size, there was no hiding that rack. Those are prime, that's for sure.

I sigh and look around my apartment, trying to figure out what to do to get my mind off things. My eyes see my helmet, and I grin. Fuck what Dr. Lefort said yesterday. I've been flexing and moving my arm for days now around the apartment, and I can handle my bike. It's not even a real crotch rocket anyway—there's no way that I could get away with that on the team—just a 650 cc Ninja that can walk it out on the freeway, but nothing extreme. Back home in Silicon Valley, I have a 1000 cc Ninja RH that can peel the paint off the road if I want.

A bike ride could be just what I need. In fact, I know just where to go, and I grab my helmet along with my leather jacket and keys. My arm is feeling mighty bare, and some new ink would help me quite a bit.

* * *

"You did what?"

Carrie's looking at me with disbelief, her clipboard in her hand and her mouth hanging slightly open, looking at the bandage that's wrapped around my upper arm. "I said I got a tattoo, so I won't be able to go too heavy today," I reply, touching the bandage. "You know, my skin being sensitive and all."

Carrie taps her pen against her teeth, and I'm struck again at how cute she is. She's still wearing ridiculously oversized clothes though, so my feelings that she's an iceberg are probably true. I mean, we're in the weight room, for fuck's

28

sake, and she's wearing pants like she's getting ready to go out in snow—and we're in the desert of California, for fuck's sake!

"Fine. Then we'll just have to modify some things," she finally says, scratching through and scribbling. "I'll make sure nothing touches the skin."

"But—" I start, before she cuts me off, jabbing her pen in my direction.

"It's not my problem that you decided the night before starting a Coach Dave Taylor-written rehab and workout protocol, of all things . . . that you decided to go out and get some ink on your arm. Personally, I don't give a damn if you do the workout shirtless to let it show off to the world and air out, but you're not getting out of your workout."

"Still—" I try, and Carrie cuts me off again. I swear, this girl needs to be put in her place, and quick. But, I catch Coach Taylor giving us a look out of the corner of my eye, and I know he's willing to try to back up his threat of breaking a barbell off in my ass if I do what I want to do, which is say fuck this and walk off.

"Still nothing. You know, I bet if we put the weights in the middle of the stadium with thirty thousand women watching, you'd be going at this gung-ho. What, you afraid of being shown up by the others?"

Now she's egging me on? Holy shit. "You know what? You've got a big mouth for a training intern. How about you back it up?"

Carrie considers it for a moment, then nods. "Fine. Give me two minutes to change into my workout clothes. You . . . don't move."

Two minutes was all I needed as I pulled off my shirt,

29

just as she practically asked me to do. Turning around, I checked out my best tattoo, a huge set of eagle's wings that stretched from shoulder to shoulder, and the beginnings of my half-sleeve on my left arm. The guys at Downtown Ink only got a little bit done. I mean, there's only so much even a good artist can do in three hours, but they had given me a sketch of what the final product's going to look like, with Celtic symbolism playing a big part in the design.

"You done showing off for yourself?" Carrie said behind me, and I turned. For the first time, I was struck dumb by her as she stood there with her arms crossed in front of her body.

Those curves.

That ass!

Holy shit, Carrie Mittel's fucking stacked! She's not skinny, but with a guy my size, she's exactly how I like it.

Her hips flare out from her trim-ish waist in a set that lets you know those hips do not lie at all, before drawing down into legs that I just want to pour some gravy over and gobble. Every man's got a body part they like best, and I've always been one for a strong, toned set of thighs, and Carrie . . . she's got the sexiest set of legs I've ever seen.

My cock twitches in my shorts, and I have to remind myself that I'm supposed to be pissed at her. "Is that for motivation?" I finally get out. "Because you know, I'm wearing less than you."

"We're not playing strip poker," Carrie retorts, but I see her eyes flicker over my torso. She likes what she sees. Still, she's all business, at least on the outside. Give it time, she can't keep this up for long. "Let's get that hex bar over there. We're

30

starting with trap bar deadlifts."

"The fuck you say?" I ask, surprised. "This is an elbow rehab session, not a full-on workout."

Carrie looks at me like I'm an idiot, and I shut my mouth again. How is she doing this to me? "Holding the weight in your hands allows you to strengthen your biceps tendon and muscles without putting direct strain on the cleared out areas. Besides, you're a football player. You guys are supposed to have strong hips and lower backs for your sport, right?"

We get started, and I'm surprised when she brings over another hex bar, sliding plates on it herself. "What's that for?"

"You told me to put my money where my mouth is," she replies. "I'm not stupid enough to try to lift the weight you can. But I'm not a prissy princess either."

I watch as Carrie grabs the two handles of the bar and starts copying the motion I was just doing, and even though I'm not as much an expert in weight training as I am in football, I know that she's barely getting started. Setting the bar down, she grins and tosses me a glance with her eyes, which I notice are strikingly pretty for their being brown. They're gleaming at me right now, and she's smirking. "By the way, pound-for-pound, that's more than what you just lifted. So how about you stop fucking around and we get to work?"

By the end of the workout, not only does my arm ache, but my entire spine aches from my neck to my tailbone. Deadlifts, hip lifts, pullups, pulldowns . . . I swear, I didn't know there were so many ways to work the back. I guess I've been taking it a bit too easy.

Through it all though, Carrie was right there with me,

31

going nearly rep for rep even if the weights were lower. She even grunts sexy, and my cock is stirring in my shorts again as I watch her in her now sweat-soaked workout shirt that's clinging to her every curve. She hits the switch on the machine that my elbow is resting in, and a low hum starts up. "All right, that oil's going to warm up here in about two minutes. You've got ten minutes in there before we get you in the whirlpool. Ten minutes in there for a general full-body soak, and you'll be done."

"Think you can hang out while I sit here in this thing?" I ask. "I'd have brought a book if I thought ahead."

"You don't strike me as someone who thinks ahead a lot," Carrie says with a smirk, but she sits down. "Or someone who reads, for that matter."

"Actually, I'm carrying a 3.2 GPA. Not Dean's List or anything, but I'm not just some dumbass ball player who doesn't know shit outside of pass routes and how to play beer pong." It's true. I'm not an idiot. If I'm going to be in control of my life, and I will be, I need to be smart enough to not get ass-fucked by an agent. Not to mention, when your father is one of the biggest businessmen in the Silicon Valley, you don't grow up without learning a thing or two. "What about you?"

"3.95," Carrie replies, but without taunting. "I'm here full-ride academic, so I've gotta keep the grades up."

"That's impressive," I grudgingly admit. "Those are the sort of grades that you hear about from the engineering geeks or something. What's your deal?"

"What do you mean?" she asks, sitting back and stretching those incredible legs out in front of her. She leans back and spreads her arms out to the side to stretch, not realizing or not caring that it's also turning her chest into twin mountain peaks that stick an impressive way into the air. I admit it to myself that I want nothing more than to get her in the sack—if nothing more than to teach her a lesson on who's the boss.

"Well, I mean, what got you into training? It's not something a lot of girls go into."

Carrie nods and sits forward, obliterating my view of her curves, but the image is still burning in my mind. "I was an athlete for a long time myself. In high school, I played soccer and softball. Unfortunately, I got injured in a collision at home that tore my shoulder up. I'm not upset about it, though. I wasn't good enough for a D-1 school anyway. I would have been D-2 at best, but in doing rehab, I really got into it. It gave me a way to channel my athletic nature, and so when it came time, I just naturally came here."

I laugh softly, and Carrie gives me a look.

"What?" she asks.

"Nothing. Not everyone can be as amazing on the field as I am."

Carrie lifts an eyebrow and gives me a look. Okay, I admit it, I'm an asshole, and I was just making a joke. Carrie doesn't take it that way, though, and she gets up, her eyes flaring in anger. "I think you can watch your own timer. When it goes off, get in the whirlpool. I'll see you Friday."

Carrie storms off, and as she does, I'm given the treat of one last view of her tight bubble butt. I bet that same ass gave her plenty of power to drive in balls when she played softball too.

So I pissed her off? Ah well, that's half the fun. Get

33

them so pissed off at me they want to scream, and then make them scream for a whole other reason. Let 'em think they're punishing me. Maybe that's just what Carrie needs.

I'm sitting in the whirlpool ten minutes later when Coach Taylor comes in, shutting the door behind him and coming over. "You little punk," he says, and I see that he's in weight room mode, not his normal, relaxed mood. "Ever thought how you'd feel if that injury caused you to never play again?"

"The fuck you worried about, Coach? She said she'd see me on Friday, and I followed your protocol. It wasn't that serious—and it was true."

Coach looks at me, then turns around, grabbing the bucket behind him. One of the things the training room always has on hand is buckets of ice water, meant for icing down injuries, and for what the trainers call 'contrast training,' where you soak the injured area in hot water and then immediately dunk it in ice cold water, only to repeat the process back and forth until your balls are about ready to retreat into your body forever.

It's one of these buckets that Coach lifts up and dumps on me. While the whirlpool absorbs a lot of the cold, my head is fully exposed, and I'm sputtering, chilled, and gasping in a second. "What the fuck?"

"Carrie Mittel is one of the smartest, hardest working, best interns I've had in this program in years. She came here in a sad state from that injury of hers, chunking up forty pounds because of all the changes, and has spent the past year and some change busting her ass. She's a better athlete, a better person than you are, regardless of whether you go to the

34

League or not. So treat her with some respect, Duncan. Don't piss me off."

"I could have your job for this!" I yell, starting to get out of the tub, but Coach Taylor pushes me back down with a firm hand, and I don't have the grip or leverage to resist and go splashing back in.

"And I could have you kicked out of school on a Title IX complaint for sexual harassment," Coach says quietly. "By the way, she didn't say anything to me. I overheard it through the intercom that is installed in here. I left it on because I wanted to make sure you behaved. You obviously didn't. Now get your shit, get dried off, and get the fuck out. Friday, you do your workout, and no shenanigans. We clear?"

"Yeah," I grumble, wiping water out of my eyes. "We're clear."

Clear that before this is all over, I'm going to break Carrie Mittel. That's for damn sure.

* * *

"Hey, Duncan, thanks for coming to the party."

I'm at the Psi Kappa Tau sorority house for what they're calling their "summer bash" for the girls who decided to stay for this summer session. That means that the house only has about a dozen girls instead of the normal twenty-six or thirty, but who cares?

"Tiffany, when you said that you ladies were throwing an event, I couldn't stay away," I reply. Tiffany Hill is going to be the president of the sorority starting next semester, and she's pretty hot, in that Barbie doll, Stepford sort of way. Perfectly styled red hair, blue eyes, slightly pointy chin, but high, most likely enhanced, cheekbones over a toned, slender body that probably never saw a workout like what I'd been through this afternoon. "How are the girls?"

"Oh, you are certainly popular around here," Tiffany says with a gleam in her eye. "However, I was thinking that I might want to keep you all to myself tonight. That is, if you're up for it?"

I chuckle and lean in. "You know what that means, right?"

Tiffany nods and hums back. "Baby, you can have me any way you want me."

I nod and give her a smile, but as I do, suddenly, Carrie's face flashes in front of my eyes. I shake my head and step back, confused. Tiffany doesn't understand and tilts her head. "What's wrong?"

"Just had a hard rehab workout today," I semi-lie. I did have a hard workout, but it isn't what's giving me pause. "Guess I need a drink to cool the nerves. What do you all have?"

"Open bar, same as always," Tiffany says. "Go on, relax and enjoy yourself, and we'll talk later."

PKT isn't as stuck up a sorority as some of the places on campus, where they all think their pussy is gold and that they deserve their places in the upper-crust of society, but it's also not a straight-up dog house, so the party is quiet but still enjoyable. Still, as I'm sitting back and sipping at my beer, chatting with the people who approach me, I can't get Carrie out of my mind.

The way her body looked in those workout clothes. Her ass stretching the fabric of her shorts when she was bent over to do her hex bar lifts, and oh my God, the way her tits looked against that t-shirt.

And best of all, she's a real woman, none of that fake shit I see surrounding me far too often. That body of hers—I could go to town on it for days and still not wear it out. The way that she challenged me makes me want her even more.

Most girls I would've had eating out of my hand in under five minutes, but Carrie went ninety minutes with me without my shirt on and still didn't want to jump on my cock to play cowgirl. I could tell she liked what she saw, but she's strong enough to resist me. I'll wear her down. It's just a matter of time.

"Hey, stud," Tiffany says, interrupting my thoughts. She has a drink in her hand, something fruity looking, but she's not too buzzed yet that she's slurring her words. "How are you enjoying the party?"

"PKT knows what to do," I say, smirking and finishing my drink. "Looking forward to the Greek Week throw-downs already."

"Mmm, I'm looking forward to about five minutes from now, if you're into it. I even decided to spice things up a bit. I've got Gemma heading upstairs too."

Tempting. Gemma Falcone is a French-Italian international student who has always given off that innocent vibe with a hidden inner slut. She's like the epitome of lady in the streets, freak in the sheets. For some reason, though, even though this should be like a dream come true, my mind is on Carrie, and I'm just not into it at all. "Sorry, Tiff, but I think tonight, I'm going to pass. New ink, and my back is already tightening up from earlier. You and Gemma have some fun though."

She pouts, and I'll admit that it probably often works. She can wrap most men around her little finger with that pout, and some day, some poor bastard is going to get taken to the cleaners by her because of it. "Aww, come on, stud. You know you want to."

Tiffany is such a nympho. I'm surprised she isn't fucking her way through the basketball team. Oh, wait—she probably has. "Not tonight. And if you keep pushing it, maybe never. You know I've got plenty of other options."

No woman likes to be told she's just one in a long line, even if she is one, and Tiffany is no different.

"Fine." She stews, then looks around. "If anything, Martin's here, and I know he likes Gemma. Hell, from what I hear, he's freakier than you anyway. See you, Duncan."

"See you," I say, and I soon make my exit, going out to my bike and getting on. I've only had two beers, and I make it back to my apartment without getting pulled over by the cops. I take a long, hot shower and sit down on my couch, wondering what the hell is wrong with me. Seriously, I just turned down a threesome with some pretty hot chicks over a woman who got twelve gallons of ice water dumped on my head.

What the fuck am I thinking?

Chapter 4
Carrie

"Hey, Carrie, got a minute?"

"Of course, Coach. What's up?" I ask, sticking my head into his office. It's the first week of classes, and I'm settling in well to my new schedule, but I'm still busy. I hope Coach doesn't have a lot to talk about. I'd like to get back to my dorm room and crack the books on my Organic Chemistry class. It's a requirement, but I'm not looking forward to it. My professor is known as a total bitch and cuts no slack at all.

"Hey, I got a request from Coach Bainridge just now—thought I'd run it by you. How'd you like to work the sidelines for the football game tomorrow?"

I'm stunned. Getting a slot for working the sidelines of a football game is considered a privilege that only best training students get. Almost all of them are seniors or grad students, and for me, a junior, to be asked is surprising. "Uh, you got the right person, Coach? I'm just a junior."

"You were personally requested by Coach Bainridge. Apparently, you did something right with Duncan."

What the hell? "Really?"

Coach smiles and kicks his feet up on the desk. "In my opinion, you've gotten under Duncan's skin, and in a good way.

I've never seen him work this hard, and according to what the football coaches tell me, he's been doing the same during practice."

"Gotten under *his* skin," I repeat, thinking about how much Duncan's gotten under *my* skin by insisting on working out shirtless unless we are doing squats or lying down for bench presses, and the near-constant innuendo he's worked into almost every conversation.

He's still been coming in to get his elbow and his wrists wrapped before every practice, and he's insisted that I be the one to do it. It's benefited me in some ways, though. I get to pour out my frustrations into the weight room more easily. "Coulda' fooled me. If you ask me, he seems to enjoy attempting to torment me."

"Well, whatever the case, you've had a positive effect on him, and everyone sees it. And don't lie to yourself—you've seemed to gain some confidence and work harder than ever yourself."

"Thanks . . . I think," I say, but I'm pleased either way. It was hard work, but I'm proud that Coach Taylor noticed my effort. "I had to push myself just to get him off his lazy ass."

"Uh-huh," Coach sarcastically says, not believing a bit of it. "Carrie, a hint. I've been in this game longer than you've been alive, and I won't lie to you. I've had more than a few workouts fueled by some attractive woman nearby. But don't let it go deeper than that with Duncan, okay? I know I'm not your father or older brother, but . . . he's bad news. He's a man's man on the field, but he's got some growing up to do off it."

I take a deep breath, knowing he's trying his best to be

40

friendly and look out for me. He does that from time to time. "So I've noticed. You don't have to worry about me. I appreciate the responsibility, though."

"Don't thank anyone just yet. It's not going to be a walk in the park. The football coaches want Duncan happy and playing hard, so if he wants you on the sidelines, well, that's probably where you'll be. Make sure you're ready to put up with his shit for the whole season."

Football. Big opportunities lay with people who get slots to work the sidelines for football. But at the same time, I have to be careful not to get tagged as Duncan's next conquest, the next in his long line of *Touchdowns*.

Still, I can't pass up the chance. "I'm ready, coach. When do I need to be here?"

"The players have to report at nine tomorrow morning. We start getting ready at eight. You get tagged with a lot of grunt work, Carrie—setting up water stations, towels, crap like that. We start tape-ups at eleven. A guy like Duncan will get his closer to game time, say noon or so, so I'll pull you to the stadium training room then. Game time is actually the easiest."

"Oh, that'll be nice," I say. "I've never seen a game in the stadium before. Too busy with my bookwork."

"Well, hold onto your hat, Carrie. Because tomorrow, you get to see your first game."

* * *

I'm nervous as the players start filing in for the game, coming off the team bus. Western does things slightly old-school, in that even for home games, the team rents a hotel and everyone comes in on a chartered bus, supposedly to get everyone's mind in the right place. I've already been working

41

for ninety minutes, setting up the sidelines. Towels, tape, ice packs, and of course, the emergency kit, although if there is anything too serious, the ambulance crew from University Hospital takes over.

"Hey, PAT," one of the players, Vonnie James, greets me as he gets off the bus. "Hope you're ready."

"Pat?" I ask myself, trying to figure out why he'd call me that. I mean, he doesn't know me that well.

"What's up, PAT?" another player greets me, and his buddies chuckle. I'm flustered, and I start to feel embarrassed when I see Jason Simmons, the head intern, come by.

"Hey, Jason?"

Jason's a nice guy, and for a while as a freshman, I had a bit of a crush on him. He's engaged to be married after he graduates next May, and my crush faded last year anyway. "Yo, what's up, Car?"

Calling me 'Car' instead of Carrie is one of the ways my crush on Jason faded away. It's stupid and I hate it, but ah well. "Hey, about three or four of the guys have called me Pat. What the hell's that about?"

Jason grimaces. "They're not calling you Pat, but PAT, as in Point After Touchdown," Jason says as he forces out his words. "It's gone around the team. They know Duncan's been gunning for you. They call every girl he's got his eyes on *PAT*."

"They . . . what?" I ask, getting angrier as I listen. "They think I'm some sort of what . . . next booty call?"

"Yes," Jason admits. "I'm not saying I agree with them, just . . . they're jocks. They're gonna talk."

"Oh, I'll give them something to talk about," I growl, turning on a heel and marching back to the stadium area. I

42

know there's nothing I can do about it until I get a chance to talk to Duncan, but it still pisses me off. It pisses me off so much, in fact, that I have to be tapped on the shoulder to go back to the training room, where I find Duncan waiting for me.

"About time," he taunts as soon as I come in. "Were the water bottles a little low on ice or something?"

"Shut up," I hiss, grabbing my scissors and tape. Duncan doesn't need a lot. The tape is mostly there to minimize the small chance he's got of hyperextension after the surgery, and it doesn't take me long. "In fact, just sit there and don't even speak to me. Let me finish and go play your stupid fucking game."

"Whoa, whoa, what's got your panties in a bunch?" Duncan asks, and I stop, looking up into his eyes. There's a hint of the guy I sometimes saw during our workouts, when it was just the two of us and there was nobody else around—a real guy, not the arrogant, cocksure asshole he is around nearly everyone else.

"They're calling me PAT," I say with a sigh. "I didn't agree to this because I want to play Touchdown with you."

Duncan nods and pats me on the shoulder. "Don't worry, I'll take care of those idiots. I didn't tell Coach to have you here because of that. I did it because you do a good job helping me get ready to play. Now, can we do the wrists, or are you going to leave the tape so tight I'll lose my thumbs tomorrow?"

I can't help it. I give him a little grin at his joke and finish him up quickly. He hops off the table to go back down the hall to the locker room. As he does, he pauses and grabs my arm, pulling me in and kissing me. His lips are amazing, and

43

despite myself, I'm practically moaning in lust as his tongue finds mine, and we grow closer before I realize what the hell I'm doing and push him away. "Asshole!"

"Yeah, I've been called that too," Duncan says with a chuckle as he leaves the training room, whistling to himself.

After he leaves, I notice that we weren't alone, and that Chelsea Brown is still in the training room, trying to look like she hadn't just seen something she wasn't supposed to. "What?"

"Nothin'," Chelsea says, grabbing the last of her towels and going to the door. At the door, she pauses and turns around. "Actually, there is something. If you just want him to rock your world, then go on with your bad self, but don't get emotionally involved. That way, you won't get upset when you're his next cut-off."

"His what?" I ask, curious despite myself. A minute ago, I was hot as hell, ready to jump Duncan's body. Now, I was in chills but couldn't stop my questions short of being smacked in the head.

"His cut-off. He grows bored pretty easily and moves on. That man's a dog. If you want to ride that cowboy, go ahead, but make sure your heart's got bulletproof armor."

I nod and hear an announcement over the stadium P.A. "We need to get to field level," I say. "Come on, it's game time. And Chels?"

"Yeah."

"Thanks for the heads up."

We get up to the field, and I'm pretty busy as the last of the pre-game festivities wrap up. Western's opponent looks pretty overmatched on paper, and I find out from listening to the scuttlebutt on the sidelines that they are. Most big schools like Western schedule a 'tune-up' game at the beginning of the season.

So it's with no surprise as I watch Duncan put on a clinic, catching three touchdown passes and getting over a hundred yards receiving. Western dominated the entire game, and when the clock ticked off the final score, the scoreboard read 77-6. A slaughter.

Watching Duncan put on a show was like watching poetry in motion—savage, hypnotic poetry that aroused your spirit for battle . . . and I had to admit, at the time, my spirit for passion. I was hard pressed to keep my mind on my duties during the game, especially when he tipped me a wink during the fourth quarter. *Damn him.*

I'm cleaning up the water tables when I feel a presence behind me, and I turn around to see Duncan standing there, his uniform soaked through in spots, turning the bright green home jerseys to nearly black. "Hey. How was your first game?"

"Interesting," I say, trying my best to not get angry. I can still feel his lips on mine from before, and inside, a little voice that doesn't get to talk much says it wants more. "You played well."

"Against these scrubs? They'd lose to our second-stringers, but yeah, it was fun," Duncan says, glancing back at the rapidly diminishing stands behind him. "Whew, that's the best part, though, but it's always sad to see them go."

"What's that?" I ask, intrigued even though I don't want to be. "The crowd?"

He nods, then shrugs. His eyes kind of open wide, and I see something that I've never seen in him before. He's

45

showing me something about himself, something that I doubt few people have ever seen. "There's something about being out there, knowing that today, there were eighty thousand people here, and there were times today when I could feel their eyes on me. They got to see me, who I am, making my name. It's a powerful feeling. I felt . . . complete."

"Is that why you do it?" I ask. "Just for the fame?"

Duncan stops, his eyes and face clouding over as he recovers his normal cocky bravado. Instead of answering, he smirks and takes my hand. "There's a party over at a house off campus," he says. "I was thinking, since you helped me so much over the summer and all, maybe I'd take you."

"You're inviting me to a party?" I ask, and despite my misgivings, I'm flattered. But I won't be a PAT. I have more self-respect than that. Somewhere, I find the resolve inside me to pull my hand from his. "Sorry, maybe another time, when I'm not some trophy to celebrate a win."

Duncan's face falls for a moment before he regains himself. He comes close, and I can't move. For some reason, my feet are frozen to the ground as he strokes a thumb down my cheek. He leans in, and his warm breath sends shivers down my spine as he whispers in my ear. "Oh no, Carrie. You're not just some trophy or a PAT. You'll see."

He takes my hand and kisses my knuckles, and I shiver again. Oh God, he's so sexy, and his words . . . is there any truth to them? "Have a good evening, Carrie. I'll see you Monday."

* * *

I'm in my dorm room, struggling to try to study after the game. I can't get Duncan's words out of my head, and

46

finally, after rereading the introduction to *The General Physical Properties of Organic Compounds* four times, I slam my book shut, groaning in frustration.

"Seriously?" I mutter to myself. "One kiss, a touch, and a whispered promise, and he's got you right where he wants you. Get your shit together, Carrie."

But there's nothing wrong with a little fantasy, a voice in my head whispers, and I know that voice. It's the same voice that came to life earlier today when his lips found mine, and his large, powerful hands pulled me closer to him.

"Argh!" I groan, leaning back and grinding the heels of my hands into my eye sockets. I look up at the ceiling, a half-smile coming to my face as I think of seeing him again.

He's interested in you. Who cares if it's just a booty call? This booty needs to be called, and more often. Besides, if you take care of these needs now, you can get back to Organic Chemistry and not . . . organic chemistry.

I can't help it. I smile at my little joke to myself. My hands drift down over the tops of my breasts, circling and stroking them through my t-shirt. I'd ditched my bra—I was in my dorm room anyway—and the sensations shot through me, electric tingles that added to the warm wetness rolling around in the pit of my stomach.

"You're beautiful," Duncan says, his eyes sparkling and his lips writing hot trails on my neck. We're in a grand bedroom, a four-poster bed surrounded by lacy curtains, limiting my view of the rest of the world, but in the distance, I can hear the crash of waves and the call of tropical birds and smell the ocean on the breeze. We're together, alone in this paradise, and I'm happy to be here with this dream of a man.

My breasts are crushed against his chest, his arms pulling me

47

against him, his hands kneading the flesh of my ass. We're rolling back and forth, teasing and running our hands over each other's body but still leaving our clothes at least somewhat on until we reach this plateau where there's no turning back, and I don't want to, anyway. I'm helpless against his strength, and I don't care. I want this man. He senses my desperate hunger and raises his lips from my neck to whisper in my ear, "Give yourself to me."

"I do," I whisper, reaching down and cupping the huge rock between his legs.

He pulls my shirt up so that he can taste the skin of my breasts. I'm lost, tossed and turned by the feeling of his tongue on my body, his lips wrapping around my nipple and teasing it.

He pushes my knees apart, and I can't resist him. My body needs him, and I push my shorts and panties down, exposing myself to him.

"Duncan . . ." I nearly sob, the feelings of his lips on my nipples and his hands on my now naked ass leaving me in overload. I throb for more of him, hungry for the dangerous pleasure that he can bring me.

Duncan lifts his head from my breasts to look down at me, towering over me as he reaches for the waistband of his jeans. He unsnaps and pushes, and there it is . . . his perfect, steel-hard cock. I've never seen anything sexier or scarier in my life. I don't know if I can take it all, not with the power and danger wrapped up in the rest of his body.

"Don't worry, you'll enjoy it."

I'm nodding, knowing that he's telling the truth. Duncan's grin tells me that he knows my thoughts, and he guides himself inside me, my pussy spreading and wrapping around his cock until he's all the way inside me.

Holy shit. Just a single, deep stroke, and I'm nearly coming already, my hands clutching at my breasts and pinching my nipples. I can't help myself. He grins and slips a finger into my mouth, and I suck while *he starts to thrust in and out, my mind obliterated with each movement of his cock inside me. I've never felt something like this before, complete and total pleasure, my body taken by this powerful man who knows exactly how to light every nerve in my body on fire.*

I'm making noises, noises I never knew I could make, animalistic and thick as he slides in and out of me, his cock sending tremors up my spine each time. "Can you take it all?" he asks suddenly, and I look to see that he's still restraining himself, his fingers shaking because he's keeping himself under such tight control.

I look into his beautiful gray eyes and nod, smiling. "Don't hold back."

The look in his eyes at my words lights a fire in my heart as much as his cock is lighting a fire in my pussy, and his hips speed up, powerfully driving his cock into me. The first shocking impact sends me into spasms, nearly convulsing as he hammers into me over and over, driving me insane with sensation. My God, it feels so good, and he's still going, those hips and legs giving him immense, overwhelming power that crushes me into the bed. He takes my other leg and pushes it up, pinning me as his cock slams over and over into me, his eyes boring deep into my soul.

"You can come now," Duncan whispers, and suddenly, I'm there, as if I was waiting for his permission, riding the immense wave of my orgasm as Duncan shudders right along with me. I'm being bred like some sort of bitch, and I know that for Duncan, I'd be his bitch if he wanted it. Anything to feel this good. "You're mine."

"Yours . . ." I whisper, slowly coming back to reality as I realize I'm not in a bed surrounded by white gauze curtains and tropical birds, and the whisper of the ocean breeze is actually the fan on my laptop. My hands are damp and my room reeks of sex, not the heady sense of real sex, but just the lonely aroma of my masturbation.

Damn Duncan Hart. Damn that cocky bastard.

Chapter 5
Duncan

Two weeks, two away games, but it doesn't matter as I run onto the field at Farmington University, our away whites gleaming in the sun. They can't stop me, and the only bad thing about coming to Farmington is that they have a smaller stadium than Western, holding only sixty thousand instead of our eighty.

"You gonna put on a show again today?" Charlie Peters, one of our defensive backs, asks as we all gather on the sidelines for the kickoff. "I've got fifty bucks saying you get two touchdowns."

"Hope that means you took two and up," I shoot back, smiling. "You keep doing that, and you'll make plenty of money this year."

"We'll see. Nobody can keep up the pace you're on for a whole season," Charlie replies. "I mean, you're going to be breaking records by Thanksgiving if you keep this up. Shit don't work that way."

"You mean it doesn't work for other people," I reply. I look around at the crowd, and feel their power soaking into me and filling my body with their energy. Nobody understands the power of the crowd that way, the rush . . . the recognition. Duncan Hart, world-beating tight end, not Duncan Hart, son of Winston Hart.

I put my Dad out of my head and focus on the game. We're going on defense first, so I slap Charlie on the shoulder as he straps up. "Go get 'em. I hate trying to play both ways."

"Yeah, right!" Charlie calls, jogging out on the field as Coach Bainridge calls for the starting defense. I watch him go and settle into the game, flexing my arm as I feel the tape. Coach Taylor did the job this week, and it feels different, not quite right, but it'll get there. Still, it's not Carrie's work, and I'm not sure I like it all that much.

Pretty soon, though, we get the ball, and it's my turn. Let's go to work.

* * *

Three weeks into the season, and Western's knocking on the door of a top ten ranking in the polls, and it's all due to me. Tyler, our quarterback, is even getting some sniffs from pro scouts, who are wondering if his play is because of him or because of the talent surrounding him. Of course it's the talent around him. "On three. Ready, BREAK!"

Tyler spreads the ball around a bit in the game. I mean, he can't just throw it to me every single time. Farmington's not a bad team. In fact, they went to a bowl last year, but they can't stop me, and because they can't stop me, they can't stop the Western Bulldogs.

I line up on the right side, squaring my feet. I look across and see that the linebacker covering me is number 47, a guy I've burned two times already for big chunks of yardage. Farmington runs a 3-4, and their outside linebackers tend to play close, only a couple of yards off the line to jam guys like me . . . if they can. "Don't worry, 47, it's all going to be over soon," I call, grinning, making sure to keep my voice low enough that the ref won't throw a flag on me. "Thirty minutes at most, and you can go crawling back home."

"Fuck you, bitch!" he yells, and I've got him. He's distracted, not playing smart, and it's just a matter of time.

I can see Tyler out of the corner of my eye smile as he starts his count. He knows what's coming, I've used it enough before. It's not a particularly original taunt, but fuck it, it works.

The ball snaps, and 47 is out of control, so pissed off he charges instead of waiting for me to come to him. I slap his outside shoulder, sending him past me while I slide my hips and body to the outside.

I'm uncovered as I turn back, just in time to catch Tyler's pass. I've gotta give it to him. He's not the strongest armed QB in the conference, but he's got laser precision, and I don't need to break stride at all as I draw his pass in and turn upfield.

I see the free safety coming to try to stick me and I lower a shoulder, taking him on my left side while I send a quick angled step that puts my entire weight into him, and the hundred and ninety-pound bitch goes flying while I spin off, already accelerating upfield again. There's only one guy who has a shot at catching me. He's got the pursuit angle, and as a cornerback, he's pretty fast. He's closing the distance quickly, but I've only got twenty yards to go.

Fuck it. We're up by two touchdowns already, one of them mine, and I want to have some fun. When the cornerback gets close enough, we're nearly at the goal line, and I lay out, diving over top of him and flipping, completing the front flip to land on my feet in the end zone, the cornerback left lying on the turf with a chunk of grass for a snack, and the roar of the fans is a physical wave that lifts me while the rest of the team comes rushing toward me.

Someone hits me from behind, and I realize that 47 isn't willing to let my taunt go, but as he drives into me, I roll with it, flipping him over and landing him on the turf underneath me, face to face.

"Don't worry. I'll seal the deal of making you my bitch after the game. Just make sure you've got lots of lube," I taunt him again as the mob of players on both sides tries to pull us apart.

The late hit costs Farmington fifteen yards on the kickoff, and 47 gets thrown out of the game. As I head off the field, the ref gives me a warning. "Watch the trash talk, 83. Any more of it, and I'll throw a flag on you."

Like I care. I've already broken their starting linebacker, gotten two touchdowns, a fucking ESPN highlight reel catch, and I've still got a quarter to pad my stats. I jog off the field and take a seat on the bench. I look around for a moment, then remember that we're on an away game, so the training staff is light. Carrie's back at Western.

"Looking for your PAT again?" Tyler asks, taking a seat next to me and pulling off his helmet. "You know she's probably back at campus, watching the game and dreaming of you. You hit that yet?"

"Fuck you, Paulson," I seethe unexpectedly for some reason. I'd already warned him once. "I told all of you to stop calling her that."

53

"What, PAT? Fuck it, man. She's just another slut," Tyler continues, his words cut off when I grab him by the shoulder pads and jerk him to his feet. "Whoa, what the fuck, man?"

"I said . . . stop calling her that," I hiss, my face inches from him. "She ain't no slut. Back off, or the only thing you'll be doing the rest of the season is learning how to jack off left-handed."

"Whoa, whoa!" Coach Thibedeau, our tight end coach and offensive coordinator yells, getting in between us. "You two, calm the fuck down!"

"Just remember what I said," I finish, letting go of him. "Not a word."

Tyler's pissed, but he lets Coach Thibs lead him away while I sit back down and stew. What the fuck am I doing? I know that sort of blowup is going to be caught by the cameras, and even if I'd told Tyler before to not call Carrie that, we'd done shit like that with each other lots of times. Coach Thibs isn't in a good mood either when he comes back.

"What the hell are you doing, Duncan?" he yells, barely restraining himself from popping me in the shoulder pads as he echoes my own inner thoughts. "Are you trying to get yourself benched or something?"

"I won't take any disrespect from anyone," I reply, looking Thibs in the eye. "Not from Tyler, not from Farmington . . . not from anyone."

"Yeah, well, if you want to catch any more balls this game, you'd better cool that shit off right now," Thibs replies, squatting down so we're eye to eye. "What the hell's gotten into you, Duncan? Talking shit to the other team, sure. Talking the same in practice, I don't like, but we can't seem to get you to stop. But you've never started shit with a teammate in the middle of a game. Don't get cocky. Farmington's a good team, and we could still lose this."

"No chance in hell of that," I say, looking up at the scoreboard as the crowd roars, contradicting me. Farmington's offense just connected on a deep pass, and they scored quickly, bringing them back within two touchdowns. Twenty-eight to fourteen, with one minute left in the third quarter. I look back at Thibs and pull my helmet on, snapping up.

"Okay, you're right. Fine. I'll keep it under control."

After the game, which we do win thirty-five to fourteen, I find Tyler in the shower area, where he's styling his surfer boy hair to perfection. He's currently dating one of the cheerleaders and probably looking forward to some quick couple time before we all get on the plane back to Western. "Yo, Tyler."

He glances over, then turns back to the mirror. His voice is tense, like he isn't quite sure how to handle me approaching him. Tyler's a tough guy for a quarterback, but I'm way too big for him. "Yo, Duncan."

"Hey man, I just wanted to say . . . my bad on the sidelines. I shouldn't have jerked you around like that."

Tyler brushes his hair one more time, then sets his comb down, turning to look at me. "Okay. Let's get this straight between us, Duncan. I know you're the biggest reason I'm putting up numbers like today. I know that, and I'm grateful for it. But that's beside the point. This girl, Carrie . . . she's getting to you. You need to get your head right. You're getting away with it the past two weeks, but come next week, we can't have it. We're playing Clement, remember? Their

55

defense is all hard core motherfuckers."

"They always are. At least they aren't as bad as they used to be," I say, thinking back to my freshman year. Back then, Clement had beasts at linebacker, especially in the middle. Biggest ass whipping I've ever taken in a game. "But yeah, they're good."

"Damn right. Unless you want to be punked in front of a home crowd next week, including Carrie, you'd better have your shit tight come game time," Tyler says, finishing his hair. "Yo, we're friends, right?"

"I guess," I reply, checking out my own hair. I'm not as picky as Tyler, but I'm not going to look like a mop coming out of the locker room either. "You know how I roll."

"Nobody's your real friend. I know. But you know what I mean. Just... make sure you're doing what needs to be done. The League's calling your name next year, while I'm hoping to get a spot up in Canada or on someone's backup roster. Ah well. No matter what, I've still got one thing on you."

"What's that?"

Tyler flips his hair and flashes me a cocky surfer boy grin. "I'm still better looking than you."

I laugh, our rift healed. "I doubt it. At least, that's not what your mom says."

* * *

"I can't believe you asked the coaches to do this," Carrie says as I meet her in the library. I hoped she'd be flattered, but instead, she's upset, but I'm not sure why. "I mean, as if having me as your personal taper isn't bad enough, Duncan—"

56

"Nobody's going to say a single word about you. I've made sure of that," I reply, setting my bag down and realizing what it is. That stupid fucking nickname. Yeah, it's pretty obvious to everyone that I'm wanting to get in her pants, but things have changed some too. I don't want her as just another notch in my belt. "I just realized a couple of things after I got that first test back."

"That you shouldn't have blown off your science requirements for three years?" Carrie says as we sit down in the study booth. Western's library is huge and has two-person booths lining the study area that are perfect for this sort of partnered tutoring. "And maybe choosing Introduction to Human Biology wasn't the best choice?"

"Well, I figured I'm already an expert in the portion on reproduction," I tease, and it makes me warm to see Carrie blush a bit before she shakes her head. She's still so shy, but she's able to be strong too. Softness and strength together . . . God, she's sexy.

"I doubt that the *Kama Sutra* is on any of the tests," Carrie says, coming around at least a little bit. "However, the Krebs Cycle is, and for a guy who uses it to build a ton of muscle on that frame of yours, you don't know how it works."

"So help me," I say, and Carrie looks around, nervous. "I'm serious, Carrie. I know I'm a jerk, and maybe I shouldn't have kissed you the way I did before the first game, but . . . well, I enjoy spending time with you. Three games, seven touchdowns caught, and it's because of your work with me. Well, I take that back. *Some* of it is because of your work with me. You're cooler than most of the assholes around this campus."

57

I'm warmed again when Carrie brushes a lock of her cornsilk blonde hair behind her ear, smiling shyly. I realize she doesn't know how hot she really is, maybe because of the weight loss, maybe because of her keeping her nose in the books too much. But as confident as she is academically or when it comes to training, she's just as shy and insecure in the social realm.

I take her hand. "Come on, Carrie. I promise I'll behave myself, all right?"

"All right," Carrie says, giving me a little smile, and we get to work. She's got a knack for explaining things, better than the teacher's aide who's been trying to get through to a lecture hall of fifty people who can barely understand what he's been saying, and the time flies. Carrie and I are both surprised when the chimes in the library ring, and we realize that we're only fifteen minutes from the library's closing. "Whoa."

"Yeah," I say, laughing softly. "This has been the best study session I've ever had. And you do make it a lot more interesting than my major courses."

"Which are?" Carrie asks, then shrugs. "They didn't tell me. Coach Taylor just told me you asked for my help on a biology class."

"I'm a management major," I reply, putting my book back in my backpack. "I figure it'll teach me enough to keep my shit together next year when I'm in the pros. A little bit of business, a little bit of leadership, you know . . . stuff that could be useful."

Carrie nods and closes up her own backpack. "You're smarter than that, though. I've seen it. Why do you insist on limiting yourself to being just a football player?"

"I'm more than *just* a football player," I reply. "I'm an exceptional football player. But as to why . . . well, tell you what. Go out with me, and maybe I'll tell you."

Carrie shakes her head. "Not interested in a team party again. I already told you that."

Carrie goes to stand up, but I put my hand over hers, and she stops. "I'm serious, Carrie. No team party, no frat house, nothing like that," I say, and I'm surprised in that I actually am being honest. I want to spend time with her, not just find a way to fuck her. "Just you, me, and maybe a pizza? Stagglione's just off campus makes a pretty mean deep dish."

Carrie considers it for a moment, then shakes her head. "Nope." She sees the disappointment in my face and breaks out in a grin. "I don't like Stag's. But, if you make it the Bangkok House on the other side of campus, I might be tempted."

I grin, and the chimes play again. We've got five minutes to get out now. "Okay, Bangkok House it is. How about tomorrow night, say eight? I'd say Saturday, but after Clement, I might not be in the mood for a date."

"A date, huh?" Carrie teases as we walk toward the exit of the library. "Why, Duncan Hart, I think I might be the first girl in at least a semester you have actually asked out on a date, and not what your reputation says you normally invite girls to."

It's my turn to blush slightly, and Carrie takes my hand when we go outside, walking down the long steps to Allen Quad, and yeah, it's the same Allen that the stadium is named after. Being stupid levels of rich means you get to put your name all over the university you give your money to. "Well, I guess you could say that—"

59

"If you can keep yourself under control, I think a date with you might be a lot of fun," Carrie says, and suddenly, she gets onto her tiptoes, kissing me on the cheek. "Have a good night, Duncan. See you for taping tomorrow."

Carrie starts to walk away, but she turns and looks back. "By the way, I wouldn't worry about Clement," she says, just on the edge of the circle of light from the library lamps. "As good as you've been doing, they should be the ones worried."

"Who knew you were romantic?" I toss back, and Carrie laughs, giving me a wave. As she walks away, I notice that she's not wearing stuff as oversized as she used to. It's a subtle change, but I can start to see the faintest outlines of her dynamite figure in her clothes, and I watch until she disappears into the night, heading toward her dorm room. I shake my head, and I'm smiling as I get on my bike and fire it up, heading back to my apartment.

A date. For Thai food. God, I feel like such a goofball.

Chapter 6
Carrie

The Bangkok House is not just a restaurant, but a cafe as well, and with the late summer heat breaking slightly to the cool of early fall, I'm glad that the waitress seats Duncan and me at an outdoor table.

"Wow," Duncan says for the second time, and I feel

60

the warmth creeping up my cheeks. I took half an hour standing in front of my closet before picking my dress, one of the cutest I own. The wide shoulder straps and relatively high-cut neckline help support the built-in light bra while I can still wear another underneath, and the tummy area is tighter than I would ever feel comfortable wearing in normal situations, but if Duncan is going to ask me out on a date, then I want to look good.

I feel buzzed, and I understand more about the personal magnetism that is Duncan Hart. "So how was practice today?" I ask as the waitress brings around our drinks, Coke for him, lemon water for me. "Sorry, Coach T had me working the training room all afternoon, doing ultrasound and contrast therapy with the girls on the volleyball team. By the way, Linda says hi."

"Yeah, I bet." Duncan chuckles and takes a sip of his drink. "It went well, but to be honest, I'd rather talk about anything but football. You'll get a whole view of that this Saturday. By the way, speaking of Linda, someone told me that I ran you over in the hallway that day when I said something to her the day before we met. Is that true?"

I nod, laughing. "You plowed me over pretty good. You were wearing your sling and never even gave me a second glance."

"Well, I'm glad you didn't hold it against me. These past few months—they've been some good times."

"Thanks, I guess . . . for me, too," I say, and I know I'm blushing, but I can't help it. "I still don't know why you asked me out, though—I'm not going to be a booty call. There are lots of girls on campus who'll be that, I'm sure."

61

I'm surprised that, instead of denying it or playing it off, Duncan just accepts what I say as a fact. "There are, but I don't want them. I'm done with that."

I'm stunned, and I blink, making sure my ears are still working. "Say what?"

"I don't want those girls," Duncan says simply, giving me one of his heart stopping smiles. I know I'm too young and in good enough shape to be having a heart attack, but damn if it doesn't feel that way right now. "I want you. Especially after you came in that dress."

"Please. It's not my best look," I say, looking down, but Duncan stops me, his fingers lifting my chin. "I mean, it's a nice dress, but I need to lose a few. I shouldn't have worn it."

Duncan starts laughing, and at first, I'm a little pissed. "You really don't know, do you?"

I sit there in silence, unable to take my eyes from his. He shakes his head, his eyes intense, and I pull back, unable to handle it. "Don't tease me, Duncan."

He reaches beneath the table and rests his hand on my thigh, just over my dress. "I'm not teasing," he says softly. "You've got the sexiest legs I've ever seen, beautiful hair, and don't get me started on your eyes," he says and starts running his hand up higher.

I don't know what to say, so I say nothing, but when the waitress comes back, he pulls his hand from my thigh. I can still feel it there, a ghost of it just about halfway up my leg, and I wish it had gone higher. It gives me confidence, and I order my Tom Yum soup without any reservations or trying to eat like a bird in front of him. Duncan orders a big plate of Pad Thai, giving me a grin. "We can share if it's more than I can

62

handle, right?"

"I doubt there are many things you can't handle . . . if you put your mind to it," I reply, and I'm surprised that I'm flirting back with him as he reads the meaning of my words.

"That's more like it. You know, when you first started working with me, you were the first person outside the coaches to get in my face and not back down around campus. At least, I can't think of the last time someone called me a lazy bastard without catching a helmet in the teeth."

"It worked, didn't it?" I laugh, sipping at my water. "You know, you surprise me."

"How's that?"

"Well, you have this public image—this cocky asshole, no offense, that is Duncan Hart. The guy who rocks the tatts, the motorcycle, the trash talker, on and off the field. That guy, by the way, I would never have accepted an invitation to dinner with."

"Yet you're here with me now," Duncan says, setting down the fork that he's twirling point-first on the tabletop.

"Because there's another Duncan Hart, I suspect," I say. "The guy who didn't go off like a child when I needled him during workouts, but just bore down and pushed harder. The guy who asked and listened when we were in the library yesterday. The guy who is taking management courses because he doesn't want to be just a dumb jock."

"Maybe," Duncan says, his hand warm as it takes mine. "But remember, I could be just doing that as an act, trying to get into your pants."

I laugh and lean in until we're close. "Duncan, in case you haven't noticed . . . I'm not wearing any pants."

63

We're so close that I can feel his breath on my lips, and I want to kiss him so badly that I'm willing to let go of my nervousness, but before we can close that last little gap between us, a voice interrupts us.

"Well, Duncan, so nice to see you!"

We part, and I look up to see a lean redhead coming up with some other girl, both of them practically wearing a designer catalog on their fashion-model bodies, all tight jeans, pearled tops that hug their size-four bodies, and perfectly coiffed hair. They both are screaming sorority with their body language, and the disdain in their eyes when they see me is evident.

Duncan, however, seems happy to see them, and smiles widely. "Tiffany! Mandy! How nice to see you. What's got you here on a Wednesday night?"

"We were invited to a new club that's opening this weekend, but the owner's having a special sneak peek event," Tiffany titters, pointing down the block. "Since Mandy and I don't have morning class, we were going to check it out. What about you? You can even bring your . . . friend."

The way she says *friend* lets me know that she's jealous, but I keep my mouth shut. Girls like Tiffany have always intimidated me. They were the ones, back in high school, who were driving new cars while I had to ride the bus or hitch a ride with some of my teammates on the softball team if my parents couldn't pick me up from practice. They had the nicest clothes, the hottest guys, and all the perks, while I had a softball bat and calluses on my palms.

Now I'm confronted by not just one, but two girls like this, and I realize that I'm out on a date with a guy who is one

64

of them. Duncan is a hot shot, one of those guys that every guy wants to be and every girl wants to be with. I'm looking at Tiffany, and she's practically got '*Fuck Me, Duncan*' written on her forehead, but he's sitting back and taking it in stride. He doesn't understand.

"We'll see. What's the name of the place?"

"Blowouts," Tiffany says, emphasizing the *blow* part. I wonder, if I wait long enough, would she get under the table and suck him off right here? "It's two blocks that direction."

"All right. For now, though, I need to fuel up from practice," Duncan says. "Check you girls later."

"Sounds good. Duncan, and . . . well, anyway, see you," Tiffany says, walking off before I can even tell her my name. Duncan watches them for a second, then turns his eyes back to me, where he sees that I'm not happy.

"What?"

"You didn't even introduce me, Duncan. That's pretty rude, you know?"

He shrugs and spreads his hands. "I figured you were going to speak up any second. You know, the way you stood up to me, I didn't think those sorority sluts would get you like that. Chill."

"Chill? You treated me exactly how they think of me—that I'm beneath them. And I saw Tiffany's face. You've given her the full effect, haven't you?" I shouldn't be getting jealous, but I can't help it.

"She's never had the pleasure of having a Hart Attack," Duncan says, and I gawk at him. He has a fucking nickname for his sex skills? What the fuck?

"You think that makes it all right?" I ask, standing up

65

and folding my napkin. "No offense, but I'm not in the mood to play invisible good-time girl for your Hart Attack any time soon. I won't be a side piece."

"Carrie, come on!" Duncan says, getting up and stepping in front of me. "We were having a good meal, and I thought a good date. Let's go back to that, okay? Listen, I'm sorry that I didn't introduce you to those girls, but what's the point? They're not the kind to take a liking to you anyway."

"So you'd rather keep your playmates separated by social class?" I ask, now fully pissed off. "No thanks, *Touchdown*." I make sure to emphasize Touchdown to let him know how mad I am.

He recoils, his face darkening as he finally feels the anger I've been feeling for the past few minutes. "Carrie, I'm not like that, and I think you know it. Sure, I'm no saint, but a lot of my reputation is built on rumor."

"Whatever. I'm not sure I believe that, but maybe we should just keep it semi-professional between us. I'll tape you up and help you in science, but other than that, I don't intend to let myself be given the *Hart Attack* any time soon. Good night, Duncan."

* * *

"Do you want to talk about it, honey?"

I'm back in my dorm room, a bowl of Honey Nut Cheerios in my left hand while I have a huge spoon in my right. "What do you mean, Mom?"

Mom is on the other end of the Skype call, her own blonde hair pulled back and her face filled with concern. "Carrie, you never call on weekdays unless something is up, and you never eat cereal like that unless you're upset about something. In fact, the last time I saw you with a bowl that big was . . . well, I think it was when Dale James broke up with you right before the prom."

"Yeah, thanks for that memory," I grump, unable to help myself even though I know Mom didn't mean anything by it. "Just . . . had a bad date tonight, that's all."

"So that's why your hair is still up." Mom chuckles. "Be glad your dad is out on the road tonight. He'd be more concerned than I am. He still doesn't understand that you're not his little girl that needs to have her scraped knees kissed away any longer."

Dad is a long-haul trucker, which is good money, but it meant he couldn't spend as much time at home as a lot of other parents. It makes him overprotective. "I'll get over it. Just a guy from the football team who thought he could play me."

"I see. He must be cute," Mom teases, and I have to laugh. Mom has always used humor to get me out of a funk.

"Mom! Okay, okay, he's gorgeous. But . . . we're just from different worlds, that's all."

She nods and goes to say something, but there's a knock at my door. "Well, honey, sounds like you've got a visitor. I'll let you go. If you need anything, give me a call, okay? And Dad should be home Friday night. He's excited to see the Western game. You guys are going to be on national TV—he's hoping that maybe he can see you on the sidelines."

I laugh. That's so him. "Okay, but the most he's going to get is a half-second side shot if he's lucky. See you later. Love you."

The knock at my door comes again, and I get up, already calling out, "Hold on, hold on!"

I open the door and see Chelsea Brown in the hallway, a smile on her face. "Hey, Carrie. What's wrong?"

"What is it? Do I have a sign over my head that says I had a bad night?" I ask, stepping back into my room.

"Your hair is up, you're wearing a pajama t-shirt even though it's barely nine o'clock, and to be honest, I didn't even think I'd find you here. I was coming to drop off some notes from Coach Taylor. I was gonna leave them on your desk. Guess your date didn't go very well?"

I give Chelsea an only slightly surprised look, then just shake my head. Fuck it. I'm just not used to this level of social scrutiny. "How'd you know?"

"Duncan was happy as hell about it during practice," Chelsea says, and I remember she worked football practice today while I was running a rehab session with Rita Smothers of the tennis team. "He even shut down a couple of the guys who tried to give him shit about it. I figured you'd still be out for another couple of hours. What happened?"

"Tiffany and Mandy happened," I say. "Couple of sorority row girls who came by with dismissive looks for me and open legs for Duncan. They practically begged him to go to some new club with them. He . . . he didn't exactly stick up for me."

Chelsea nods, as if she's seen it before. "I know what you mean."

"You too?"

"Not with Duncan, but yes, I know what you mean. It's in the past, and I'd like to keep it that way, no offense. By the way, here are the notes. See you tomorrow?"

"Yeah," I say, taking the notes. "See you, Chelsea."

It's about twenty minutes later that I hear a motorcycle rev its engine outside, a Kawasaki, I know for sure, and I finally let a tear trickle down my cheek.

Chapter 7
Duncan

I can't believe it.

"Dad?" I ask, seeing the familiar silver-streaked hair and broad shoulders that I hadn't seen in at least six months. "Dad!"

My father turns around, and there's a look of surprise on his face. "Duncan? What are you doing here?"

I shake my head and approach him. We're outside the team hotel, and everyone is getting ready for breakfast, but I have a few minutes. After the past few days, I could use some good luck. "It's the team hotel. We're going to have breakfast before heading over to the stadium. You know, the Clement game is today?"

"Oh, no, I didn't," Dad says, and my mood immediately darkens. Why else should it be any different? He hasn't been at any of the other forty starts I've made for Western over the past three years. "I'm in town on business. Meeting with investors, you know. New project upstate."

That's Dad, always looking for a new angle. I see he's wearing a wedding ring again. I hadn't been notified.

"So, what's her name?" I'm cold, my mood going from glum to black, and I can hear the excitement draining out of my voice as I look him in the eye. "You know, you didn't send me an invitation."

"I didn't? My mistake. I remember telling my secretary to send out the invitations."

"What's her name, Dad?"

"Tawny," he says with a leer that tells me exactly what Tawny Hart looks like. My father has very consistent tastes: tall, long hair, and a body you could bounce a quarter off any part of it, even if it is surgically enhanced. In fact, to him, a girl just isn't a woman without a little silicone somewhere.

"Where'd you meet her?"

"She was a massage therapist at a club I frequent," he says, and I try not to roll my eyes. Great. He met her at a rub-n-tug. Wonder how much she charged for a handy. "She and I just clicked."

"Uh-huh. Well, if you have a chance, think you can make it to the game? I'm sure I can get you in if you don't have tickets."

Dad shakes his head and looks at his watch. "Don't think so. Meeting's going to run all day, so . . . another time. Really, though, I've gotta go. See you later, Duncan."

"Yeah, Dad . . . bye."

* * *

The reporter is in my face, and it's not the day that I want to do any of this shit. The past two days have been terrible, and it's only because the Athletic Director insisted that

70

I'm doing this.

"I'm telling you, college football fans, what a game we've got for you today. The Western University Bulldogs host the Clement Golden Spartans, in what a lot of folks are calling the biggest game in the first half of the season. Western and Clement have traded the conference championship back and forth over the past few years, with whoever wins this game normally going on to clinch the conference title."

Yeah, yeah, yeah. Last year, we took Clement, and two years ago, they took us. Big fucking deal. The yapping announcer goes on.

"Things are a little different this year, as the Pacific Football Conference has followed in the footsteps of many of the other major conferences and implemented a championship game system. That doesn't make this game useless, of course. There are still major impacts for the national championship at stake, as well as the fact that whoever wins this game holds the edge for the conference championship, as the team that finishes the regular season as the conference champions will host the championship game."

Will this guy hurry the fuck up? I need to get taped. I need to see Carrie. The past two days, she's barely said anything to me, and I'm not able to focus. I can't get past Wednesday night, and I want this to be over with. Then there was my Dad . . . fuck this. I need outta here. *Now.*

"With us now is Duncan Hart, the star tight end of the Western Bulldogs. Duncan, thanks for joining us. I know you're going to be getting ready to play soon."

"I'm always ready to play," I say into the mike, just letting my mouth go. I don't care any more. "But what's up?"

71

"Well, Duncan, in pregame analysis, it's going to be a tough battle between Western's spread offense, and Clement's vicious defense. In speaking yesterday with Nick Hostler, the Clement defensive captain and linebacker, he says that he's looking forward to it. It seemed very interesting. He was quite interested in you, in particular. Any idea why?"

Because last year, I smoked his ass . . . not that I would use those exact words in an interview. I know I'm a trash talker, but I try to be smart about it. "Nick's the sort of player who wants to test himself against the best. It's one of the things I like about him."

"You say one of the things. What's the other?"

"He keeps testing himself against me, and he keeps failing the test," I say with a smirk.

After the interview is over, Coach Bainridge pulls me aside. "Really, Duncan? Did you have to bad mouth the other team two hours before kickoff?"

"Don't sweat it, Coach," I reply, brushing him off. "It wasn't that bad—just a little gamesmanship. If anything, it should get the fans riled up. Hostler knows I hate him, and he hates me. Some kiss-kiss words before the game won't change that. Besides, I need to get ready."

"You'd better," Bainridge says, giving me a look, "because your practice the past two days has been garbage. Get your head right."

I'd like to get my head right, but it seems that I've got everyone and their fucking brother trying to stop me from doing it. I go to the trainer's room, where Carrie is finishing up taping Tyler's ankle—he rolled it a little on Tuesday—then she turns to me. "You know, you don't need the elbow tape

72

anymore. That thing's stronger than it was before your injury, by this point."

"Just give me my security blanket and let me have some peace of mind," I reply, holding out my arm. Carrie goes to work, wrapping the first layer of pre-wrap around my elbow, totally silent. I fume for a moment, then launch in. "Well, Duncan, why yes, I have had a great morning. In fact, I was just enjoying a wonderful conversation with my friends about whether to have granola or pancakes with breakfast tomorrow. How's your day been? Oh, I'm doing fine, Carrie. I saw my father before breakfast, where he blew me off, and I've just completed an interview with a national cable network, where I probably came off as an asshole, pissed off Coach Bainridge, and now, the one person I really want to talk to won't even speak to me. Other than that, my day's going to hell!"

"And that's my fault?" Carrie asks softly, looking up at me. "It's my fault that you treated me like shit on our date and came off as that cocksure asshole that I just got finished telling you I didn't like? In case you didn't notice, you're the one causing your own problems by not being able to think about what the hell comes out of your own mouth. Before our date went south, I was having a good time, because I told you, there are two of you. There's the you who's intelligent, one hell of a ball player, and a guy I happen to like. Then there's the you that, like you said, is an asshole. Your choice, Duncan. I hope to see the first guy more."

Carrie leaves the training room, and I'm left alone, steaming in my own anger. Finally, in frustration, I punch the supply locker next to me, putting a dent in the metal side, but doing nothing to relieve my frustration. I head into the locker

73

room and get strapped up, still not sure what's going on inside me.

We get the kickoff, and jogging out to the huddle, I'm off balance. Normally, I'm the guy who's settled down while the defense are the ones who are pressed out of control, but this time, I'm the one bordering on the edge, seeing red, and we haven't even started.

"Duncan? Hey, Duncan!"

"What?" I ask, growling. "Just get me the fucking ball," I hiss, going up to the line. I drop my hand down and look across to the Clement defensive end, sneering. "You're my bitch."

"We'll see," the end sneers back, and suddenly, the ball snaps. I'm caught off guard. Isn't the play supposed to be on two? The end fires off the line and plasters me, driving me back and down to the turf before I'm barely out of my stance. Tyler, who was expecting me to release to the outside, is forced to throw across his body to our split end on the other side, who at least caught it for a three-yard gain. "You're gonna have a long fucking day, boy."

The words are no joke, as at halftime, I have no catches, and I've spent more time on my back than I have since freshman year. Jogging down the tunnel to the locker room, I'm pissed, and we're losing, fourteen to ten.

"Duncan, you okay today?" Tyler asks me after Coach Bainridge gets done chewing out the offense's collective asses. He's quiet, and the long streak of dirt on the front of his shirt shows that he's not the only one who's taken a few hits out there so far. "Seriously, you sick or something?"

"Or something," I say, and Tyler nods. He opens his

74

mouth, and I hold up my hand. "Don't ask."

"I won't, but I need to know. If you're fucked up, I need to check down faster, go to the other options," Tyler says. I feel kinda bad for him. His stats are nearly as horrible as mine, and our only touchdown is because our special teams ran back a punt to the four-yard line, so close a child could have punched it in for a touchdown. "Do I need to check down?"

"You do what you need to do," I say, still pissed. "We'll take care of it in the second half, okay?"

"All right," Tyler says, but I can see he's not convinced. He moves off and starts a discussion with Coach T and some of the other guys for the rest of halftime while I stew.

The second half starts, and our defense stuffs the Clement offense for a three and out, so we're ready to go soon. Going out to the huddle, I can see it in the eyes of everyone in the huddle. They're not confident in me, and it pisses me off more.

I line up, ready to go. Tyler's called the same play that got me injured in the Green and White Game. The problem is that my route is a crossing route right over the middle of the defense, supposedly at a depth that is too deep for the linebackers but too shallow for the safeties to jump on things. If I run it right, it's a great seam route. If the linebackers are on it, I can get laid out, especially if the pass is high.

The ball snaps, and I cut across the middle. Tyler takes his three-step drop and releases the ball, just a little high, but you expect that with a pass over the middle of the line. I go up for the ball. It's still a few feet from me . . .

I get blasted in the chest and chin, throwing me to the turf so hard and fast, the wind is knocked out of me. I look up to see Nick Hostler grinning at me, but he takes off before I can do anything, and I realize that Tyler's pass has been intercepted and we're scrambling to stop the free safety who caught the ball from doing anything.

My sights are on Nick Hostler, who's trying to block for his teammate. I charge at him, but he's too far ahead, and the Clement safety goes in standing up for a touchdown. I see the ref raise his hands, and I can't hold it back any more. "Touchdown? What the fuck do you mean touchdown?" I scream into his face. "Were you so fucking blind you missed the pass interference?"

"Back off, 83," the ref says, giving me a warning. He's a home ref, even if he is paid by the conference, and he's not going to throw a penalty on me unless he has to, not after we already gave up a touchdown.

"That's bullshit!" I scream. "You're fucking blind!"

The ref tosses his penalty, blowing the whistle, and I feel hands pulling me back, but I don't care. I lose my cool, going at him even more, and it's obvious to me even while I'm yelling at him that I'm not even mad at the missed call. I'm pissed that things in my life aren't going how I want them and looking for a scapegoat.

The ref throws another flag, blowing his whistle twice, and I'm ejected from the game.

I stare at him, ready to charge, fighting against whoever is holding me back, when Coach Thibedeau comes around and throws a cup of water in my face. "Duncan! Get a fucking hold of yourself!"

I stop, shocked. What the hell did I just do?

"Get to the locker room," Coach Thibs says, his voice

gentle now that I'm at least a bit under control. "You got ejected. You're not allowed on the sidelines. We'll talk about this after the game. Coach Taylor?"

"Yeah?" Coach Taylor says, and I see he's already there, probably ready to physically escort me from the field if he needs to. Hell, he was probably one of the people holding me back.

"Walk Duncan back to the training room. And make sure he's calmed down, okay? Just . . . ditch your gear and calm down."

The fans, for the first time in three years and four games, are booing me as I leave the field. I cringe, and I feel like running, but my pride keeps me walking as I reach the tunnel, even as I feel some joker spray me with a cup of ice and probably Coke, since the stadium doesn't allow beer. I feel Coach Taylor behind me, but I'm empty. I don't feel it any longer. I just make my way to the training room, unstrapping my shoulder pads as I walk.

"You need anyone to talk to?" Coach Taylor asks when I pull my gear off and sit down on the padded training table.

"I'm fine." But I don't feel that way. "I'm just frustrated. You're not pissed, Coach?"

"Oh, I'm pissed, but remember, I'm not a football coach. Besides, you're talking to the man who got so fired up and pissed off for an event that I head butted an Atlas Stone and knocked myself out. So I can kind of understand, even if I don't like it. Chill out here, and I'll have someone check on you later."

I lie back on the table, staring at the ceiling, trying to figure out where I had been for the past three days, when the

77

door to the training room opened again. I look over, my heart catching in my throat when I see Carrie before I sigh and put my head back down. "Sorry, nice guy Duncan isn't here. The asshole just got done making an idiot out of himself."

"Actually, it was me who came down here to apologize," Carrie says softly. "I shouldn't have spoken to you that way when you came to get taped up. I screwed up your mental mindset—threw you off."

There's a part of me that wants to agree with her, to shift the blame. But I look at her face, and another part of me, perhaps the stronger part that might actually be a decent guy, speaks up instead. "No, Carrie, you don't need to apologize. I've been this way for days. And it's all my own fault. All you did was tell me the truth."

"What happened?" she asks, coming over and hopping up on the table next to me. "Seriously, you looked ready to burst a blood vessel out there."

"I was," I say, sighing again. "It's been a lot of things, but what you said, when you were pissed off at me in the Bangkok House, I've been kicking myself about it ever since. I guess I finally realized that I'm too much like my father. Then I saw him at breakfast today, and it didn't go well, and then . . . well, I was just a time bomb waiting to go off."

Carrie stops, looks into my face, then puts a hand on my shoulder. "We've known each other since June. That's what, almost four months now? I don't think you've ever said a thing about him. I think this is the first time I've ever heard you use that word in a conversation, in fact. Lots of momma jokes, but nothing about your father."

I nod. "I don't talk about him often. He and I . . . we

78

don't get along very well. Probably has something to do his lifestyle."

"What kind of lifestyle is that?"

I chuckle darkly. "Check it out yourself, but I'll save you the creepy research. Winston Hart is one of the bigger venture capitalists in Silicon Valley, never the public figure, but high enough in the group of investors that he has swing, before he cashes out and takes his money elsewhere. He's worth . . . well, put it this way. I'm not here on scholarship, and my apartment in the Vista Apartments is fully paid for by him. He probably doesn't know or care what it costs. It's his way of showing *familial relationship*."

"Not a very affectionate father, I take it?"

"Not a very affectionate man," I say. "I mean, he's in town today for business, and he didn't even know about the game! I think he was surprised I'm even on the football team. And well, let's see . . . since I was born, he's on . . . yeah, wife number four. And for three days, those two words have been swirling around in my head. Seeing him just brought that out more."

"What words?"

"Side piece," I whisper, uncovering my eyes and turning my head to look at Carrie. "Carrie, I know I can be a bastard. I'm selfish, and maybe even rotten to the core, from time to time."

Carrie swallows a pained expression, then nods and looks at me calmly. "But?"

I sigh. "Maybe the past four months . . . I'm starting to change. Maybe . . . I don't know. I just know that I'm sorry. I'm sorry I treated you without the respect that I really feel for you.

79

Seeing my dad reminded me of what I don't want to be."

Carrie surprises me by leaning over and giving me a kiss on the lips, soft and delicate, and when she lifts her head, she's smiling. "Then maybe I should give you a chance to make it up to me. But it's going to be your last chance, Duncan. Pick me up from my dorm at seven tonight. You only played half the game. I think you've got enough energy to take me out for dinner."

I'm smiling, and I reach up to stroke her hair. "Why?"

"Maybe because over the past four months, I've come to like you. And if you're willing to make the effort to become a better man, I'd like to stick around and see who that man could be. From what I've seen so far, he's going to make a name for himself. He's going to be a better man than his father, at least from what I've heard."

I nod, and Carrie gives my hand a squeeze. "All right. Let me go tell Coach Taylor that you're not destroying the place, and go help clean up with the aftermath of the game. I hate to tell you, but I think we just lost our first game of the season. Clement's kicking our asses right now."

I sigh and sit up, nodding. "Guess I have something else to make up for."

"First test of this new man you want to be. I'll see you at seven."

I'm waiting quietly when the team starts filtering in, all of them glaring at me. Nobody comes into the training room, though, dressing and walking out without a single greeting. I understand, and I wait quietly, not even saying anything when the trainers start hauling their gear into the room, nobody speaking to me until Carrie carries a bag over her shoulder. She holds up her fingers, telling me the bad news. 27-10.

I nod, and she puts her stuff away, her eyes full of emotion, but before she can say anything, Coach Bainridge is in the doorway. "You're suspended from the team for the time being," Coach says, his anger burned out at least for a while. "Come by my office Tuesday to discuss what happens next. I need that long to calm down and figure that out myself. Now go get dressed and get out."

Great. Great game.

Chapter 8
Carrie

After getting suspended from the team, I wasn't really expecting Duncan to arrive for our date. I mean, if anything is a mood killer for an athlete, it's getting at least temporarily tossed off the team. But, it wasn't until five thirty that I realized that in the four months we'd known each other, I had yet to exchange phone numbers with him. He knows where I live, but that's because it's listed for every player and intern, at least those who live on campus. He knows the dorm building, but not the room number.

So I am surprised when, at six fifty-four, I hear the now familiar sound of a Kawasaki motorcycle pulling up into the parking lot of the dorm, and I stick my head out of my window to see Duncan getting off his cycle. "Hey!"

"Hey!" Duncan calls back, waving. "You coming down, or am I coming up?"

"I'll come down!" I call, closing my window. I make sure to lock the door when I leave, and I head down the stairs and out the doors, a skip in my step. I feel like a cloud has lifted off me—maybe because of the way his face lit up when he waved, maybe because of the memory of our kiss in the training room. I don't know what it is, but when I reach the parking lot, I'm happy.

It looks like Duncan is too, especially when he sees what I'm wearing. "Jeans and a jacket? What, is your dress still dirty?"

I laugh and shake my head, wrapping my arms around his neck and giving him a quick peck on the lips, surprising me, but in a good way. "Not at all. But, last time we tried the classic dinner date thing, and that certainly didn't work. I was thinking, maybe tonight . . . we could just get away from it all for a little while? Besides, I didn't know if you'd show, and you don't have my phone number!"

"You're right. I don't. We'll have to remedy that, won't we? But I like the outfit," Duncan says, wrapping his arms around me. It feels good, and my heart speeds up a bit in my chest. "Where do you want to go?"

"I don't know," I reply, looking over at his bike. "But that looks like a two-seater, and I was wondering, maybe you could teach me how to ride that thing?"

Duncan's grin is all the answer I need, and he takes me by the hand, leading me over to the bike, where he unlocks the seat and pulls out another helmet. "I keep an extra brain bucket in here, just in case," he tells me, looking sheepish as he hands it over. "Climb on, and be careful about the vibrations."

"The what?"

"I put a sport suspension in this thing," Duncan says as he climbs on, helping me on after him. It's a weird lift of the leg, but I manage it, and I find that in order to keep my balance, I have to lean against his back, and I naturally wrap my arms around him, enjoying the scent of his leather jacket. "Handles bumps well, but the engine vibrations can go right through the frame and up the seat. You can guess where they go next."

"So, you're telling me that the throttle won't be revving just the bike's engine while we ride?" I ask, leaning back to put on the helmet, which I find is just a bit big, but not too bad

83

while Duncan laughs. "I bet you designed it to do this, didn't you?"

"Nope, but I'll try to keep it under control," he says as he glances back.

I lean in and whisper in his ear. "Say that again."

"What?"

"Keep it under control. It's . . . sexy, coming from you."

Duncan looks back at me, his eyes twinkling, and pulls his helmet on. "I knew there was a reason I wanted to ask you out. Come on, let's go find some fun."

Duncan starts his bike, and I can feel exactly what he means, as even with my legs on the back pegs like Duncan points out, I can feel the power of the bike's engine rumbling between my legs. We ride off, Duncan taking it easy at first so that I can learn to adjust on the curves and turns, but I can sense that he really wants to unleash the bike's power, and I pull myself in tighter, holding onto the amazing torso that is in front of me.

I can't see much. Duncan's back and shoulders are so wide, so everything is caught in side glimpses that slide past too quickly to really do much more than hold on, but as we continue, I realize I'm becoming more and more turned on. Duncan's body in front of me, the throb of the engine between my legs, the smell of the rich leather of his jacket in front of me, but most of all, the knowledge that his strength is keeping us safe and secure. Even if he wants to rev the bike up to a hundred miles an hour, I feel safe holding onto him.

Duncan slows, and we pull off the road into a parking lot, and I see that we're at a miniature golf center, of all places.

84

I can't help it. I laugh. "Fun?"

"Sure," Duncan says, taking my hand. He helps me off with my helmet, then helps me off the bike's saddle. My legs are a little shaky getting off, partly because of the throbbing itch between my thighs, and partly because I just wasn't used to riding a bike. "Sorry."

"No," I get out, laughing again and leaning against him. "You warned me, and besides, it was one of the most fun rides I've ever had."

"I thought you hadn't ridden on a bike before."

"Wasn't talking about bikes," I purr, and Duncan stops, brushing the hair out of my eyes. "What?"

"You've shut me down for four months, except for some flirting, and now you're dialing it up to eleven."

I stop and look him in his eyes and put my arms around his waist. "Because I've seen you at your worst now, and you've been through hell, and yet . . . you still apologized for your behavior. You showed up tonight, and I half expected a depressed, down in the dumps guy who I'd have to spend the night comforting for his issues—if you showed up at all. Instead, you showed up with a smile and a wave, like you really want to spend time with me."

"Of course I do," Duncan says, stopping when I hug him tighter, and he wraps his arms around me, holding me close. "That's exactly why I'm here."

"I know," I say softly, pulling his head down for another kiss. I didn't tell him, but the idea of kissing him has gotten more and more attractive to me since our shared kiss in the training room, and as our little pecks grow more and more, I pull him in, our tongues tasting each other, his hands so powerful on my back. Finally, I pull back. "Come on, let's go have some fun. It's been years since I played putt-putt."

We go inside, and I see that there's more than just golf, but a decent-sized arcade center, pizza, the whole nine. "Wow, and you've been here before?"

"Yeah," Duncan says with a laugh. "I like to sometimes get away, and it's fun. Not at all like when I was growing up, you know?"

"Not really," I say honestly, taking his hand. "But I'd like to find out. Where do we start?"

We start with the arcade, where I find out that Duncan is actually a crack shot, at least with a light pistol. His hands move amazingly fast as he shoots down horde after horde of zombies, his eyes flickering side to side. "How'd you get so good at this?" I ask after my forearm cramps up and he's still firing away. "Jesus, watch out!"

A super-zombie, one of those types that are put in these games expressly to make you eat up your tokens, pops out of nowhere and hits us both, ending the game. I'm tempted to drop another token in to continue, but Duncan holsters his pistol and takes my hand. "I learned to shoot when I was a kid. My Dad felt that it was important I learn supposedly 'manly' habits like that, and not end up, and I quote, *one of these Silicon Valley, pansy ass, sissy boys.*"

"Yeesh, what a moron," I exclaim before blushing. "Sorry. Guess that's not something you say about your date's parents."

"Except that it's totally true. Come on. I may have only played half a game, but I'm starving. Let's eat."

We get an extra large pizza with sausage, bacon, and

86

bell peppers, along with Cokes, and find a seat. Just as we do, I hear someone call out Duncan's name again. "What is it with us and food and getting interrupted?"

"I don't know," Duncan says with a laugh. We look over, and I see a guy wearing a frat shirt, Alpha Tau Epsilon, along with what you'd expect a frat guy's girlfriend to be on his arm. "Hello, Joe."

"Good to see you," Joe says, pulling his Barbie-doll date along with him. "Man, after that game . . . you're the last person I expected to see. What happened?"

"Just had a bad day," Duncan says, and I can tell he's not wanting to talk about it. Joe, however, doesn't catch his tone of voice and plows ahead. I've known it for years, but intelligence and the Greek system do not always go hand in hand.

"Seriously, like, you were going Captain Caveman out there. Missy and I were fuckin' stoked to see you here though. Hope, you know . . ."

"No worries," Duncan says. "By the way, this is my date, Carrie Mittel. Carrie, this is Joe and Missy."

"Uh . . . hi," Missy says, surprised as I offer my hand. She shakes before pulling back with an over-the-top shake of her wrist. "Geez, that's a strong grip."

"Carrie's strong," Duncan says, giving Missy a measured look. "She's a great trainer, and one hell of a girlfriend."

I'm too stunned to catch her reply as my mind whirls around Duncan's words. Girlfriend? Did he just really call me his girlfriend? Somebody pinch me, please.

Joe and Missy soon leave, and Duncan turns back,

87

shaking his head. He sees that I'm still staring at him, open-mouthed, and blushes. "Sorry. I swear, that shit doesn't happen everywhere I go."

"It's not that," I say. "Just . . . you just called me your girlfriend."

"I know," Duncan says, smiling, grabbing a slice of pizza and taking a bite. He chews slowly, considering his next words as if he's wondering if he should keep up the cockiness. "For four months now, since the day we met, I haven't been the same. I spend my days hoping to get down to the training room faster and to the library after practice in order to spend time with you. I may have jumped the gun to put that prissy princess in her place, but I still meant what I said."

I nod, a silly grin breaking out on my face, and I take my own slice of pizza. "I think I could get used to being Duncan Hart's girlfriend."

A smile breaks out on his face, and we finish our pizza in a warm haze of dreamy happiness. When we're finished, I'm already ready to ask Duncan to take me back to his place, but instead, he clears away our plates and holds out his hand. "Have a round with me?"

"Careful," I tease, getting up. "Remember, I'm a former softball player. I tend to do well with sports with sticks and balls."

"Then maybe I'll get put in my place," Duncan chuckles, the two of us going out to the course.

I've never seen miniature golf as an exercise in seduction, but then again, I've never played a round with Duncan Hart before. We don't even keep score, just having fun with each other and playing the holes. With each stroke, I'm finding myself laughing and exchanging looks with him, the rest of the patrons or people forgotten as it seems the two of us are sharing our own little private space. When we come to the eighteenth hole, I move in to the ball, and I feel Duncan behind me. "Looks like a difficult shot."

"It is," I agree, looking down the green fake grass, which is lumpy and rising with fake hills. "Think you can lend me a hand?"

Duncan comes closer, his hands coming around to cover mine, and I gasp when his hips snuggle against mine. He's hard, oh, so hard, and I can't help but push back into him, both of us wanting and needing the double layers of denim between us to disappear. "Shh," Duncan says, his voice warm and seductive in my ear. "Let's just do this together."

I'm barely looking at the ball now, instead feeling Duncan's hands on mine, his body pressed into my back, his, oh my God, his cock pushing against my hips. I don't even notice when I bring the putter through, striking the ball and sending it down the course. Without even caring, I drop the putter, turning around to kiss Duncan, only barely noticing when I hear the sound of my ball dropping into the hole. "A hole in one. Nice shot."

"I had help," I whisper in between kisses. "And lots of inspiration."

"So where to now?" Duncan asks, his left hand resting on the upper curve of my ass. "More pizza? Zombies? Another round?"

I shake my head and kiss him again. "Take me to your place," I say with my most sultry look.

The entire ride back, my body is humming, and I can't

wait until we're at his place. He pulls up in front of his apartment building, and while I know it's an upscale, I don't care, my eyes only on him as he lifts me off the bike and into his arms. I wrap my legs around him as he carries me, so strong that I'm no more strain than a feather in his arms, to the elevator and up to his apartment. "Carrie, are you sure?"

"It's okay, Duncan. I trust you," I say, letting go of his body long enough to push off my shoes and strip off my jacket. "I trust you," I repeat.

Duncan stops, his eyes full of emotion. "Carrie—"

"Shh," I say, kissing him again. I peel off his leather jacket and run my hands over his chest, shivering in anticipation. "We can talk afterward. I have only one request."

"What's that?"

I pat his chest, feeling the muscles underneath. "I'm a big girl. I don't break. Show me your strength."

His triumphant, ecstatic growl as he lifts me and carries me back into the bedroom is all the answer I need. We land on the bed in a tangle of arms, legs and bodies, his mouth hot on my neck and his hands needy, demanding as he pulls my t-shirt up and off, leaving me in just my bra and jeans. As he's kissing down, I'm trembling as his lips find the tops of my breasts, his fingers massaging the soft flesh. "Duncan . . ."

"You're perfect," he whispers as he pulls the strap of my bra off my shoulder, flipping the cup down and exposing my breast to him. He stops, and a smile spreads across his face as he sees me exposed to him.

"Yummy." He chuckles before nearly devouring my breast, sucking and licking on my stiff nipple. He rolls it around with his lips, his tongue sending lightning bolts of pleasure through me with every brush over the tip, and I can't believe it feels this good. Even in my fantasies, it wasn't this good. I claw at his shirt, until finally, it pulls free of his jeans, and I can feel the muscles and skin that I've watched flex for so many workouts under my hands. His skin is remarkably soft, while his hands are just slightly rough as he kneads my free breast with his left hand while his right hand does the same to my ass.

When I get Duncan's shirt up high enough, he pauses and sits back, allowing me to peel the shirt the rest of the way off and throw it across the room. I reach back and unhook my bra, freeing myself totally, and then, I unsnap my jeans. I lie back on the bed, starting to take them off when Duncan stops my hands, taking over to peel them the rest of the way down and off. He marvels at my legs, running his hands up and down them, and then, in a total surprise move, kisses my toes. "They're so cute, I couldn't resist."

I giggle and spread my legs slightly, beckoning him forward. "You can kiss anywhere you'd like."

He chuckles and gets off the bed, unsnapping his jeans and going over to his dresser, opening the drawer and coming back with a condom and lubricant. "Safety first."

"Would you like a hand?"

"A hand . . . or a hand?" Duncan says while I start to rub myself with my fingers. My body is already on fire, and I can't resist. He sets the condom and lube on the edge of the bed and reaches for the waistband of his jeans, pushing them the rest of the way down, revealing himself totally to me.

He's perfect. It's the only word that can describe him as his cock hangs in front of him, heavy and huge. I hold my breath as Duncan reaches for the condom next to him, and I suddenly can't. "Wait!"

"What's wrong?" he asks, his eyes suddenly worried. I nod and get to my knees, crawling across the bed and taking the warm, sexy cock in my hand.

"I wanted a taste," I hum before I kiss the tip of his cock, licking around his flared mushroom head, marveling at the taste and texture. I spread my lips around him, swallowing him until his shaft is buried deep in my mouth, pulling back and worshipping his cock. With a gleam in my eye, I swallow him deeper, all the way until the trimmed hairs at his base press against my lips. He's stretching my lips, but my throat has no problem massaging the head of his cock until I pull back, letting him out with a loud pop. "Delicious."

"Holy fuck," Duncan marvels, stroking my face with his hand. "How did you—"

"Never did have much of a gag reflex," I reveal, turning around and pushing my panties down halfway. "Now, I think you can take care of the rest, can't you?"

I hear the foil packet of the condom rip, and then a little squirt as he smears lube on his cock, even though I'm dripping wet and ready for him. He reaches between my legs, rubbing my pussy, and I can't help it, lowering my head and pushing back into his questing digits. He hasn't even penetrated me yet, and I'm on the quaking edge of coming, when I stop, feeling the head of his cock at my entrance. "Oh, yes . . . yes."

Duncan eases his way in slowly, which I'm grateful for. Still, I push back, encouraging him to keep going until I'm at the limits of my ability to stretch, and he pulls back, giving my body a chance to adjust.

92

"So perfect," Duncan whispers as he eases in again, deeper this time, pulling out and pushing in with slow, tender strokes until I feel his thighs settle against my hips. All the way in, and I'm split nearly in half, lost in the sensations and pleasure. "Carrie."

"Don't hold back," I remind him, pulling forward and pushing back onto his amazing cock. "Give me all of it."

Duncan growls again, his hands pushing me forward, crushing me into the bed as he mounts the mattress behind me, my hips in the air and my back bent nearly in half as he starts driving himself into me mercilessly, powerfully, each thrust of his hips smashing into me, obliterating any resistance I could have put up even if I wanted to.

Instead, I'm in heaven. It's never felt this good, each nerve exploding with his punishing thrusts, my body trembling on that heady mix of pleasure and pain that feeds off each other, elevating both. I'm helpless, groaning and lost in the waves of pleasure that shoot through my body, pushing back and begging for more, more, more from him.

Duncan increases his pace and his power, jackhammering into me hard and fast, taking my body to heights of pleasure I've never felt before. I should be coming, but I'm not. There's not enough time between one thrust and the next for the chain reaction to even start, and instead, his cock smashes through any concept I have of sexual ecstasy, my universe coming down to two things. One, that Duncan is the one I've been looking for. And two, that I need to give back to him as good as I'm getting.

The competitive athlete inside me comes forward, and I'm pushing back into him, growling with him, telling him to

93

give me more, harder, to fuck me as hard as he can. We're building, higher and higher, the bed crashing against the wall in front of me, and I'm dripping with sweat, my body exhausted, but I won't give in. He's given me so much, I want to show him that I can take it and give it back to him.

"Carrie . . . I'm going—"

"Come!" I growl, my own body exploding as I feel him swell inside me, and he's coming, his last powerful thrust driving me into the mattress and into oblivion as I climax. I'm crushed beneath him, sandwiched between his powerful body and the mattress beneath me, which is good, because I've lost control of my body. My feet drum on the mattress, my hands scratch at the blanket, and I scream out, unable to control myself as I come harder than I ever have before in my life.

When it finally passes, Duncan pulls me into him, and I feel him shaking behind me, his shoulders quivering as he spoons and holds me. I turn and see there's something in his face. "What is it?"

"You," Duncan whispers, stroking my face. "That was fucking perfect."

"Couldn't have said it better myself," I reply. "Think we can do this again before I leave? Or should I just stay? You're too good to only have once."

Chapter 9
Duncan

Staying the night becomes staying the weekend, and we end up staying in bed most of the day Sunday too. Finally, on Sunday night, I'm taking her home.

"I want to invite you up, but if I do, I don't think I can ask you to leave," she says with a regretful chuckle. "And I've got a test in Organic Chemistry this week. Mid-terms, you know. My teacher's a total pain in the ass too."

"I know," I reply with a smile. I've been smiling all day, it seems, and I can't stop it. Not that I want to. "That's not as crazy as the thoughts going through my head right now, though."

"Which are?"

"Ditch the dorm room. My apartment is a two-bedroom place, though of course, I'd rather you stay in mine. We could turn the other into a study room or something."

Carrie smiles and kisses my cheek. "That sounds

amazing, but let's not move too fast. If things are going well after mid-terms, we can talk about it. I'll see you tomorrow, right?"

I shake my head sorrowfully. "Nope. At least, not at practice. I'm suspended, remember? I meet with Coach B on Tuesday."

"What are you going to do?"

I smile and stroke her hair. It's so beautiful, pale gold and silky, and I've spent all day marveling at it, whether spread out on a pillow underneath me or flung into the air as she rides on top of me. "I'm going to do the right thing, or maybe, just what I know you would want me to do, and what I should do. Don't worry about it right now, though. Go crack those books. I'll see you Tuesday, maybe. We're still on for a study session Tuesday night, right?"

"Right," Carrie says. "Good night, Duncan."

"Good night, Carrie."

I get back on my bike and ride away, stopping by the athletic complex. I don't know why, except that I want to look on the stadium again, even if I can't go inside the Pavilion. I shouldn't even be here. I'm suspended from the team, and I can't even be in the building until Tuesday.

I see someone else outside when I pull up, and as I get closer, the street lamps reveal that it's Alicia Torres. I respect her, even if I've never told her as much. She's got too much heart as a basketball player not to.

"Hey Chicha," I say as I take a seat on the big concrete steps that lead to the upper levels, where you go into the Pavilion in order to get tickets and go to the big arena inside. She hates the nickname. It's one that her big brother gave her

96

when she was a baby, and I'm the only person she lets get away with it. Probably because she knows I don't give a damn if she wants me to use it or not. "I figured basketball would have the day off."

"We do. I came in for some personal work," Alicia says, setting her bag down. "You know, hanging around here isn't the smartest idea. I think there's about a hundred people who want to kick your ass right now."

"Yeah, I figured the same thing. The whole football team, even the scout team Rudys. But . . . well, I've never been the smartest person."

Alicia chuckles and takes a seat on the steps beside me, her bag between us. "You said it—not me. I can understand it though. I mean, I've gotten tossed out of three games myself, and Coach has made it clear that if I get tossed for techs again, I'm sitting out a week."

"You certainly picked the right school to go to, with your personality." I chuckle, and Alicia joins in. "But?"

"But, I've never heard of you losing control like that. I was in the stands, and I'll be honest, it scared the hell outta me watching you. You were about ready to kill someone, I think."

"At the time," I sigh, looking at the distinctive arcs of the lights of the football stadium curving up into the night, dark but still visible against the background lights of the city. "I probably was. You're right. I've never lost control like that before."

Alicia hums, as if she'd expected it. "I don't know what caused it. Honestly, I don't really care, either . . . no offense."

A car pulls up before I can reply, and Alicia grabs her bag. "That's my ride. Take care of yourself, Duncan, and get your head right. Good luck with Coach B on Tuesday."

Alicia jogs down the steps and climbs in. In the dome light, I see that the driver is a guy, and she gives him a kiss on the cheek as she slides into the passenger side before the door closes and they drive off.

After she leaves, I lean back, looking up at the moon, my mind spinning at what she said about me losing control. My dad really has done a number on me.

Up to this point in my life, as much as I disliked him, I've been just like my father. I've been Winston Hart, recast in a younger, slightly more athletic frame. Hell, Dad was a basketball player in college, and Mom, at least before she got tired of his shit and took off, was an athlete as well. She was wife number two for him, about five years younger . . . and he cheated on her soon after I was born, at least from what I've heard. I wish Mom had stuck around longer, or at least to see me, but after Dad's lawyers got done with her, she moved back to New Jersey, where she was from. I'm not even sure how that happened, but with money, I guess I shouldn't be surprised. I haven't heard from Mom in years.

I'm just another bastard, I guess. But I don't want to be. Maybe there is a good guy inside me, a guy who can be worthy of a woman like Carrie. But when is that guy going to come out? When am I going to be able to move past the mental fuckeduppedness and become that man, and not the overgrown, horny boy I am now?

Too late for Carrie, that's for sure. I don't want to hurt her. She's too special. If I can't be a good enough man for her, there's no reason for me to string her along. Next time, after we get together again, I'll make my move. I'll give her the Hart

98

Attack and then break it off. Sure, it'll hurt in the short term, but it'll be better for both of us in the end.

I walk over to my bike and climb on. Riding home, I only wish I could break it off with Carrie faster—save her the pain.

*You mean save **yourself** some pain.*

Fuck you, conscience. Where were you the past four years?

Still here, but you didn't listen to me before. You just pushed me away.

What the fuck was I supposed to do?

Stop being a coward, is what you need to do. Man the fuck up. Talk to Carrie. She deserves that much.

I rev my engine, and instead of going back to the apartment, I turn right, heading for the freeway. I need speed, and right now, the freeway is exactly what I need.

Chapter 10
Carrie

"No, really Mom. I have a boyfriend."

Mom's looking at me like I'm nuts, and I guess it has been a while since I've been this excited to share the news with my parents that I'm seeing someone. Then again, when you compare Duncan and the weekend we just had to any other guy I've ever gone out on a date with . . . there's no comparison.

We made *love*. Oh, sure, we didn't use those words, and there wasn't any mention of the L-word between us, but hey, a girl can hope.

Mom, however, isn't so optimistic. "Honey, that's nice to hear, I guess. Who is it?"

"Duncan Hart. He's one of the guys on the football team. We kinda met that way."

"I see," Mom says, and there's movement in the

background, and Dad comes into the field of view. "Vince, Carrie's seeing someone."

"Oh really?" Dad says, taking a seat next to her. They're in the living room of our house, it looks like, and Dad looks tired. He must have just gotten back from another run. "Who is it, sweetheart?"

"Duncan Hart. He's the tight end for the Bulldogs."

They both look less than pleased, and I lean back, crossing my arms. "What is it? I figured you guys would be happy for me. You know, two years without a boyfriend and all?"

"It's not that, honey," Dad says, looking over at Mom. "It's just that . . . well, he's a football player. And I think I know that name."

"He's got a good chance of going pro next year. First round, even."

Dad nods, then sighs. "Carrie, football players tend to be . . . well, they tend to have egos and personas that aren't exactly our style."

"You mean you think because he's a star on the team, that he's a superstar in real life?" I shoot back, getting angry. How could my parents be upset like this? "He's a good guy. Perfect? No, but a good guy. And he's making something of himself."

"Yeah, a million-dollar contract and a trophy wife," Dad gripes, then winces. "Sorry, I shouldn't have said that."

"No, you shouldn't have," I say, then take a deep breath. I don't want to blow up with my parents, especially over a video chat. Any time you get mad at someone over the Internet, you just end up feeling like an ass later. "Listen, I need

101

to study. I've got a mid-term tomorrow. I need to crack the books on it. I'll talk to you later."

I hang up before they can reply, and turn away, frustrated. I don't really need to study. After my initial struggles with Organic Chemistry, I've gotten the hang of it pretty well. A lot of it is that I'm able to connect it back to my training studies, and to be honest, tutoring Duncan. Which, I think as I smile to myself, he hardly needs. He could pass that class with or without my help, but it's nice to be able to spend time with him on what I guess we can now call study dates.

Something I look forward to more and more.

* * *

"Okay, class, you will have exactly ninety minutes to complete the test and turn it in. Please make sure you show your work on any mathematical calculations, and fill out your test papers legibly, please? I'm not going to go back to try to figure out any chicken scratches, so if I can't read it, it gets marked wrong, regardless of what you mean to say."

"Good luck," I hear whispered behind me, and I turn, surprised to see Chelsea Brown sitting there.

"What are you doing in this class?" I ask, surprised. "I've never seen you before."

"Don't let it get out, but I took this class when I was a sophomore," she whispers back. "I only pulled a 'C' though, so I was hoping to audit the course and maybe get a better grade this time. Unfortunately for me, I forgot that I have my capstone course exactly thirty minutes after this class starts, so I've been mostly just reviewing the online lectures and the notes. At least I can't get lower than a C this time!"

I chuckle and turn back forward as Professor Vladisova

comes by, passing out the test papers face down on the desk. She's a major pain in the ass, but I can deal with it. Science is science, not a matter of whether you like your professor or not, and as she comes back around to the front of the classroom, she looks over everyone with her cold, dark eyes. "You may begin."

* * *

As I'm coming up on the last ten questions, I feel my phone vibrate in my pocket. I know I should leave it alone, but if I do, then the tone on my voicemail is going to go off. It's a weird setting, I know, but it works for me, and I pull the phone out, seeing that it's Duncan. "Miss Mittel?"

"Sorry, Professor," I say, hitting the *Call Cancel* button. I quickly type out a text message. *What?*

Can you talk? Please.

I look at the clock, and see that I still have plenty of time, thirty minutes with only ten problems remaining. I stand up, setting my pencil and paper face down on my desk. I leave the room and head into the hallway, calling Duncan as I go.

"Hey. How was the test?"

His voice sounds a little strange, and I frown. What's wrong? "I still have thirty minutes on it. I probably shouldn't have left class to call you . . . you know I'm in the middle of the test, right? It must be important."

"Oh, damn, I forgot. Listen, can you meet me at the stadium right after your test is finished? It's important."

I'm still getting this weird feeling about his voice, but maybe it's just the stress that he's feeling. After all, he is supposed to be meeting with the football coaches today about his suspension. "Sure. At one?"

"One is good enough. Thanks, Carrie. See you."

Duncan hangs up, and I put my phone back in my pocket. I'm worried. His voice just sounded . . . weird. Like he was upset about something, or maybe sad? And I still don't understand how he could've forgotten I was in my test, but I don't have time to think about it. I still need to finish my test.

Professor Vladisova is giving me a strange look when I come back in from the hallway, but I brush it off, sitting down and turning my test back over. I'm lucky the last ten questions are easy. I'd crammed them last night, and they are almost direct copies from the book. I finish them just as the Professor calls out the five-minute warning, and I check my paper for last-minute mistakes or stupid errors. "Time."

Going up, I hand in my paper, and she's still looking at me strangely. "Sorry, Professor," I say, thinking maybe she's upset about me taking a personal call during test time. "I had a personal issue. My boyfriend."

"I see, Miss Mittel," she says and sets my paper down. I turn to leave. I have just enough time to get to the stadium by one o'clock if I hurry. I rush back and grab my bag, heading out the door with a quick goodbye to Chelsea, who's still sitting calmly, a little smile on her face. She must have done well on the test.

I get to the stadium just a few minutes before one and see Duncan by the tunnel that leads from the outside to the inside of the stadium. It's currently locked, but it's a common meet-up point, and I wave as I see him. Rushing over, I jump into his arms, giving him a big kiss. "Damn you! You nearly got me in trouble, but it's so good to see you!"

"I missed you too," Duncan says, his voice still strange,

104

but his hands are working their magic again, and I feel the warmth spreading through me. "Yesterday was so hard without you."

"I'm sorry about that," I force out between kisses, trying to think, but his lips are nibbling on my earlobe, and it's so hard to think. He cups my ass, and I groan deeply, unable to help myself. "What are you doing?"

"Needing you," Duncan says, pushing me up against the concrete wall. "I need you so much."

"Duncan, slow down," I reply, pushing him away with effort. I'm breathing hard, my nipples are aching inside my bra, and my body is aching for him . . . but why is my heart not into this?

I see it in his eyes. Oh no. Oh, fuck no.

"Carrie, I need something special before the meeting," Duncan says, his eyes dead even as his voice drips with desire.

He comes toward me again, and I put my hands up, pushing him away. "No. You're not going to do it."

"Do what? I just need you," Duncan says, and I let my anger give me strength. I shove him back, away from me, and he takes a full step backward before stopping.

"What you need is to stop running away," I state, stepping away from the wall. "I know what you're trying to do. For some reason . . . I've had this gut feeling ever since that call. For some unknown fucking reason, you think that you need to *Hart Attack* me, don't you? Don't you?"

"Come on, Carrie," Duncan says, his voice desperate. He's tormenting himself, and for some reason, he's not thinking clearly. "It's the only way. I don't want to hurt you."

"You think a quick romp and then cutting me loose will

105

make it any better? I see it written all over your face," I yell, jabbing him in the chest. He takes another step back, but I follow, staying right in his face. "Well, Duncan Hart, I'm not going to let you do it. Do you understand me? I won't let you run away this time."

"What do you mean?" Duncan asks, his voice trying to play it off, but falling far short.

"This weekend, it wasn't just some weekend sex marathon. I saw it in your eyes when you dropped me off Sunday. I don't know what's changed since then, since you told me you wanted to become a better person. And I don't know what inner demons are telling you that you need to do this, but you need to choke them down, kill them! Kill those demons, because they're tearing you apart. You don't really want to do this. You just want an excuse."

"An excuse for what?" Duncan says, his eyes shimmering with emotion and pain. "For what?"

"An excuse to not fight those demons. Here's what's going to happen—I'm going to walk away right now, and you're going to stay here and think. Have your meeting with the coaches and find out what's going to happen. I'm going to go down to the weight room, do my workout for Coach T, and wait. I'll wait as long as you need me to, because I care about you."

"What if I can't fight them?" Duncan asks, backing away to lean against the concrete on the far side of the tunnel. "What if I can't fight it?"

"You can. I know you can. I'll help, but you have to take that first step yourself. When you're ready, call me. I'll be there, I promise you. I want to be a couple, not a threesome

106

with you, me, and your inner demons."

I stand up and walk away, trying not to cry, but the best I can do is force one foot in front of another, crossing the street and going down the steps to the basement of the Pavilion. Once inside, I find the nearest bathroom and have the cry that I've needed, and I blow my nose loudly before standing back up. I have work to do.

Chapter 11
Duncan

I'll help, but you have to take that first step.

I feel Carrie's words swimming in my head, and I should be angry, pissed off. I've never been turned down like that before. When it comes to bedding girlfriends, Duncan Hart bats a thousand, and each time, it's a home run.

This time, though, I'm not. I'm crushed, and Carrie's words rip through my mind, hot knives through butter. I'm not supposed to be this way. I'm supposed to be the guy who breaks the girl, not the guy who gets broken. I'm the alpha, the stud . . . and I'm sitting here speechless as she walks away.

The demon, the voice that Carrie was just telling me about, pats me on the shoulder, chuckling and whispering in my ear.

Fuck it. Go find another bitch, clear your mind. New pussy does wonders, don't you know?

Fuck you. You're the son of a bitch that got me in this mess. You're the one that keeps bringing me back to square one. I'm sick and tired of being sick and tired. Because for once, I have someone who isn't going to run away, who can be strong when I'm not.

. . .

There's no answer, and I know that at least, for a moment, I've beaten the inner demon back. I know it's temporary, but I need to build on it. I look at my watch and see that I have ten minutes to get to my meeting with Coach Bainridge. I don't want to waste a minute of time, especially with my temporary reprieve.

I knock on Coach's outer office, and I see Coach Thibs sitting down at one of the other desks, reviewing something on his tablet. "Duncan. I didn't expect you for another ten minutes. You're five minutes early."

I nod, stepping inside the office. "I know. Is Coach Bainridge here?"

Coach Thibs nods and stands up. "He got done with the AD about half an hour ago. He asked that I come in with you, so that we have a witness. You okay with that?"

I swallow and nod, and follow Thibs into Coach B's office. He's sitting down, waiting. Obviously, he heard me and Coach Thibs out in the other room. "Sit down, Duncan."

"Yes, sir," I say, and I see Thibs give me a double take. Bainridge, however, has probably seen players pull the penitent act before, and he isn't buying it. He's been around the coaching game longer than I've been alive, after all. He's not going to listen to some sob story. Nope, it's time to man the fuck up.

108

"Duncan, do you how much damage your little outburst cost?"

Of course I have. Not only the inside track on the conference title, but seven spots in the polls. We went from knocking on the top ten, to barely hanging out in the polls at all. I've already read two stories calling Western the 'paper Bulldogs' after that loss. I know the damage.

"Yes, sir," I say again, choking off the inner demon before he can get a word out. I clamp my hands down on the armrests of the chair, squeezing until the wood groans under my fingers. "I hurt the team."

"Damn right, you did," Coach says, leaning forward. "Duncan, I've lost a lot of games. Even the best coaches do. But one thing I've always tried to do, even with prima donnas like you, is make sure that you got the concept of team first, individual second. I thought we talked about this back in the summer."

"We did, sir. Right before my elbow evaluation."

Coach nods and taps his pen on his desk, looking at me. "I thought you'd gotten that message. You kept up your smack talk, but you put in the work. I even tried to meet you halfway, asking Coach Taylor to assign that trainer you worked with over the summer. You certainly responded, and put up games that finally spoke of the talent that I've seen in you for four years. Then comes Saturday . . ."

"Yes, sir. I have no excuse for my actions. I was out of line."

It's Bainridge's turn to be surprised, I think he expects me to argue with him about this. But he's right, and in my mind, I keep telling myself that this is for Carrie and for myself. *For us.*

"All right. The Athletic Director wants me to give you a verbal warning. At the end of the day, you put asses in seats. We lose again, and we've got no chance at the conference championship. If it were up to me, I'd have benched your ass for the rest of the season, conference championship or not. However, I think I will go with Coach Thibedeau's suggestion."

"Which is?"

Coach Thibs speaks up for the first time. "One game suspension, provided you do two things. First, you behave yourself. Second, you help me work with coaching Carlson, who's going to be playing tight end this Saturday. You will not dress for practice. You'll be in track pants and a t-shirt. Coach him in the video meetings. The kid's a freshman, and he's raw."

I think about it, then shake my head. "No. I need one more thing, coach."

Bainridge raises an eyebrow, his voice full of threat. "You're not in a position to demand anything, Duncan."

"Hear me out, Coach. I think you'll approve of this."

* * *

A hundred sets of angry eyes stare at me as I get onto the short stand that Coach Bainridge likes to use to look down on practice when we're running drills. He's got another tower, one he uses when we're doing full team practices, but that thing's too high for this.

"Duncan Hart has something he'd like to say," Coach Thibedeau says to the group. "Take a quick knee. Duncan?"

I look around and clear my throat. If I'm to be honest, I need to do this right. "I'm sorry," I call out, making sure my voice is loud enough that even the kickers screwing around in the back can hear me. "I'm sorry, and there's no excuse for what I did. I thought only about myself, and I've been doing that for too long. I've been a bad teammate, a terrible leader, and an even worse friend to some of you. Coach Bainridge has suspended me for this Saturday's game, and I've accepted that. But I know that whatever Coach says, it's you guys who will really decide when my suspension ends. I just want to be a Bulldog again. I want to be part of the team. I've asked Coach, and he's agreed to let me help out in practice, but I can't dress. I'll do what I can to help."

I turn toward Coach T and step down from the stands. As I pass him, he says something quietly, and I turn to him. "What was that, Coach?"

"I said, good apology. Let's see you back it up. But it's a good first step."

First steps. Maybe today is all about first steps.

I'm standing with Coach Thibs for most of practice as he gets to work with Carlson. I've barely given the kid the time of day all season so far. He was just some scrub underneath me, but now, I'm forcing myself to focus on him, watch him as he sets up, drilling, running routes, trying to step up to the first team offense level.

About fifteen minutes after passing drills start, I watch Carlson try a flag route, but his cut step is sloppy, and if he does that in the game this weekend, it won't be pretty.

"Carlson!" I yell after the play is over, pulling him over. He's trying hard, I can see that, but he needs to focus. "All right, you've gotta make sure—make all of your steps razor sharp, got it?"

"I am," Carlson says, and he's sucking wind. He doesn't run this much in practice, normally, and he's nervous. "He's

111

just too fast."

"You're bigger and stronger, so if you stick him at the line, then make your cuts sharp, you'll get the separation you need. Like this."

I turn to Coach, who's looking at me, intrigued. "One more time?"

Coach shrugs and turns to Tyler. "Run it again!"

"Watch me," I say, lining up in slot like Carlson is supposed to. The defensive back, a senior named Joe Manfredi, who also has some potential pro-level skill, is giving me a look like I'm crazy. Today is Tuesday, full contact day, and that rule applies whether you're wearing a helmet or not.

The ball is hiked, and I grab Joe's shoulder pads before he can make contact with me, snapping him down and to the side, knocking him just enough off-balance to give me half a step on him. I take off, losing that half-step quickly as my tennis shoes don't grip the turf as well as cleats, but I cut hard anyway, turning just in time to catch Tyler's pass. I turn to go upfield when I get hit from the side to land painfully on the turf, seeing Joe looking down on me.

"Good route," Joe says before offering me a hand. "Think you can get Carlson to do that?"

"We'll see."

* * *

"You what, Coach?"

"You heard me, Duncan. For four days, you've worked your ass off with Carlson, telling him every hint you can think of," Coach Bainridge says. It's already five thirty, we have a primetime kickoff in an hour, and I feel like I've just been smacked in the head. "I've been watching. You've taken the

112

comments, you've cut out the trash talk, but most of all . . . you've tried to be a good teammate."

It's what I want to be. It's what's stopped me from calling Carrie. I have to prove to myself that I can take this step alone. She's never been far from my thoughts, and my sleep has been spotty at best, but I have to make this step if I'm ever going to be the man she deserves.

"I . . . I want Carlson to do a good job, that's all. I want the team to win."

Coach studies me for a minute, then reaches beneath his desk, pulling out my jersey. "Here. I notified the AD and the game crew. Your suspension is reduced to the first half only. I know you haven't practiced, but you're still the best tight end in the conference. Think you can get suited up and join your teammates for warmups?"

I can't believe my luck, and I catch the tossed jersey, turning and running back to the locker room. One of the equipment managers must have gotten the message as well, because my gear is sitting there, my pants already prepared, my helmet gleaming. "Holy shit."

"You gonna sit there and curse, or get your shoulder pads ready?" Tyler asks behind me, and I turn to see him giving me a smile. "Bainridge won't tell you this, but a group of us went to him and asked him to let you play today."

"Why? Who?"

"Why? Because we need to win, and you help us do that. Who? Everyone, Carlson included. Now go get ready."

I quickly get my things together and run down to the trainer's room, wishing for the first time all week that Carrie was there. Instead, I find Chelsea Brown. "Hey, Chelsea, can

113

you help me with my hands?"

"No elbow?" She asks, and I shake my head. There's no time for it, and Carrie's words echo in my brain.

"Just the hands. Besides, you guys know that I've only worn it as a crutch for a while."

"Okay," Chelsea replies, grabbing the tape. "So they're going to let you play?"

"The second half. But I want to be ready in case."

Chelsea starts wrapping my hands the way I like, running the pre-wrap over my wrists but leaving the backs of my hands bare. She does my left hand first, then my right, and she kind of lingers like she wants to say something, but she doesn't. I don't give it a second thought.

I give her a quick thanks and rush back to the locker room to grab my helmet and gloves, getting up to the field just as the team starts group warmups. The sun is almost down, and the lights are bright as I run out, dazzling me for a moment, and I feel the familiar rush of adrenalin. I hear a surprised roar from the crowd, but this time, I don't care about it. I'm totally focused on the team and take the rearmost position in the warmup lines.

We run through things, and I continue to coach Carlson throughout. We rehearse a move I showed him, something Coach Thibs borrowed from the Western Judo Club, and we finish warmups. Going back inside, Carlson stops in the tunnel, grabbing my shoulder pad. "Hey."

"Yeah?"

"Thanks, Duncan. For everything this week."

The first half of the game is tough. Western's hanging in, but the Silverados have a very stingy defense. Carlson's fighting his ass off, but he's just not able to hang in there, and with the offense unable to get anything going, the defense is getting tired. The breakthrough happens with five minutes left in the second quarter, when the Silverados hit a deep pass that puts them up by a touchdown, and then, just before halftime, he nails an amazingly long field goal.

The horn goes off, and the team runs back into the locker room. After his few words to the team as a whole, Coach Bainridge comes over to me. "You ready to go in?"

"Whatever you need, Coach."

He nods, then drops his bomb. "I want you on special teams too. They're burning us on kickoff and punt coverage, and I need someone who can form a blocking wall for the runners. Can you do it?"

Special teams. The suicide squad that is normally made up of second-stringers or crazy dudes who don't care about their health. If running routes and getting tackled is like getting into a minor car accident, special teams is like a car accident on the freeway going high-speed.

"Get me out there. Whatever you need."

Coach nods again, and the trembles start. I haven't felt the trembles since high school, and I know what they are. I'm not scared. I just want to get on the field, to play and fight and win.

* * *

One minute left. No more timeouts. We're down seventeen-thirteen. We need a touchdown, and it's seventy-two yards away.

"All right, guys, this is where we make ourselves famous," Tyler jokes in the huddle, looking around. I look

115

around, too, and see my teammates. They're exhausted, beaten up, and just a little way from crumbling. We need to get fired up, and Tyler's trying.

He calls a run play, risky at this point in the game, but the Silverados aren't expecting it either. If we toss it to the outside, we have a chance to gain yards and still get out of bounds.

I pop the defensive end before releasing to the outside. I see the defensive back coming on a collision course with our running back. I lower my shoulder and crash into his side, my body already aching from blocking on punts and kickoffs, but I don't care. The guy is blasted off his feet, and as I go tumbling down with him, I see our runner scamper for eight yards before running out of bounds, stopping the clock.

"All right, all right!" Tyler yells when we reform the huddle. Forty-nine seconds left. "That's what the fuck I'm talking about!"

"Tyler," I groan, and I'm feeling something grating in my elbow. I don't care. They'll have to chop off my arm to get me out of the game right now. "Let's close it out. I don't have two minutes left in me."

Tyler pulls me up and looks me in the eye. "Think you can do it, Touchdown? Or do we get Carlson in here?"

I nod. "I got this. After this, though, nobody calls me Touchdown."

"You catch the ball, and I'll make sure of it. Don't fuck this up, Duncan."

"See you in the end zone."

We line up, and I can see the defense running through their schemes, adjusting to our formation.

116

I release quickly, praying that our right tackle can give Tyler enough time to get the ball off. I cut out on a flag route, turning my head to see the pass already in the air. Tyler's let it go just a little long, and I urge my tired legs to go just a bit faster, to cover the space a bit quicker.

It's on my fingertips, and I pull it in, knowing that my hectic pace sent me off-route. I'm in the defensive back's zone now, and he's closing from behind fast, the free safety coming up fast on my left. I juke, spinning off one guy to feel the other hit me.

I bounce, refusing to go down. No fucking way, not with everything on the line. I run, as hard as I can, my arm screaming from that last hit but my fingers refusing to let go of the ball. I've been sitting on my ass nearly all week, and I'm tired, forgetting how much football hurts.

The goal line is only ten yards away . . . eight . . . five . . . two . . .

Someone hits me from behind, and I reach out with everything I have, praying I'm close enough. I can only hope the ball doesn't tumble from my fingers as I reach, pulling my knees up to prevent the ball from being blown down from an early touch.

I hit the ground and hear a whistle. The wind's been knocked out of me. I can't do much more than move my head, which is jammed into the turf enough that I can barely breathe. I turn my head to the side to see the side judge standing, his arms over his head signaling the touchdown, highlighted against the bright glare of the stadium lights and the black of the night sky beyond. It's the best touchdown I've ever scored, even if it's not the prettiest.

117

Twenty-four seconds left, and we're up, nineteen to seventeen. Someone pulls me to my feet, and I see it's Tyler, who's grinning. "How's it feel, hero?"

I look around, seeing the stadium still exploding in cheers, and my chest is heaving, I'm so winded. I hope I'm in better shape next game, or I'll die by the third quarter. "I need some fucking Gatorade."

Tyler pounds me on the back, laughing. "Done. And then?"

"I want to call Carrie."

Chapter 12
Carrie

I wake up on Sunday, and I'm feeling good. I'd caught the game on television, and I have to admit that I cheered when Duncan caught his touchdown pass.

I'd kept up to date with what he was doing, even if I was intentionally keeping myself away from football. Coach Taylor could tell Thursday that something was up, and he told me what Duncan had been doing. I prayed, as I slipped off to sleep on Saturday, that he'd call me soon.

Waking up Sunday, I know that I need him. My arms ache, and more importantly, my heart aches as I think of him, the sight of him hugging his teammates after his touchdown. The talking heads after the game were, of course, heaping praise on him, saying that perhaps the half-game benching helped him.

My phone rings, and I'm excited, thinking that perhaps it's Duncan, but my excitement fades when I see that the number is a landline, although one I don't know. "Hello?"

The voice on the other end is a bit stuffy, officious, but unconsciously so, like someone who has been doing it for so long, they don't even realize it. "Miss Mittel? This is Lawrence Friar, Vice Dean of the Academic Board."

Vice Dean of the Academic Board. The Honor Committee. They're one of the staples of Western, and one of the reasons I'd selected the school. Modeled after the successful and long-running boards in the Ivy League and at the military academies, the Honor Committee has one purpose: to eliminate cheating. Even the athletes aren't exempt. An athlete at Western might get tutoring, might get easy classes, but they do have to turn in their own work and take their own tests.

"Good morning, Dean Friar. How can I help you?"

"There's no easy way to say this, so I'll cut straight to the point. Miss Mittel, there's been an accusation of cheating."

"Oh no! Well, of course, I'll be happy to help the Board in any way I can. Who is the accusation against?"

"It's against you, Miss Mittel. Would you mind coming to the Board offices?"

I'm shocked. What the hell is going on? "Of—of course. When?"

"As soon as you can would be best. We'd like to clear this up as quickly as possible."

"Y—yes, of course. Me too. This must be some sort of misunderstanding."

"I hope so, Miss Mittel. Please, as soon as you can."

I roll out of bed and grab the nearest set of clothes I can find, pulling on some jeans and a t-shirt. I walk across campus, trying to figure out what the hell could have caused someone to level an Honor charge against me. I mean, I make sure to list all my sources for all my papers, which I know is the biggest thing that people get rapped for by the Honor Board.

The Board has its own separate building on campus, a small, octagonal building that's made of granite, with a peaked roof that gives it an intimidating air, and the only windows are narrow slits on the upper floors. Frankly, I've always thought the Honor building looks like a cross between an old-fashioned jail tower and a rocket ship and has a sort of Gothic intimidation that would be complete if they would put the stocks or a gallows out front. I walk up to the heavy front doors and pull, finding them locked. Before I can think that perhaps I just got punked, the intercom next to the door buzzes. "Miss Mittel?"

"Yes, the doors are locked."

"I'll be right down."

I stand at the front of the building, feeling my nervousness grow with each second that passes. I start shifting back and forth, not sure what is going on, but I can't help my jitters. Finally, just when I'm about to hit the button on the intercom again, the heavy doors unlock, and the door opens up. They're bigger than normal doors, at least ten feet tall, and I see as they're pushed open that they're thick, too. In fact, if there's ever a zombie attack, the Honor building is a very good place to take cover.

"Miss Mittel, I'm Dean Friar. Please, come inside."

He's probably a little over fifty years-old, with a big shock of white hair on top of his head that looks slightly curly, like maybe he should be the sort of man who always keeps his hair short in order to keep it under control, but he doesn't. He's probably been in academia his entire adult life and cut his teeth on the wild days of the seventies.

"Dean, I would love to know what this is about. I mean, I've never cheated on anything in my life." Now that I have someone to talk to, my jitters stop, but my nervousness doesn't. If anything, I'm getting more nervous by the second.

"I understand, but we need to go through the process. Follow me, please."

We go upstairs, where I see Professor Vladisova sitting in a conference room. There's only one conclusion that comes to mind—my organic midterm. "Professor? Do you think I cheated on the test?"

"You left the test room for several minutes," the Professor says in her heavily accented English, tapping a paper in front of her. "You come back in, sit down, and rattle off the rest of your questions at nearly impossible speeds, scoring them perfectly. Too perfectly, in fact."

"What?" I don't know what to say other than that. I'm being accused of cheating because I answered the test questions too perfectly?

"The Professor suspects that during that time you left the room, you looked up course materials," Dean Friar explains, gesturing me to a seat. "Now, this is just a preliminary questioning. Maybe we can clear this up. If so, then no formal paperwork will be started against you. It's also why I called you on Sunday. I hope we can clear this up without any disruption to your academic schedule. I've been doing this for a long time, and I don't like disrupting the lives of good students."

"Thank you, Dean. Professor, I swear to you, I didn't cheat on the test. I studied the night before, and those last questions, I noticed they were lifted almost totally word for word out of the book. Since I had just studied them, I was able to answer them quickly, that's all."

"Is it true that you left the test room with your cellphone?" Dean Friar asks. He's taken a seat at the table, his fingers folded in front of him, and I suspect that somewhere, something is recording what we're saying.

I nod. "Yes. I got a text message from someone, and it

seemed important, so I stepped out to call them back. I explained I was still in the middle of a mid-term—they'd forgotten. After saying goodbye, I went back into the test room and went back to work."

"So you deny using the phone to look anything up?"

I nod my head vigorously. "Dean, if there were any benefits I got from that phone call, it was that I was somewhat distracted and got my out of my own way with the answers. I was kinda in another frame of mind after getting the call."

Dean Friar nods, then looks over at Professor Vladisova. "Is there anything else to your suspicions, Professor?"

She nods, and taps the paper in front of her again. "This. I was made aware of Miss Mittel's cheating by another student. I have a written statement from that student saying that she saw Miss Mittel using her phone for cheating purposes during the test time."

"What? No way!" I yell, caught off guard. "Who is making up lies like that?"

"The complaint came from Miss Brown, who was sitting behind you in the test. She says she saw you pull your phone out to access the Internet multiple times."

"No! She's lying! I—" I try to defend myself, but the name just hits me in the gut. Chelsea? Why is she saying I cheated? What the hell is going on? "The phone stayed in my pocket until that message. You even noticed the first time I pulled it out."

"This can be easy to clear up, then. Miss Mittel, does your phone have Internet capability?" Dean Friar asks. "I mean, not everyone has a smartphone, but many do."

"I do, sir," I reply, taking it out. "Here, take a look at my logs. I didn't access the Net the entire time. I only had the one text message, and then a phone call."

Dean Friar nods and turns on my phone. He swipes at the screen for a second, then turns it back around, handing it back to me. "Would you mind unlocking it?"

"Of course, sir. Just a minute."

I enter my password and hand the phone back to him, who taps at my screen. I don't know what this proves, though. I could've easily just erased my browsing history. Instead, the Dean's face goes more pinched a minute or two later, and he sets the phone down to look at me. "Mind explaining this?"

I pick up my phone and see that the Dean's pulled up my data usage statistics for the phone with some app. The log shows . . . data usage during the test? What the fuck? "I . . . I can't explain this, sir. I didn't use the phone during that time, except what I've told you."

"Well, your data logs show that you accessed over twenty megabytes of usage on the day of the test," Dean Friar says. "Did you happen to use the phone to browse the web during that day?"

"No. I have my laptop, and my data plan doesn't cover anywhere near that much."

"Well, let's check your browser history then," Dean Friar says, taking the phone back and tapping away. How in the hell does this man know how to pull up all this stuff on my phone? *I* don't even know how to do that.

"Trust me, there's no—"

"Access of the course notes and lectures in your browser history?" He asks, showing me the phone. His wintry

124

smile has totally disappeared, and Vladisova is looking like she's about to burst a blood vessel, she's so pissed off. "Miss Mittel, you seem to be digging yourself a deeper and deeper hole."

"No. There must be a mistake. I didn't cheat, I—I studied." That sounds pathetic, even to my ears. I might as well have *Liar & Cheat* on my shirt.

"I hope that's the case. Miss Mittel, based on this, I still have to notify you of your rights under the Western University Honor Code . . ."

* * *

I'm in a daze as I walk back to my room, my fingers numb, and twice, I trip over random things in my path.

I get back to my room without killing myself and sag into my chair, still trying to figure out what the fuck just happened. I reach into my pocket to call Coach Taylor. He's always been sort of a mentor, but then I remember that I left my phone with Dean Friar. He said that the Honor Board would return my phone to me by Tuesday. I could have fought that, but what's the point? I'd look even more guilty than I do right now.

My computer beeps, and I see that I'm getting a call. I don't want to, but I get up and go over anyway, hoping that maybe this day could have at least some good news in it. I see that it's Mom and Dad, and I open the call. "Hey guys."

"What's wrong, sweetie?" Mom asks immediately. That's Mom. I can't put anything past her. She's always been able to read me like a book. "You look upset."

I think about lying but decide against it. I mean, what's the point? "I've run into some trouble, Mom."

"What kind of trouble, Carrie?" Mom asks. She turns

125

her head and hollers over her shoulder. "Vince! Come here!"

"Mom!" I protest when she turns back around. "I'm not in preschool any more."

"No, but you don't need to repeat yourself either. Might as well let him hear you the first time," she counters, and I can't argue. Mom works as an office manager, and she's always been a person who focuses on efficiency. Then again, when you have to measure your family time in blocks between your husband disappearing on the road for a week or more at a time driving a truck, and you're balancing a full-time job and a young daughter, efficiency is important.

"What's this about trouble?" Dad says, coming into the room on the other side, and he takes a seat. "What happened?"

"I've been accused of cheating on my Organic Chemistry mid-term," I said, trying to control my emotions. "The Dean of the Honor Board asked me some questions today."

"What? I mean, I assume you didn't cheat, but why would they think you did?" Dad asks, and I take a deep breath, trying to think of what to say.

"Of course I didn't cheat. I got a single text message and stepped out to call Duncan back, then went back and took my test. But they're saying that I was pulling up course notes and lectures during the test time. My phone apparently even says so—it says I cheated. All I did was talk to Duncan for like . . . two minutes."

"Duncan," Dad says. "That's the football player you were seeing, right?"

"He is, but he didn't have anything to do with it. Another student, a girl I thought was a friend, accused me, and

126

my professor went to the Board. Now I'm in deep shit, and I don't know why she'd accuse me."

Dad gets angry, and I can see he's about to go off. His face is getting red. "I can tell you exactly how. I'll bet you anything that slime ball had something to do with it."

I try to force myself to stay calm, but it's getting increasingly difficult. "I think I know him a little better than you do. I've been on the training intern staff for a year and a half now, remember? I've been working with him daily since June. We took a long time before we decided to start seeing each other."

Well, that's on pause right now, but I'm not going to tell you guys that, but that's beside the point.

Dad, though, is already in full-on rant mode. "That may be true, Carrie, but he's scum. After you called, I checked up on him—just Google him, and it's like a bad tabloid story. Parties, off-campus incidents, and a list of girls on his arm that stretches for pages. I thought I raised you better than that!"

I take a deep breath and close my eyes for a few seconds before I look at the screen again. "I understand you want to protect me, but I'm an adult, and I know what I'm getting myself into with Duncan. But let's get one thing straight—Duncan had nothing to do with this. He isn't the one accusing me of cheating . . . so let's just stop talking about him."

Dad turns redder, and I get a little worried about him. The last thing he needs is something to run his blood pressure up. Mom looks at him, and then interjects before any more stress can be built up. "So what happens now, Carrie?"

"Well, effective immediately, I'm suspended from the

training staff and all my extracurricular activities," I say, which is probably the most painful part of what has happened. If I could at least go down to the training room or weight room, I could talk it over with Coach Taylor, maybe release some stress on the floor. "So that's going to give me a lot of free time that I really don't want."

"What else?"

"I can still go to class so I won't fall behind, but all my grades and GPA are in limbo until the Board has its full hearing. That's in a month."

"What? Why a month?" Mom asks. "That's a long time to keep someone in limbo."

"Supposedly, they want to make sure that things are done right."

Dad fumes, calming enough that he's at least not turning purple any longer. "If you get found guilty, I assume that means you lose your scholarships?"

I nod. "I know you guys can't pay for a school like Western, but I'll make it happen, even if I have to take out student loans or get a part-time job."

"Damn right, we can't pay. You realize I just signed the papers on a new truck?" He asks, and I wince. Dad drove an old Mack for years, and by now, it has to be at least twenty years old. God knows how many miles he's put on it. "Now this."

"Dad, stop," I beg, trying not to cry. "I'll get through it. I didn't cheat, I swear to you."

"It's this Duncan's fault," Dad repeats, his voice dropping. "I just know it. Somehow, it's his fault. Of course it is. He's a *Hart*, right?"

128

"What's that mean?"

He shakes his head and gets up, leaving the camera view while Mom looks up and watches him. "Sweetie, we'll talk later," she says, looking back at me. "I'm sorry you're having trouble. Make sure you keep us up to date."

"You know I will. Take care."

I hang up the call and lean back. Great. Just great. Like I need anything else in my life right now. The only relationship I've had in far too long to admit is on indefinite hiatus, I'm accused by a supposed friend of an Honor violation, and now, my parents are stressing too.

I can't even go talk to Chelsea about this, because I was told by the Dean that I'm not allowed to approach her until the hearing. What am I supposed to do?

The only other thing I can think of right now. *Duncan.*

Chapter 13
Duncan

Post-game activities, including a meeting with Coach Bainridge and the Athletic Director, took until nearly eleven o'clock, so I didn't get back to my apartment until midnight. I thought about calling Carrie then, but I decided against it. She was probably already asleep, and besides, what I needed to tell her, I wanted to be well-rested and ready for it.

Waking up now on Sunday, I stretch, wincing when my elbow sends out a wave of pain. I remember that last hit from the Southern Nevada safety. His face mask hit me right in the elbow, and now, I can barely move it.

I grab my phone from off my table and pull up Carrie's number. I notice that it's already noon. I guess I was more tired than I thought. "Come on, pick up, pick up."

Carrie's phone rings twice, then a mechanical voice cuts in. *"The number you have dialed is temporarily unavailable. Please leave a message at the beep."*

"Hey, Carrie? It's Duncan. Listen . . . we need to talk. I have something I want to tell you. I need to go down to the Pavilion. I dinged up my elbow and could use some ice and maybe a whirlpool on it. If you get this message, could you give me a hand? If not, let's talk later. It's important."

I hang up and grab my bike keys. The ride to campus is painful, but I take it slow and pull into the parking slot without a problem. I go inside and downstairs, where I find Coach Taylor going at it with his own personal workout.

The barbell comes crashing down as Coach T hits his limit for that set, and after he takes a few deep breaths, he sees me in the mirror. "Duncan. Thought you'd be chowing down on some pizza or still sleeping. Whatcha need?"

"Took a shot to the elbow. I thought I'd get some treatment. You got anyone who can see me today?"

He turns around, his hands and shins nearly ghost-white with lifter's chalk, and shakes his head. "Sorry, nope. But give me about forty-five minutes to finish this up, and I'll take a look. Where'd he hit you?"

"The facemask hit me right in the funny bone. I thought it was just that, but I woke up this morning and had a lot of problems moving it. Figured some contrast or ultrasound might be good."

Taylor nods and puts me out of his mind as Pantera thunders through the speakers and he gets back into his workout. I take a seat on a machine and watch in amazement

131

as 'DT' Taylor goes into an intense, focused fury on the weights, battling them like they're his worst enemies, until finally, with a primal scream that would intimidate your average male gorilla, he drops his dumbbell on his last set of rows.

"Damn, hope I can do that when I'm your age."

'DT' is gone, and Coach Taylor is back, and he laughs as he kick-rolls the dumbbell back to its place in the rack. "If you get to my age, here's some advice. Take up bike riding, do some yoga, and sit back and enjoy life. Don't be middle-aged and crazy like I am. Give me five to change shirts and mop up."

"I'll help out with that," I say, going over and getting the sponge mop in the corner and bringing it over. "Besides, middle-aged and crazy sound like where I'm headed. Too many inner demons I'm fighting."

"I've heard," Coach Taylor says. "You seem to have done a good job with it so far this past week, though."

"I have a good reason to," I reply. "For her."

Coach goes into his office while I get the ghost of lifter's chalk up off the floor and put the bucket back. I follow him into the training room, where he flips on the heating element for the whirlpool and pours ice into the bucket.

"She's worth it," he says simply. "Now, show me the arm."

We're both surprised by the bruise that's grown in my elbow. It looks bigger and darker than when I woke up this morning, and Coach whistles. "And you didn't drop the ball?"

"Lucky, mostly. Had it in two hands at the time."

Coach has me flex and bend my arm a few times, then nods. "Okay. Let's get it into contrast for thirty minutes, two-

132

minute switches. Then when you get home, take a few Tylenol." He sighs. "I'm going to recommend to Coach Bainridge that you go no-contact on Tuesday. Run your ass off if you want, but you should avoid hits on that arm for a while. Why wasn't it taped this past game?"

"Carrie wasn't there," I said simply. Coach Taylor raises an eyebrow, but he only nods at what I say.

"Well, next Saturday, when she does tape you up, make sure you wear a neoprene sleeve on top of that elbow as well. The equipment guys will get you what you need. You good?"

"Yeah, I guess," I say. "Thanks."

* * *

With no contact, I didn't worry about taping at all, instead running routes and reviewing tape with everyone and getting used to my new elbow sleeve, which, to be honest, I don't like but will at least pad my elbow some for a while. We actually have a strange game this week, a Monday night game, so Coach Bainridge gives us a lighter workload. I'm still sweating, though, after ninety minutes of running routes and some light blocking, so the early stop is nice.

The only dark cloud over the day is that Carrie still hasn't returned my calls. I tried two more times yesterday, and today, I couldn't find her at all. I think about stopping by the training room, but decide instead to do what needs to be done. I can soak my elbow at the apartment later. I climb on my bike and ride to her dorm, pulling up outside. I look up to her room and see the light is on, so I go inside, ducking up the stairs and heading to the third floor, making my best guess as to which is her room.

Knocking, I feel nervous. "Carrie? It's Duncan. Please,

133

open up."

It's a scene that I never thought I would be in, standing outside a girl's dorm room and asking nervously to be let in. My fears evaporate to be replaced with concern when Carrie opens the door and her eyes are dull, lifeless. "Duncan. Come in."

I walk in, leaving the door open like you're supposed to in the dorms, a rule I have routinely broken, but this time, I'm not worried about following. Carrie's in some sort of trouble.

"Carrie, what's wrong? I tried calling you the past two days, and you didn't pick up. I thought you were mad at me or something."

Carrie sits on her bed, more like flops onto it really, her head hanging and her blonde hair hanging limp—and it looks unwashed. She's still beautiful, but not the Carrie I'm used to seeing. "Sorry. I don't have my phone. I got a call from the Honor Board yesterday. I've been accused of cheating."

"What? You'd never cheat! You're too damn smart!" I protest, and Carrie looks up. "It's true. What did they say you did?"

"When I called you during my orgo mid-term, they said that I was looking up test answers on my phone," Carrie says, taking a deep breath. "I—I don't know how, but my phone has a data trail that says I cheated."

"No way," I reply, taking her by the hands and helping her up. "What can I do to help?"

"Duncan . . . I'm suspended from the Pavilion because of this. I can't even get within fifty yards of Chelsea, since she made the statement against me."

"Chelsea?" I ask. "You mean Chelsea Brown? She's

134

involved with this?"

Carrie nods, and I'm pissed. Not at Carrie, but at myself. "I—I have to apologize to you, Carrie. Chelsea and I had a little history a long time back. She didn't take it well at the time, but it seemed as if she'd gotten over it. My guess is, she's jealous and trying to hurt you."

"But the phone? Her lies may have started the ball rolling, but my phone . . ."

I stroke her chin. "It doesn't matter. Chelsea's clever. She probably found some way to make it look like you cheated. Don't sweat this. We'll get through it. Besides, we've got time before the hearing, and there's a lot to do between now and then."

"Like what?" Carrie asks, and I give her a kiss on the forehead.

"Let's get off campus for a little while—try to get your head right before you go back to class tomorrow. And we've got *us* to talk about."

Carrie nods. "Where do we go?"

I push back and look down at her frumpy shorts and oversized t-shirt. "First, how about we get you dressed in something more appropriate, then we'll figure it out?"

For the first time, Carrie smiles and nods, snapping me a mock salute. "Yes, sir!"

She grabs some clothes from her dresser and runs off down the hall to the bathroom, coming back with her hair pulled back into a ponytail, a light green sleeveless blouse, and some jeans on. "Better?"

I pull her close and kiss her, letting her know exactly how I feel. "Much. Anything else you need?"

135

"Let me grab a few things, throw them in my backpack, grab my jacket, and let's go," Carrie says. "Duncan . . . I'll go anywhere with you. I really do need to get out of here."

I nod. "Let me go get the bike ready and grab your helmet."

"Okay. I'll see you down there. And Duncan?"

"Yeah?"

Carrie kisses me, and I'm tempted to change plans, to close the door to her room and take her to bed, but I don't, slapping that inner demon away and just returning the kiss. Man, sometimes, I regret trying to be a *good guy*. "Thank you."

I head downstairs in a haze, waving at the few people who call out my name. When I'm in the parking lot, I see Chelsea Brown walking toward the entrance to the dorm, and I set Carrie's helmet aside. "Yo, Chelsea!"

She turns her head and smiles, walking over. "Duncan! How are you?"

"That's close enough," I say when she's about ten feet away.

I pull out my phone and turn on the video camera. In this world of accusations and campus culture, I'm not going to fuck around any longer. She's obviously a vindictive bitch with how she's lying on Carrie. "I'm just letting you know that I know what you accused Carrie of. I don't understand why you decided to result to such lies, especially something as damaging as that . . . but I'm not going to let you get away with it."

Chelsea sees my phone, then looks at me and turns, stomping off without a word. I turn off my video and put the phone back in my pocket. A few minutes later, Carrie emerges and she's smiling. Her backpack is stuffed, and I give her a

136

questioning look. "I don't plan on coming back here tonight," she says simply. "Think you have space for me at your apartment?"

I grin, not needing to say more as I pull her in for a hug. "Hey, does Chelsea live in this dorm?"

Carrie shakes her head, confused. "No. Why?"

"She just went in a few minutes ago. Maybe I should talk to Coach tomorrow."

"No," Carrie says, shaking her head. "You don't need drama—you have your own demons to deal with. Remember, this is about us, right?"

"Any idea where you'd like to go?"

Carrie nods and kisses my chin. "Take me up to the foothills. We can watch the city for a while from Mission Park. Then, we go back to your place."

Chapter 14
Carrie

I didn't expect Duncan to react the way he does when I tell him I want to go back to his place. I mean, it doesn't take a rocket scientist to know what that means. Instead of looking excited, he looks pensive, but he nods and hands me my helmet. I climb on behind him, and we ride off, getting on the freeway and heading up to the hills. Mission Park overlooks most of the city, where we can sit on a picnic table and look down on the lights twinkling below us.

"Hmmm, this is nice," I say as I lean into Duncan. "I've never been up here at night before."

Duncan puts an arm around my shoulders. His hand is warm, and the summer has officially ended in California, fall is starting to take hold, and the air is just a little chilly. I hum, but Duncan's still stiff. "What is it?"

"Just . . . I guess I don't want to rush you into something," he says, and in his voice, I can hear restraint, tenderness, and a hint of doubt, something I'd never expect. It's touching and warms me as much as his hand or his body. "I didn't come by to end up repeating the same mistake I made last time."

"You aren't," I reassure him. "This past week has been

138

hard for me, and I know for you too. All week, the conversation we had has been replaying in my head. I kept hoping and praying that you were getting on top of your demons, and watching you Saturday, I thought you were."

"I tried to call you yesterday, but I got home too late to call," Duncan says quietly. "But you didn't pick up. I guess I know why now. When you didn't call back again today, I couldn't stand it any longer. I need you—I need you for your strength, for your tenderness, for everything that makes you who you are. Because the fight's not over."

"It never will be," I say, leaning in and nestling against him. "And you're worried that if we do what we did last time, that you're going to lose that fight."

Duncan nods, and I take his free hand. "I don't want to hurt you," he says.

"I can take care of myself, if you haven't noticed," I reply, chuckling. "Duncan, you're more sensitive than you let on."

He cocks an eyebrow, flexing his unoccupied arm into a pretty decent bicep pose. "Who, me? I'm the Western University bad boy, remember?"

I laugh and scoot over, sliding down the table until I'm laying on it, and rest my head on Duncan's lap, looking up at the stars. "That's true," I quietly muse as I look at him against the outline of the overhead stars, "but you're more than that too. We can be strong for each other, right?"

Duncan nods, and we sit quietly, him stroking my hair while I watch the stars and he watches the city. "Carrie?"

"Yeah?"

"Remember when I told you about the crowd and why

139

I love it so much?"

"A little. I thought there was more you wanted to say, but you didn't."

"It's one of the things I've been thinking about. I know why I want the crowd, the fame, the adoration."

I hum, and his hand moves in slow, lazy circles over top of my blouse, not really stroking my breasts, but he's skirting around them. "Why?"

"It's not them I want attention from, at least not just from them," Duncan says, looking down into my eyes. "I wanted attention from my father. He has never really given me much attention. A shitload of money, but attention . . . no. You know who taught me to throw a football as a kid?"

"Your mother?" I ask, and Duncan shakes his head.

"No. Mom had taken off by then, tired of Dad's shit. Actually, the gardener taught me to throw a football. My first games, Dad was never there. He was always off making some next deal, some new score. In fact, thinking back, I can only remember of a handful of games he's ever been to. None since I came to Western, that's for sure."

Suddenly, Duncan laughs and smiles. "I thought the girl was supposed to be the one with the Daddy issues?"

"Well, if you want, I can dress you up and start calling you Sally," I tease back. "But only if I get to dress like a guy, too, and you call me Sir."

Duncan laughs again, and his hand finds the curve of my left breast and massages it gently, causing me to moan. His hands are bewitched, that's all there is to it. "I think I like you as Carrie much more."

I groan as Duncan finds my nipple and pinches it

140

lightly through my blouse, bringing it to pebbly hardness. "I like you as Duncan a lot more too."

I shift around, and he brings his other hand to my right breast, warm waves of pleasure rolling through me as he massages each breast gently. "You are so beautiful."

"With you, I *feel* beautiful," I whisper back, looking up at him. "You don't know how much that means to me."

Duncan leans down, and though he can't kiss my lips, he finds the hollow of my throat, kissing my neck softly. He whispers something, so soft I can't hear it, but I know what I want to hear him say. "Here?" I ask.

Duncan shakes his head, smiling wistfully. "As wonderful as that sounds, I don't have a condom on me. I wasn't exactly expecting this."

I think about it for a second, then grin. "I know what to do then . . . the *Hart Attack*."

He stops, frozen, unsure. Before he can say anything, I cover his hands that are still resting on my breasts and begin kneading my breasts and his hands at the same time. "Yes, I've heard the rumors of what the Hart Attack is."

Duncan's hands begin to move again, his right hand drifting to the buttons of my shirt, unbuttoning my blouse slowly. "What about . . . well, lube?"

I laugh and reach up, rubbing the big muscles of his right arm. "I had the idea when I was packing. Look in my backpack. I didn't expect to do it out here, but hey."

Duncan finishes unbuttoning my blouse and carefully opens it, taking me in. There's barely any light at all, just the moon overhead, and he becomes a pale, ghostly version of himself, like an old-fashioned movie or something. I lift my

141

head and roll up to a sitting position before coming closer and kissing him. "Duncan, I trust you. I'm clean, I promise."

"I know you are, as am I. I'm usually pretty *anal* about protection." He chuckles. "I need to get you ready," he says, reaching for my backpack. He opens it and finds the tube of lubricant, taking a look at it in the moonlight. "How long have you had this thing?"

"A while. My freshman dry spell left me kind of desperate, and I ordered some things off the Web that I'm never going to let my parents see."

Duncan laughs and uncaps the tube, squeezing just a drop onto his finger before rolling it around. "It's still good. We're going to need a shower together at home after this."

I nod and unsnap my jeans. "I like the sound of that."

"What, a shower?"

"No . . . *we* and the words *home* and *together.*"

Duncan chuckles and gets off the table. "I like the sound of it too. Next semester, think you'll take me up on my offer?"

"We'll see, mister." I get off the table and bend over, my feet on the grass but my hands planted on the edge of the wood. I feel sexy, powerful, and vulnerable all at the same time, and I love it.

Duncan gets behind me, finds my waistband and eases my jeans down, the cool air causing goosebumps to break out on my flesh as I step out of one leg. "The key is to relax," he says softly as he starts to massage my ass. "Have you ever done this before?"

"No, but It's been a secret fantasy of mine since high school," I admit.

142

"Girl next door Carrie with a fantasy like this?" Duncan teases, his hands powerful and gentle on my ass. I spread my legs more, and he brings his right hand between my legs and rubs at my panties, his fingers finding the lips of my pussy, sparks shooting from every caress. He curls three of his fingers in a wave motion, and I'm assaulted with pleasure, my thighs trembling with each amazing stroke.

Duncan eases my panties down, and I hear the cap of the lube open again, this time hitting my ass and dribbling down, in between the cheeks. I open myself in anticipation, breathless as his left hand brushes deeper, deeper . . . and I feel his finger on my asshole, electricity filling me. It feels so good, the soft massage. I never thought it could be like this.

He opens me slowly, slipping a finger inside to my gasp, barely inside, so tight, but he keeps his massage going until I'm open more, his finger slipping the rest of the way inside almost effortlessly. I'm caught up in the wave of sensation as Duncan's fingers on my pussy work in concert with his finger in my ass, bringing me higher and higher, but never letting me come.

"Duncan . . . no more teasing. I want you."

"Patience . . . just a little more, to be sure."

There's a moment of pain as he slides another finger in, but it's gone in an instant, replaced by the deep, primal pleasure of his fingers inside me. Fantasy is being brought to life, and I can only wait, helpless to him, as he finishes opening me up. When his fingers pull out, I'm left empty, and it's soul-crushing for a second before I hear the sound of his zipper going down, and I realize he's preparing himself. "Take a deep breath," he says quietly. "Then when I start to push, exhale and push back into me."

I nod and realize what he's asking. It'll help relax my muscles. I take a deep breath, nearly letting it go when I feel the thick head of his cock rub between my ass cheeks. I'm so ready for him, I want to come already. Then his cock lines up with my asshole, and I tense. "Relax . . . and breathe out."

He pushes slowly while I push back, and the pain is big, bigger than I thought it would be after so much massaging. I grit my teeth and keep pushing back, not willing to give in.

The head of his cock pops through, and suddenly, all the pain washes away in an explosion of accomplishment. I did it! And oh, God . . . it feels so good.

"Duncan . . . oh, fuck."

He hums, his breath short and choppy, and he pulls back, keeping the head of his cock inside me before thrusting in again. This time, his thick, warm cock slides all the way inside me, and I'm his . . . fully.

"Carrie," Duncan whispers, pulling back and beginning to pump in and out of me. I can't believe it. It feels so good, and I feel full, complete, and the waves of pleasure that wash through me are deeper, different than anything else I've ever felt. I grip the table, pushing back as best I can, and this time, Duncan is gentler, not with the animal ferocity and power of our first time, but tender as his cock slides in and out.

It doesn't stop the wave of my orgasm from building, and I'm soon gasping, groaning in need and want as it builds inside me. "Duncan, I'm going to come . . ."

His hips speed up, and his cock is blurring the lines between fantasy and reality as my body is taken over and over by this man that I want and need. Duncan grabs my waist and holds me tight as he thrusts harder, faster, until he's also

144

trembling, both of us right on the edge.

I feel him swell inside me, and with a shuddering groan, he pulls out as I hear him cry out, pushing me over the edge. I feel a tightness in my chest as I come, my breath stopping and the entire world ringing as I come hard. I can't breathe, but if I die right now, it'd be worth it to feel this amazing sensation.

When it passes, I almost collapse onto the table, unable to hold myself up any longer. Sweat rolls down my face, and I'm smiling even though I'm spent. Duncan's still behind me, his breath ragged in the darkness. "So that's why it's called a Hart Attack."

"Hmm?"

"It felt so good, I swear my heart stopped for a moment," I whisper, looking back over my shoulder at him. "And it's addictive as hell, too."

Duncan smiles, helping me stand to turn around and kiss him before he drops to a knee, stopping my heart again for a moment before I realize he's trying to help me with my jeans. "You scared me there for a second."

"Huh?" he asks, and I feel warmth spread up my neck to my cheeks.

"Because for a second there, I thought you were going to ask me to marry you."

Duncan stops, realizing before he laughs. "A little too fast for that, don't you think? But I did have another idea in mind."

"What's that?"

"Why wait until next semester to move in with me?"

I think about it, and I nod. "Tell you what, maybe I'll just stay with you on the weekends," I say, unable to hold back my smile. "I've still got residence in the dorm for the rest of the semester, and my parents would shit themselves if they knew I moved in with you. My dad already kind of hates you. But weekends for sure."

"And tonight," Duncan says, gathering me in his arms and holding me close. "Don't tell me you're changing your mind about tonight."

"Yes, of course, tonight."

My stomach grumbles, and Duncan laughs. "Come on. Let's go home, and I'll see what I have in the fridge."

Chapter 15
Duncan

Monday night. An away game. It seems strange to be saying that, but it feels good at the same time.

"Hey, get used to it," Tyler says to me as we jog onto the field. The lights are bright, and it's our second night game in a row. "Starting next year, you're going to be playing a lot on Sunday and Monday, right?"

"Damn right," I answer, smacking him on the shoulder. "Let's take care of these guys first."

When our schedule was first determined, a matchup of the Western Bulldogs versus the Carolina Swamp Foxes sounded like a hell of a fight. West Coast against East Coast, Western Conference against the South Atlantic Conference. There was even star power, as Carolina was bringing back not only a star quarterback, but two All-American defensive players.

Unfortunately for them, but great for us, one of the Carolina All-Americans, outside linebacker, Marcus Winston, tore up his shoulder in the second game of the season, and with him out of action, their other All-American on defense, tackle Jerome Lattimore, was more easily contained. Tyler is still going to have his hands full, but we've got the advantage.

"Man, I'm just glad you're not doing suicide squad again this week," Tyler says as we wait for the kickoff. "You were sucking wind at the end of last game."

"Don't sweat it. I've got inspiration tonight."

Tyler nods, then leans in. "Hey . . . just to let you know,

147

a lot of the guys aren't happy about the way the Honor Board is treating your girl. You notice that Chelsea ain't around."

"I noticed," I say, looking at the staff that came with us. Since this is a televised game, the network popped for the extra three tickets, and some of the training interns came along this time. Still, none of them were Carrie, and I flexed my elbow in response. "It'll work itself out. I'm making it my mission to make sure things are set right."

"Well, let's roll. Our ball!"

Tyler and I run out to the huddle with the rest of the starting offense, feeling it. The Carolina crowd isn't friendly, booing us loudly, but we expect that. "Time to be the bad guy," I yell as we huddle up. "Let's go ruin someone's night."

I line up, and Tyler sends me in motion, and I 'wiggle' across, cutting upfield as soon as the ball snaps into a ten-yard out pattern, catching the ball off a perfect lead by Tyler. I turn up field and gain another seven yards before getting tackled, and it's on.

We line up again, and I grin at the Carolina player on the other side, who's dressed in his black and light blue and still feeling like there's a chance. "What, no shit talk?" he asks as we get set. "Thought you were famous for it. I was looking forward to shutting you up."

"Don't need it anymore," I reply, and when the ball snaps, I blast him with a double-punch to the shoulder pads before cutting across the middle. I'm actually the second option on the play, but when I turn my head back, I see Tyler already releasing the ball in my direction. It's a little high, but not too bad, and I can take it in with a running jump, landing and cutting up the field with a step on my defender. Forty-seven yards later, and Western is up by a touchdown, and the noisy Carolina crowd goes, at least temporarily, quiet.

Unfortunately, the Carolina offense fires back quickly, and we find ourselves in a Monday night shootout. Great for the stat monkeys, that's for damn sure, because by halftime, we've combined for sixty-six points of scoring between us, and we're up thirty-five to thirty-one.

"Fuck, it's a goddamn Madden game out there!" Tyler gasps as we sit in the locker room. "Defense, give us at least one fucking stop!"

"Tyler, chill," I say, putting my hand on his shoulder. "We've got this."

Tyler looks at me for a moment, then laughs. "You're right. Okay. Go spread some sunshine and rainbows, Hero."

It's my new nickname from the team after Tyler spread the word that 'Touchdown' was forever retired. I shake my head and pick up my helmet. "You guys have to think of a new one. That's even worse than the old."

After discussing some adjustments, we head out for the second half, and I see Joe and the rest of the defense go to work. The adjustments they made are effective, and for the first time tonight, the Carolina Swamp Foxes punt the ball. We return the ball to our forty, and as the offense goes out, we know there's a chance to start to stretch our lead.

We line up, and as the ball snaps, I explode across the line, directly into the side of Jerome Lattimore, who was passed by our guard and tackle. He's huge, and has nearly fifty pounds on me, but I've got speed and surprise, and as he gets driven to the turf, I feel something jump over me and hear the roar of the crowd.

149

I scramble up to see our running back off to the races, nobody in front of him, and we go in with one play for a sixty-yard touchdown.

"Nice block," Coach Thibedeau says when I have a seat. "The old Duncan wouldn't have hit that hard."

"You think?" I ask, smirking. "Remember, Coach, if I throw some pancakes out there, that gets me a better draft position too, you know."

Coach shakes his head and chuckles. "Right. Well, get ready. See if this stays together."

In the end, we take Carolina's heart and win the game handily. Afterward, in our locker room, you'd expect that we'd sound like a party was going on, but we are all just too damn tired—jet lag and the idea that we have a Saturday game coming up—and we're quiet as we change and get back on the bus to take us to the airport.

"I know you're all wishing we could fly home tomorrow morning, but we've got a short week, gentlemen," Coach Bainridge says as the bus starts rolling. "Try to get some sleep. Tomorrow's a no-pads day."

"Thank God it's an easy game Saturday," someone behind me grumbles.

It is true. NMAE is one of the worst teams in our conference, but we can't slack off. I feel still at least a little awake, so I pull out my phone and fire up my text messenger. It's still only a little after seven back in California.

Hey, how's it going?
Carrie: Just got done watching the post-game. Congrats.
It was a tough one, but fun. How was ur day?
Carrie: Pretty terrible. Word's gotten out, and I felt like ppl were

staring at me all day.

> *Ouch. U OK?*

> *Carrie: I will be when U get here. I'm at ur apt.*

> *No Dorm?*

> *Carrie: Didn't want to b there. At least here, I can wear ur t-*
shirt.

> *Oh my.*

My phone goes silent for a bit before buzzing again. It's a picture from Carrie, and I open it to feel my mouth drop open, as she's posing in my bedroom with just one of my team t-shirts on, and from the looks of it, nothing else, her blonde hair flowing around her shoulders and a devilish-angelic smile on her face, her doe eyes glinting in amusement. There's a caption.

> *Go Bulldogs.*

Looking down, I realize that I'm scared absolutely out of my mind. I'm wearing my most professional looking clothes, a black pencil-ish skirt and white blouse that makes me feel more like I'm showing up for a job interview than a hearing that could change my entire life.

You really should have taken Duncan up on his offer to stay the night at the apartment.

Maybe, but I was too worried that I wouldn't get any sleep. Of course, I still didn't, as I stayed up most of the night worrying about the hearing. Now, standing in front of the Honor Building, I'm still sleep-deprived and nervous that Duncan isn't by my side.

"Don't worry," he told me this morning as we talked over the phone. "I've got a nine o'clock class, then I'll be there. The hearing starts at ten, so at most, I'll miss the opening statements. Don't worry. I have your back."

I take a deep breath again and open the door, going up to the second floor where the hearing room is located. Outside, I'm trembling, and my shakes increase when I see Chelsea coming down the hallway. "Why?"

Chelsea gives me an evil look and smiles. "It's nothing personal."

She goes inside, and I give her a minute to get settled in before I go in. I look around and grimace at the setup. The Honor Board has a history that stretches back over a hundred years, and as such, the hearing room has an aura that is straight out of the Inquisition. As the Concerned—we're not Accused, and of course, since this technically isn't a legal proceeding, we're not Defendants either—I sit in the middle of a semi-circle that wraps around the outer walls of the octagonal room. The Honor Board has a "Hearing Officer," what should really be called the Prosecutor, and then the Board itself, nine members made up of five students and four teachers who sit on the semi-circle.

"Nobody expects the Spanish Inquisition," I mutter to myself, but the old Monty Python joke doesn't help lift my spirits. I go to the table and set my bag on top of it, taking out the notes that I'd written up yesterday to help me. Not that there was much I could do. I couldn't figure out anything that could explain away the information that they had.

I take a deep breath and sit down, looking around as I see Professor Vladisova come in, dressed for class. She comes over and puts her hand on my table. "I'm sad that we have to do this . . . because you are a brilliant student, and having you in class, even after this, has been enjoyable. I hope you can grow and learn from it."

I look up at her, and she has an almost kind expression on her face. "I didn't do it. I hope after today, you will believe me."

"Miss Mittel, I grew up in the Soviet Union—the one thing the Soviet people came to know after so many years under the Communists was that lies can be told with a very straight face."

"You should also have learned that innocent people are often unjustly accused," I reply, feeling my inner fire heat up.

Good, get angry. Harness it. It's better than being afraid. "Or were Stalin's purges not taught when you went to school?"

Vladisova looks at me, then nods. "Good luck, Miss Mittel."

She takes her seat in the rear half of the room, which is reserved for witnesses and visitors. Honor Board hearings are open to any member of the University, student and instructor alike, although I don't know anyone who's ever come to watch one of these things for entertainment.

At precisely ten o'clock, as the big grandfather clock in the corner strikes the hour, the door of the hearing room opens up again, and the Honor Board walks in. The Hearing Officer is Kent Prescott, a pre-law student, from the little I found out about him. He and I had a single meeting, where he confirmed what I'd told the Dean, but that was about it.

Once everyone is inside, the Hearing President, an old man that I didn't recognize, raps the Hearing to order.

Kent stands up from his little side desk and approaches the middle of the circle. He's dressed in a charcoal gray suit, and I bet he practiced his opening statement quite a few times. He's in pre-law, after all, and wants to be a lawyer. For him, this isn't my life. It's just practice. He doesn't even care if I'm a cheater or not.

"Members of the Board, the accusations against the Concerned are quite serious. On the morning of October twelfth, Carrie Mittel sat down, along with the other forty-two members of her class, for an Organic Chemistry mid-term examination. Except, she had an advantage over the other students. She had her smart phone with her, and she used it to access class notes. She was even so blatant about it as to get up

154

and leave the room for a minute, for purposes that I will show to you. She then completed her test and turned it in as if she'd done nothing untoward. In fact, if it weren't for the observations of another student, she would have gotten away with it. Today, I intend to show how the Concerned blatantly cheated on her exam, and how she did it. Thank you."

Prescott sits down, and the Hearing President looks to me. "Miss Mittel, as the Concerned, you have the opportunity to speak. Do you have a statement?"

I nod, stand up, and say my peace. It's not as eloquent as Mr. Prescott. I'm not a pre-law student who's practiced this many times, after all. But I get my point across—that I'm no cheater, and I have no idea how this *evidence* came to be.

I sit down, and Prescott starts his case. The first person up is Professor Vladisova, who tells about what she saw, and how she was approached by Chelsea Brown after the mid-term. "At that point, I remembered Miss Mittel leaving the room with her phone at one point, and staying outside the room for about five minutes."

Next up is Chelsea Brown, and I'm shocked at the fairy tale she spins. By the time she finishes, I know I'm screwed. I literally have nothing in my defense other than my word and the fact that I already had an almost 4.0 GPA. The rest of the proceeding is merely a formality, at this point. I would need a miracle.

And in my miracle walked. Duncan strolls in, wearing a suit of his own, something custom-tailored, charcoal gray, with a white shirt and a silver-gray tie that is knotted perfectly in what Dad calls a double Windsor. He walks up to my table and sets a briefcase down, and I wonder if he bought the whole get-

155

up just for this. "Excuse me for being late."

"Excuse me?" Prescott asks. "What is Mr. Hart doing here?"

"Hi," Duncan whispers. "Sorry I'm a little late. How's it going?"

"Can't get any worse," I reply. "Nice suit, though."

Duncan winks and turns around to face the Board. "Is Carrie not allowed to have a student Advocate?"

The President thinks about it for a second, then nods. "With Miss Mittel's approval, of course."

"Of course," I quickly reply.

"Then so be it. Mr. Hart, please have a seat. Mr. Prescott, proceed."

The final piece of evidence that Prescott offers is the flash image of my phone, along with printouts of my browser cache. When I go to get up for my *attempt* to defend myself, Duncan puts his hand on my arm and shakes his head, smirking.

Duncan gets up and reaches into his attaché case. "Members of the Board, everything Mr. Prescott has presented here today sounds very compelling. I mean, if I were in your position, I'd be filling out the paper to throw Carrie out of school already. Why not? Let's hurry this up. I hear the cafeteria is serving pot roast today, and let's face it, as a football player, I love me some good pot roast."

There are a few chuckles, and Duncan has them in the palm of his hands. I guess all the press conferences he's forced to do makes him a natural. "The problem is that everything Mr. Prescott has said today . . . well, it's just not true. It's not his fault—he's just been misled. Let's start with the accusation of

156

phone usage, which this whole thing hinges on."

Duncan goes back to his briefcase and takes out a thick brown folder, the kind that you sometimes see people turn in reports with. "I'd like to submit this report, from NuTech Labs."

"What is this, Mr. Hart?" the President asks as Duncan hands it over.

"I just got this report twenty-five minutes ago. It's why I was late. The report's pretty long, and it's got a ton of technical jargon and stuff, but the summary on the first two pages is so simple, even a football player could understand it. NuTech is one of the best firms in California in the realm of computer forensics, and their experts have testified in over two hundred cases in California courts. I'm sure you can verify this easily enough."

"We'll take your word for it. Continue."

Duncan nods, and he turns back and walks to me, ready to spring his play. "At hearing what Carrie has been accused of, I hired NuTech to do a full analysis of two phones. First, hers. Second, mine. Carrie has stated that when she left the classroom, she was making a personal call. That call was to me, as well as the text message that preceded it. I know Carrie's phone was looked at by the Western Computer Science Department, but no offense to the comp sci majors. They can't do what NuTech can. The summary essentially says that Carrie's phone was manipulated, and that all of this *evidence* is planted."

There's a muted mumbling around the room as the President finishes reading the summary. "I'm calling a pause to this Hearing to confirm this report. Miss Mittel, during this pause, your restrictions to activities are still in place. This Hearing is temporarily adjourned."

Professor Vladisova comes up while Duncan packs his briefcase. Chelsea has already slunk out of the hearing room without a word. "I apologize, Miss Mittel. I'll reinstate your grade, and I look forward to seeing you next week in class."

I nod and shake hands with her. She's not a bad person, just trying to do her job, and I understand that. I look around and see that the only people left are Duncan and me. He closes his briefcase and turns around. "Like I said, I'm sorry I was late."

"I'm sorry I doubted you. I admit, I was starting to get a little gloomy," I say, wrapping my arms around him and pulling tight. "For a moment there, I was scared."

"I know," Duncan says, hugging me back. "I didn't tell you about NuTech because I didn't want to get your hopes up. They were slow on getting back to me, or else I would've told you. I barely had time to print out the report and get over here."

"But you did," I reply. "Thank God for that."

Duncan chuckles. "Come on, let's go get some lunch and change clothes. I hate wearing a suit."

As we walk out of the Hearing room, I turn and look at him. "I don't know. I think you look handsome in a suit."

Duncan looks over, his gray eyes twinkling in the dim light of the hallway. "Take it in while you can. I don't like wearing this monkey suit," he says, rubbing his belly. "I'm starving."

"Me too. Let's go. You said something about pot roast, right?"

"Last time, seniors. This is your day. Enjoy it," Coach Bainridge says as the other members of the team form two lines that stretch all the way from the tunnel to the big Western logo in the middle of the field. "Just keep your heads right for the actual game."

Coach runs out of the tunnel with the other coaches, leaving just us twenty-five seniors. It's our last home game, and Coach dressed a couple of guys from the scout team who busted their asses the past four years, giving them their time in the sun. The crowd is nuts, with big cheers even as these guys go out, their helmets glittering in the fall sun.

"Sucks that your girl can't be sideline for this," Tyler says as the defensive starting seniors are introduced. "You know, being part of the cordon and all."

"Nah, she's got seats at the fifty-yard line. I offered to her parents, but they said no, so I think she gave them to a couple of her classmates. I don't know. Either way, she's up there, so it's all good."

"From Monte Sereno, California. Tight end, number eighty-three, Duncan Hart!"

"Excuse me, time for my entrance."

The PA system is playing music, a remixed version of

Queen's *Princes of The Universe* that somebody picked out because of my first name and my dark hair, but I can't hear anything over the physical roar of the crowd as I walk out, my arms crossed over my chest, walking out a few yards before throwing my arms out, letting the joy and roar of the crowd move me. It's different now than before, and talking with Carrie has helped me so much. I still love the crowd, I love the feeling, but I know there's something even more important out there. When I get to the logo, I turn to the home side, where I pick out Carrie in her seat and point to her.

She sees me, and she points back, her words lost in the roar before it's Tyler's turn, and the rest of the offensive seniors. We get ready, and it's game time.

We take the opening kickoff and start from our twenty-seven.

I line up tight and drop into a three-point stance. We're playing against Washington Poly, a good team that's got a bowl berth already, but it isn't in the mix for the conference title anymore. If we win, we play Clement for the conference title next week. If we lose—well, we don't.

The WP defensive end is nearly bug-eyed as he gets into his stance, growling at me. "I'ma fuck you up today, pretty boy."

The ball snaps, and we crash into each other, helmet to helmet, and I'm trying to drive him. I get my shoulder to the inside like I need, at least, and I push the end out, away from the run before the ball is blown dead on a four-yard gain. "Just wait, bitch. I've got your ass."

"Who the fuck is that guy?" I wonder as I go back to the huddle. "Is he trying to be *me* or something?"

160

"Don't you remember?" Tyler asks, laughing. "You showed him up pretty bad last year, and I'm sure you rubbed it in good after. I think he's got it in for you."

"Oh, yeah," I recall, thinking back to last year's WP game. It was a night game, though I didn't quite remember the specifics. It was just another game for me.

Dropping into my stance, I get ready to run my route, a release to the flat that could net us good yardage.

I fire off, spinning off the defensive end who overextended himself trying to fight me, and into the flat. Tyler sees me open and tosses it nicely. I snag the pass and turn up field, getting tackled by two men for a twelve-yard gain. We're off to a good start, and as Tyler comes over, he's grinning. "We've got this. Clement, here we come."

The drive continues, and I line up on the left side, standing up as we spread the field, and when the ball snaps, I pop the linebacker covering me, going over the middle on a crossing X pattern. I turn and see the ball and catch it, going up before the free safety hits me, stopping my momentum. The ball blows dead, and I get to my hands and knees when suddenly, a huge weight crushes into my back, and I feel my elbow give way in a crunching snap that causes me to scream. A scuffle breaks out between the teams, but I can't do anything but lie on the turf, holding my arm and trying to stop screaming, it hurts so damn bad.

* * *

"How is it, Coach?"

We're at University Hospital, and I'm still in my game pants, but they took off my shoulder pads, although I wish they hadn't cut my jersey off. I liked that jersey. It lasted me through

161

a year and a half without being replaced.

Coach Thibedeau shakes his head. "We don't know yet, Duncan. The doc's going to get the X-rays back in a few minutes and—"

"Not me, Coach. The game. Did we win?"

Coach swallows, then shakes his head. "Thirteen to seventeen. We couldn't punch it through for one last touchdown."

"Who did it? I never saw who hit me."

"The defensive end . . . Petersen. He got ejected for it, at least."

I chuckle mirthlessly, then look out the window. "So Clement and Willamette for the conference championship."

Coach Thibs nods, then comes over and puts a hand on my shoulder. "Don't sweat it. You did everything possible, all season long. Twelve hundred plus yards receiving, twenty-one touchdowns . . . those are conference records that'll stand for a long time among tight ends."

"We've still got a bowl game to worry about," I reply when the curtain pulls back and the doctor comes in. "Well, Doc?"

"I wouldn't be looking for a bowl game, if I were you," Doctor Lefort says. Guess I'm lucky he was on duty tonight. "I can't confirm it until we get an MRI tomorrow, but you aren't using that elbow for a while. You're going to need surgery."

"What's the deal? Rough guess, Doc?"

He looks at me, curious, then continues. "Nothing's broken, bone-wise. But you've at least partially torn the anterior band of your elbow joint, and it's my guess, the biceps tendon too. That crunch you told me about was your elbow bending the direction it's not supposed to bend."

Coach Bainridge comes in, his face grave. "How's it going, Duncan?"

I force a smile to my face and sit up. "Not bad, Coach. Just need to rub some dirt in it, and I'll be good."

Coach Thibedeau is looking at me like I'm out of my mind, and even Dr. Lefort is shaking his head. "Duncan, did you hear what the doctor said? You need surgery."

I look at Coach Thibs and shake my head. "No. What I heard is that I have partial tears of a ligament and a tendon. *Partial* tears. Not total. So it's something that can wait until January. We've got a bowl game to win, and I intend to help the team do it."

Coach Bainridge looks at Thibs and gives him a thumb. He gets the message and gathers up Dr. Lefort to leave the exam room. Once we have privacy, Coach B sits on the edge of the bed. "What's going on?"

I take a few seconds to think about how I want to say what I want to say. Finally, the words come to me. "For four years, I've been an arrogant, greedy, selfish asshole. I've hurt this team as much as I've helped it, and I can't make up for that. For these last few games, since my suspension, I've tried, and I've found something out."

"What's that?"

I look at him and smile. "I love football. Not the fame—I mean, that's cool too—and not the money that might come in the next few years. I love the game. I've loved being part of this team. And I won't let this team down again. So if that MRI says I can move my elbow at all, that I can even bend my arm, then I'm going to be out there. We can worry about

163

the surgery afterward."

Bainridge shakes his head. "Duncan, if you go out there in a bowl game, you're putting your entire future at risk. One wrong hit to that elbow, and your biceps tendon gets fully torn off the bone. You lose at least a year to rehab, and nobody's going to draft a tight end with a bad bicep in the first round. You'll be lucky to get a third-round pick—if you can even play at all."

"It's my career, Coach. Besides, there are things—" my voice catches, and emotion chokes at my throat. "There are things more important than football. That's why I have to do it."

"Tell me. Tell me why, or else I put you down as unable to play in the report to the AD."

In my mind, I see Carrie, and the words come easy. "Because I love her. Because I need to be a good man for her. A *good* man . . . he'd go out and fight with his team."

Coach studies me for a minute, then nods his head. "Okay, fine, but you could be making a huge mistake. I guess I get to tell you now that the team got the invite right before I came to see you. We're going to be playing in the Sunshine Bowl."

I nod, somewhat pleased. "Sunshine, huh? That's in Florida, right?"

"Yep. Not a New Year's Bowl, though, but right after Christmas. It doesn't give you a lot of time to heal up."

Chapter 18
Carrie

*

"Are you insane?"

Duncan shifts the sling strap around his neck to get a
better seating for the padding and chuckles before reaching out
and taking my hand with his good one. "You're about the third
or fourth person to ask me that exact question this morning.
Can we at least get back home before I have to answer it
again?"

I roll my eyes and nod, carrying his bag over my
shoulder. We get on the bus from the hospital to his apartment,
and as we ride, I can't help but feel better. Seeing him down on
the turf, holding his elbow and trying not to scream, I'd been
so scared. What made it even worse was that, as Duncan's
girlfriend, I couldn't get past the nurses at the front desk. I
wasn't family, and I wasn't one of the coaches. I was just some
girl. Thank God Tyler saw me and snuck me in a side door.

"I owe a date to a very star-struck nurse for this one, so
make it good," he whispers as I go by. "I have a feeling I'm
going to regret the date."

It was helpful to see Duncan in the hospital, and now,

riding the bus next to him, I'm even happier, even if his plan is crazy. "So are you gonna tell me why you're thinking of sacrificing yourself and your future for this?"

Duncan thinks about it, then nods. "I've got a laundry list half a mile long. I can't begin to name them all. When Coach B first came around, I said it was for me, to become the man that I want to be instead of the person I am. I told him it was for you for the same reasons. But that's only part of the truth."

"What do you mean?" I ask, already moved by what Duncan said.

Duncan puts his arm around me and gives my shoulders a squeeze, smiling. "I do want to be a man who's good enough for you. That's not a lie. But when you don't have a model to base yourself on, you have to base it off what you *don't* want to be. So, I looked at my father. Did you know he used to be an athlete?"

"Not really, no. Was he a football player too?"

Duncan shakes his head. "Nope, or else, I never would have gone near the game. He was a basketball player, actually. From what I heard from my grandfather before he died, he was a pretty good shooting guard. Not pro-caliber, but when you add that to Mom, you get me. She was a near-Olympic level heptathlete. I double-checked recently. Anyway, I looked to Dad. And what I said to myself was, what would Winston Hart do?"

"And what would he do?"

Duncan pulls me closer. "He'd take the easy way out. He'd take the surgery, cruise past the pro combine or the school's pro day, and then cruise into a rookie contract if someone offered it to him. You see, for all his venture capitalist act, he's always cut and run when the going gets tough. So skipping the Sunshine Bowl—that's something he would do."

I nod, not liking Duncan's thinking, but at least understanding it. The game is as much about personal development as it is the team, and there's nothing wrong with thinking that way. After all, being a team player doesn't mean you need to be a masochist. Just partly so. "Then can I ask you a favor?"

"What's that?"

I raise my head, whispering into Duncan's ear. "Can I help out?"

The bus stops, and Duncan and I get off, walking the half-block up to the Vista Apartments before taking the elevator up. Duncan's thinking the entire time, and when we get inside, he closes the door behind us and goes into the living room. "Carrie, it's not that I'm not happy that you offer, but you know with the Honor case still pending against you, that you're technically under suspension. If some jealous bitch like Chelsea Brown catches you working any sort of rehab with me, you're putting your future of getting back into the intern program at stake."

I nod. "I know that. But I know something else, something you haven't thought of yet."

"What's that?"

"*Us.* What you're doing could be dangerous, and I want to do whatever I can for you. Besides, after I'm cleared, I really doubt they'd ever do anything to me. It's a risk *I'm* willing to take. Actually, I'd like to go one better."

"What do you mean?" Duncan asks, and I point to the

bedroom. "I think I'm a little banged up for that."

"No, you horndog," I say with a laugh. "Look."

Duncan goes into the bedroom, where I've fully made the bed and cleaned, something that he, despite being neater than most men, didn't do a great job of before. I set a bag next to the dresser, where it sits face up. "Two sets of pillows. Nice, and I appreciate the cleaning job, but what are you saying?"

"What I'm saying is . . . maybe you'd like a live-in rehab specialist?"

Duncan turns to me and shakes his head. "No . . . but I'd love to have a girlfriend who wants to live with me for as long as she wants. How about that?"

I swallow the lump in my throat and nod, blinking away the tears that are forming in my eyes. "You have no idea. Actually, there's one more thing, if you don't mind me being positively domestic."

"Huh?"

I laugh again. "Actually, I was thinking . . . after we talk, would you like to meet my parents? Skype, of course . . . at least for now."

Duncan nods, then his face clouds. "I get the feeling from what you've said, though, that your parents don't like me."

I nod. "Dad doesn't. Mom's just . . . Mom."

"Why?"

I sit down on the bed, and Duncan takes a seat next to me. He undoes the strap on his sling and slowly lays back, resting his arm on the bed while he begins to slowly curl and relax the arm. He's gritting his teeth. It has to be hurting him, but I know he's trying to keep his joint mobile, not stiffening

168

up on him.

"Dad's a long-haul trucker," I tell him as I shift sideways, sitting cross-legged next to his arm. "But he used to be an athlete too. Baseball player, actually. I guess I take after him that way. At his high school, at least my grandmother told me, baseball was a very distant second to football, and the players at his school were, in general, assholes."

"Hmm, asshole football players. Never met one," Duncan jokes, and I teasingly slap him on his chest. "Ouch. Now, you have to be fully moved in before you can do whips and handcuffs, but spanking is okay already, got it?"

I laugh and pat him on the chest again. "Careful. I may have a side to me you haven't seen yet. But, as to Dad . . . long story short, one of the football jocks stole his girlfriend. Of course, he has a grudge against *all* football players. Perfect logic."

"Ooh, ouch," Duncan hisses. "Sounds about right."

"Well, that's half the reason he doesn't trust you. The other half has to do with his trucking."

Duncan sits up some, confused. "What do I have to do with trucking?"

"He's an independent long hauler, doing cross-country runs about two to three times a month. This keeps him on the road a lot, but it wasn't always that way. When I was a little girl, he was part-owner of his own trucking company, Longstar Consolidated."

"What happened?" Duncan asks, and I shrug.

"He got bought out. Some bigshot came in when Dad was looking to expand the fleet and pushed him out the door. Now, it wasn't your Dad directly, but he was supposedly one of

169

the investors."

Duncan thinks about it, then nods. "Well, this is going to be fun. Tell you what. How about I finish up these arm flexes I'm doing, and in the kitchen, there are two buckets under the sink. We can get some contrast baths going to help out . . . and then when I'm done with that, let's call them."

"Really?" I ask. I'm surprised. I didn't think he would want to jump into the fire that quickly.

Duncan nods. "Really. If we are going to be *us*, then I guess we need to get it over with sometime or another. As for my father, I don't give a damn if he ever meets you. For now, he's done with my life until he reaches out to me."

* * *

After the call, which had none of the rancor that I thought it would, Duncan sits back and smiles. "See, not so bad?"

I nod and give him a kiss. "Nope, I think the most difficult part of moving in with you is going to be the next part."

"Which is?"

"Stopping kissing you long enough to actually get some studying done. We've both got class tomorrow, remember?"

The next day, I go to the student union during lunch, where I meet up with Coach Taylor. "Hey, Carrie. It's good to see you."

"Thanks, Coach. Thanks for meeting with me on such short notice. I know you're busy."

He shakes his head and cracks open a can of coffee flavored pre-mixed protein shake, a disgusting concoction that only a guy like Coach could love. "No problem, Carrie. You're looking good. You keeping up with your work?"

I nod. "The regular gym sucks compared to what the weight room is like, but I can still get something done there. Like you say, if it has a barbell and a squat rack, you can get work done. I'll be truthful, though. I can't wait to get back down in the basement with everyone."

"Yeah, a lot of folks are telling me the same thing. Alicia is about ready to go to the Honor Board and beg them to hurry up. Since you've been suspended, she's rolled her ankles twice."

I sit back and shake my head, chuckling. "You and I both know that it's more due to bad luck than anything. Who was taping her up?"

"Freddie Maxwell. He knows what he's doing. In fact, I'm giving him a letter of recommendation when he graduates. But yeah, Alicia's about ready to kill him." Coach Taylor takes a long drink of his protein shake and grows serious. "By the way, Chelsea quit the program. Bunch of rumors swirling about that one."

"I bet. I can't say I'm upset about that, though. You know, since she lied about what I did . . . let's not go there though. I sent you an email because I'd like your advice."

"Advice is always free for you," Coach says. "At least, monetarily. What's up?"

"Well, let's say, hypothetically, of course, that someone wanted to do some home-based rehabilitation on an injured elbow."

Coach sees right through me. "Like, say, a biceps tendon that is seventy-five percent torn and a nearly fully-torn anterior band?"

171

"Something like that. Not quite a Tommy John surgery candidate, but certainly someone who needs to go under the knife."

"But who refuses to for another three weeks or so. Well tell me, Carrie. You're pretty smart. What would you have this person do?"

"Mostly range of motion work, lots of contrast treatment, and in their sport, limited contact along with a limited range of motion brace. Once the swelling goes down in the elbow, light work, mostly to retain as much of the overall body muscle as possible without stressing the injured joint."

Coach Taylor nods and sits back. "My prognosis exactly. Now, if you had access to an ultrasound machine, I'd add that in, but most *houses* don't have that. Even ones in the Vista."

I nod somberly. "Think we can keep this under our hats?"

"Unless someone makes a direct request, sure. What you do with your boyfriend in his apartment is none of my business."

"*Our* apartment now. I'm moving my stuff this week."

Coach Taylor nods and gives me a smile. "Congrats. I know I warned you about him way back when, but I'm happy to have been wrong in this case. And don't worry, Duncan will get the best treatment Western can provide."

Chapter 19
Duncan

For most of the guys, being away from home for
Christmas week is hell. Some of them have always gone home
for Christmas, and until this year, Western's been lucky, getting
December 31st or January 1st games, giving everyone at least a
chance to eat dinner and open presents with the family. So for
a lot of the team, it's strange being in Tampa for a football
game. Then again, we're getting a longer Christmas break
because of it since our vacation isn't being interrupted by
football practice. We just start later than most students.

Personally, though, I don't really mind. Christmas for
most of my life has been just another day, perhaps with some
presents thrown in, but no real feeling behind them. But when
you can buy pretty much anything you want, except the
attention of your father, Christmas and those presents are

mostly meaningless.

This Christmas is different, however, in that I have Carrie. She went home to spend the holiday itself with her parents, and while I miss her, we can't spend the nights together the way we want anyway. We're in a team hotel, after all.

"Merry Christmas, Duncan!"

"Merry Christmas, beautiful," I say into my computer. I made sure to bring my laptop along with me, and the hotel has a good enough Wi-Fi connection. "How are things?"

"Dad's relaxed some," Carrie says, pointing toward her right, "especially after that back massager you got him for a present."

"Oh, did I put the wrong tag on that? That was supposed to be a, ahem, 'massager' for your mom."

"Duncan Hart!" I hear off-screen, and Carrie leans back, laughing. I join in as Vince sticks his head in the screen. "Tell me you did not just say that!"

"Sorry, Mr. Mittel," I apologize, still laughing. "I couldn't help it. Carrie's laughter was too worth it to worry about you being upset."

"Well, okay then. By the way, we saw you on TV today. Nice interview."

"Thanks. I felt like an idiot the whole time." I did, too. It's something I've been surprised with, as I've gone through finding the *new* me. I've gone from being a glory hound camera hog to being a bit shy in interviews. I guess when you can't hide behind talking shit, it's a lot more difficult. "So did I look okay?"

"You looked amazingly handsome," Carrie says, smiling.

174

"I'm looking forward to seeing you play tomorrow. How's the arm?"

"As good as it could be," I answer, flexing it for her approval. "The team docs shot me up with a cortisone injection two hours ago, so it hurts like hell right now, but it'll feel much better tomorrow. At least until the pounding starts."

Carrie nods, and Vince sticks his head in again, taking a seat. "Duncan, are you really sure about this? I mean, Carrie explained to me why you're doing it, but it still seems awfully risky."

"It might be, but it's what I want to do."

Vince strokes his chin and nods. "Well, I guess it's your choice. Still, be careful out there. I'd prefer if my daughter's boyfriend spends as little time in the hospital as possible, okay? She's already talked my ear off for three days about all her ideas for your rehab after your surgery."

I laugh, and my stomach rumbles. "Deal. Hey, my stomach is kicking me for missing the team lunch—because of the interview, in fact—so I'm going to have to take off soon to find some grub."

Carrie smiles and nods. "We're going to be sitting down in a couple of hours ourselves. How about we catch up after the game?"

"Sounds like a plan," I say, and Vince looks at his daughter before giving her a kiss on the cheek.

"Okay, I see you two want to share your goodbyes, and you don't need some old man getting in the way. We'll be watching tomorrow, Duncan. Good night."

Vince leaves the camera, and Carrie and I just look at each other for a little bit. "I've missed you," she finally says, smiling.

"My arms have felt pretty empty too. Have they asked you about it?"

"Mom refuses to acknowledge it. She just asks if my bedroom at the apartment is comfortable or not. Dad . . . he's totally avoided it. You know how it is. There's a part of them that knows, but it's like Schrödinger's Cat. As long as the question isn't answered, their daughter both is and isn't sleeping with her boyfriend."

"We were raised totally different. Maybe just because I'm a guy. I don't know, but I can guess. Carrie . . . I love you."

"I love you too. And thank you for the present. I was actually a good girl and waited until Christmas day to open it, too. It's beautiful."

"Are you wearing it now?" I ask, and Carrie nods. "Show me?"

She reaches into her shirt and pulls out the white gold necklace with a gleaming emerald chip in the center. The chain is a simple link chain, and the emerald is small. I didn't want to overwhelm her with a huge stone, and besides, it fits Carrie's personality. "I wear it next to my skin always. All right, I'll let you go grab something to eat, Duncan. I love you."

"Goodnight, Carrie. Love you."

She hangs up, and I close my computer and go downstairs. It only took us saying the L word once, and after we did, neither of us can stop. The restaurant for the hotel is open until midnight, and while I'm not looking for anything heavy, a good Caesar salad or something might do the trick until tomorrow's team breakfast.

When I get downstairs, I'm crossing the lobby when I

hear someone call my name. "Duncan! Wait up, son!"

I stop, shocked. Turning, I see Dad walking quickly across the lobby, a huge smile on his face. "Duncan! Good to see you!"

"Dad? What are you doing here?" I ask, confused. "Aren't you supposed to be back in Cali?"

"I realized that this is going to be your last game in college, and well, I also realized that I couldn't get another chance to see you play college ball, so I made the trip down. I know it's a bit of a surprise, but I was kind of hoping . . . well, I was kind of hoping you'd be willing to have dinner with me."

"Um, sure . . . I guess. I was just going to get a salad here in the restaurant."

We go to the restaurant, where the wait staff seats us immediately. I'm wearing my Western track suit, which gives us pretty much carte blanche in service, and as we sit down, I notice that Dad's looking at my arm. He's looking thinner than before, showing his middle age for the first time. "How's the elbow? I read about your injury."

"I'll make it. I've already scheduled the surgery for December 30th. That'll give me just over eight weeks to rehab for the Combine, but I'll probably pass on that for a Pro Day at school in March, if I can."

Dad hums and looks over the menu. The waitress comes by, and I order a chicken Caesar while he orders the pork chops with hummus. After the waitress leaves, I take a sip of my water. "So when did you get into town?"

"Just a few hours ago," he replies, giving me a shrug. He sounds different too, it seems. Nervous, or just stressed. I wonder if Tawny's left him. I mean, I didn't even get a chance

177

to meet her yet. "I just closed a deal, but I wanted to make sure that I got here in time. Duncan, I know I haven't been the most attentive father, but I do care about how you're doing. It hurt that you didn't at least give me a call when you got injured. I only found out because of cable sports."

"No offense, but you haven't exactly given a damn about my playing for about the past six years or so. I was talking about it with Carrie the other week, and I realized the last game of mine you ever saw was my freshman year in high school. You didn't even go to the Shrine Game."

Dad nods, then sighs. "I know. It's been tough, that's all. It's why I need your help."

"My help? What the hell type of help could I give you?"

Dad looks around, and leans in closer. "Duncan, I haven't exactly been honest about my finances. After the Cupertino Mafia started really going lawsuit happy, I got hammered in a lot of deals. To finance this most recent one, I had to take out some loans."

"Okay, big deal. You've done that before."

He shakes his head and sighs. "These weren't with a bank, Duncan. The banks won't extend me any more credit. Between maintaining Tawny's lifestyle, my own image, and everything else, I'm tapped to the gills. And this deal, it might not pay off for six months or more. So I went to some men I know in San Francisco. They loaned me the money, on a few conditions."

"What conditions?" I ask, a sense of dread washing over me. If he's broke, what the hell have I been paying for my lifestyle with for the past year or more? Credit cards that aren't getting paid? Wishes and rainbows? Unicorn piss? What?

178

"These men, they made a deal with me. They put a very large sum of money on the Sunshine Bowl, and if their bet pays off, then my markers are wiped clean. If not, they collect. Everything."

I sigh, shaking my head. "You're fucking kidding me."

Dad shakes his head now, his eyes intense. "Duncan, I mean it. Everything. The house, the cars, everything that isn't paid in full already. The banks are screaming for my neck, and the San Francisco men are only going to give me the money to get them off my ass if they collect on their bets. So I need you to help me out. Western needs to lose."

"You want me to throw the game?" I ask, horrified. "Are you out of your fucking mind?"

"Son, I'm not saying you need to really throw it . . . just, don't do as well as you might," he says. "You already have a banged up elbow, so just don't go as hard as you might normally. Think about it. An injured performance won't hurt your pro prospects, and you can take it easy, reduce your chance of injury."

I don't know what to say. Seven years of ignoring my football, and now he wants me to throw a game? Never mind that if I do, and it's discovered, I get banned from the game forever. I shake my head, trying to comprehend how I ever called this man my father. "Excuse me. I need to go."

The waitress is approaching the table, so I stop her and ask for my salad to be sent to my room. Dad starts to get up, then stops when I point at him, gesturing down with my finger. I leave the restaurant and go out into the lobby, leaving the hotel and sitting out by the pool. I need someone to talk to. There are so many thoughts whirling in my head. Thankfully, my phone is in my pocket, and I pull it out, dialing from memory.

"Hello? Duncan?"

Carrie's voice is a balm to my mind, and I let out a shuddering breath. "Yeah, it's me. Sorry, I know we just got off, but I had to call."

"Aww, how sweet," Carrie purrs. "What's up? You sound troubled."

"I just ran into Dad," I say, finding a chaise lounge chair and sitting down. The pool is lit right now, the water swirling in patterns of light in the night, casting weird little swirling beams all around. "He says he came to watch the game."

"That's a good thing, isn't it?" Carrie asks. "So why don't you sound happy?"

"He wants me to throw the game. Apparently, he owes a lot of money to some men in San Francisco . . . and not exactly the sort of men who wait to collect their debts."

Carrie hums, then clucks her tongue. "Let me ask you—in your entire life, what has remained pure, unsullied?"

"You," I immediately reply, and Carrie's warm hum helps me relax a little.

"Thank you, but I'm hardly pure, and in the grand scheme of things, you haven't really known me that long. What else?"

"Football," I answer, seeing what she's trying to say. "It's always been pure."

"Then keep it that way. Duncan, you're a man now that you weren't even six months ago. You're a man that I'm proud to love. Be that man. You know what to do."

180

I do. I know exactly what to do. "Thank you, Carrie. I . . . I think I should go do that now, and go get some sleep. Thank you."

"Sleep well. I love you."

"I love you too. Good night."

I go upstairs, to the fifth floor of the hotel. There are ten rooms per floor in the hotel, and this one is just for the coaches and university staff. I go to room 503, Coach Bainridge's room, and raise my hand, knocking. "Yes?"

"Coach? It's Duncan Hart. I have to talk to you about something."

* * *

My elbow's killing me. I swear, every drive, I'm getting hit in the arm at least once. The defensive ends are even using the elbow against me when I try to block them, pushing my left elbow across my body to torque it, putting more pressure on it. It's not a dirty move. It's the same move I use to get a linebacker or defensive back off me to run routes, but it still hurts all the time.

If there's any saving grace, it's that my biceps tendon isn't getting strained. Most of playing tight end is pushing, not pulling, and my triceps and chest are more important than my biceps for that. Still, the biceps is used when I catch, if anything, to pull the catch in and to cradle it against my body.

"How's it feeling?" Tyler asks, sweat dripping off his face. Two minutes left in the second quarter, and it's still a tight game. We're playing Georgia A&M, and they're a tough bunch of Southern boys. To our disadvantage, they are also used to this heat and humidity, and we're not. December, and it's still eighty-two degrees and nearly ninety percent humidity. What

181

the hell? At least it's not trying to play them in August.

"I'll live," I hiss, flexing the arm. I took a punch to the elbow that last play, and I'm aching. "Let's just play."

I line up in slot and square myself for the jarring impact I'm going to need to deliver. GAM has been playing me man to man all night, making me use my arm as much as possible.

The ball snaps, and I yank, pulling the cornerback forward with my right arm. He doesn't expect it, and I'm off, running ten yards before crossing with our split end and turning to look for the pass. I've got a step, and Tyler puts it in my hands perfectly. I take off up the field, just inside the sideline, and cut back when I see the GAM safety coming on a pursuit angle. A juke move, and I'm past him, angling across the field for the last ten yards and going in untouched for the touchdown. I toss the ball to the ref and exchange shoulder smacks with my teammates.

"That's what I've been looking for!" Tyler yells. "Damn right, baby!"

"Let's keep it going next half," I respond. "I want the damn record. What's this bowl's record for TD catches?"

"Fuck if I know. But we'll go for it anyway."

Unfortunately for us, GAM isn't as accommodating as we'd like, and after a short three and out drive by us to start the third quarter, GAM starts to eat up the clock by grinding out yardage in short, brutal chunks, three and four yards at a time. Their linemen have that farmer strength, big 'hosses' that can grind it three and four yards at a time over and over and over. They pound it out for a touchdown, and we're behind again, with ten minutes left in the fourth quarter.

"Well, there goes the TD record," Tyler jokes as we

182

start off our next drive at our twenty-three. "Time to give the D a rest and grind some ourselves."

"I'm not grinding with you, Tyler. Just 'cuz Carrie's at her parents' house . . . I'm still not grinding with you," I joke back, and everyone laughs before growing serious.

Tyler calls a swing screen pass to the flat. He tosses the ball to the back, and I clear traffic. I collide with a linebacker, and my elbow pops inside again, pain exploding through my arm, but we get the yards we need.

I'm shaking my arm when the huddle re-forms, and Coach Bainridge sees it. He sends in Carlson to give me a rest and to bring in the next play, and on the sidelines, he pulls me aside. "How is it?"

"It'll hold together for another few minutes," I reply, looking at the game clock. "I'll make it."

"Sit out two plays, shake it out, and then get back in there," Coach says. I nod and kneel, focusing and catching my breath.

After the two plays, Coach sends me back in, and we're looking at third and seven. Carlson's doing his best, but he's not quite there yet. Give him a year, maybe. He's still young.

In the huddle, Tyler's happy to see me. "Glad you're back. Think you can catch something?"

"You throw it, I'll catch it."

I drift out into the flat, just beyond the first down marker, and go up for a high pass, stretching out to catch the ball, only to get upended by a linebacker who hits me in the legs, flipping me over to land flat on my back. I hang onto the pass, though, and it's just enough for the first down.

"That one hurt," I groan as I get up off the ground and

183

get back to the huddle. We run the ball once, taking the ball to the fifteen, but more importantly, starting the clock again. Coach's plan is simple. If we punch it in, we're not going to give GAM enough time to get the points back. We end it now, one way or another.

A minute and thirty-one seconds left. I drop down hit the defensive tackle in the side while our guard and tackle pop out on the old power sweep play, taking us down to the ten. Third and two, and the clock is still running. Twenty-seven seconds left.

The ball snaps, and I smack the defensive end in the shoulder before releasing and starting my route. The linebacker sees me coming, and he's going to stick with me. We're jostling, at the limits of what the refs will allow before they call pass interference, but with less than a minute left in a bowl game, they're letting a lot more go than normal.

I turn my head back, and Tyler's scrambling, the pass rush starting to get to him. He rolls out to his right, and I cut back, reversing course to try to give him options. The cut gives me just enough space, and Tyler sees me, letting the pass go just as a big defensive end nails him in the back. The ball's a wounded duck, wobbly and high, but there's no other choice. I go up, reaching, my left arm screaming, but it's on my fingertips. I pull in, still on my feet, by some miracle, and cut upfield. Four yards, two men in front of me. They go low, I jump . . .

Somehow, I don't know how, my body clears the goal line. With eleven seconds left, Western has taken the lead, up by two.

I get up off the ground and hug my teammates. Tyler's

getting up himself, and I tap helmets with him. "Good throw."

"Bullshit. Great catch."

We go over to the sidelines, everyone quiet while we watch the kickoff after the extra point. The Georgia A&M team elects to not try anything stupid on the kickoff, and they have one desperate Hail Mary pass that falls short before the final seconds tick off, and we've won. Tyler turns and hugs me as the team celebrates. "Thank you, man. It's been a hell of a four years."

As the team celebrates in the middle of the field, I find myself exchanging high fives and handshakes with dozens of people. I have no idea who they are, but it doesn't matter. We're happy, and the only thing that could make my mood better is if Carrie were here with me.

"You did it, Duncan," Coach Thibedeau says, yelling even though he's only a foot from my ear. The noise is so overwhelming. "You came through. Now, the focus goes to you."

I shake my head and clap Coach on the back. "Never again, Coach. Never again. Now, the focus is on Carrie."

Coach claps me on the shoulders again, grinning. "Let's get you back to Western first, get that surgery done."

He moves on, and we go back into the locker room. After I get my gear off, I put my track suit back on and go back out to the field. There's a sense of nostalgia already, looking around at the grass. Regardless of whether I get drafted, or if my surgery is successful or not . . . my amateur football career is over.

I sense someone coming up behind me, and I turn, seeing Dad standing there, looking at me with pain in his eyes.

"Why, Duncan? It was just one play, one game."

"Because it was the right thing to do. That's more important than the money."

He goes to say something, but a couple of men in suits call out. "Mr. Hart. Winston Hart."

He turns his head and goes pale. The men come closer, taking Dad's arms. "Mr. Hart, Mr. Salvatore would like to speak to you about your business loans. If you'd come with us."

The mobsters lead him away, and as I watch my father get led out of my life—maybe forever now, I don't know— another person approaches. It's Coach Bainridge, who's just completed the last of his press interviews. "Duncan."

"Coach. Guess you saw that."

He nods, watching as my dad disappears into a side tunnel of the stadium. "Coach, you didn't have to trust me. Even after telling you last night, I could have thrown the game."

Coach nods and pats me on the shoulder. "The player I had at the beginning of the season, I wouldn't have. The man you are today, I trust."

We walk off the field, and Coach laughs softly. "You know, I'm going to have to send someone to clean out your locker. You're going to be in the hospital. Is there anything in there that you'd be embarrassed to show?"

"Not that I can think of . . . but if there are any phone numbers or pictures in there, can you just burn those?"

"Wise decision."

Chapter 20
Carrie

After six hours of sitting in the hospital waiting room with nothing but a book to entertain me, I know one thing for certain: I hate hospital waiting rooms, and reading *The Silence of The Lambs* is not the way to relax in one.

"Miss Mittel?"

I look up and see the surgeon, Dr. Lefort, pulling off his little cap. He's not covered in blood, so at least that's a good thing, right?

"Is he all right, Doctor?"

My face must be too easy to read or something, because his smile is immediately comforting. "He's fine. In fact, if you want you can go see him in about fifteen minutes, he's in recovery. Just give him some time to finish getting everything cleaned up and a shirt on. After all, I can't be guilty of encouraging the delinquency of college students."

I blush and chuckle, shaking my head.

Dr. Lefort smiles. "Anyway, you can go back in a few minutes. A nurse will come get you."

"Just a minute, Doc. How'd the surgery go?"

He nods. "Good. The anterior band tear wasn't as bad as I feared, and the bicep tendon's still there. If he wasn't an athlete, I'd have passed on the tendon, but you know how Duncan is. He's got bigger biceps than most people, and he puts more stress on them."

It's a long five minutes, but when the nurse finally leads me back to the recovery room, Duncan's there, looking a lot more perky than I thought he would. "Hey, beautiful."

"How are you feeling?" I ask, coming over. Duncan's arm is in a splint, and it will be for a few days before he shifts to a sling when he's not doing rehab.

"Not too bad. They used a local anesthetic instead of putting me all the way under, so I got to watch. That was creepy-cool, like watching a zit vid on YouTube or something."

"Ew. Don't tell me you watch those things," I say, coming over and giving him a kiss.

Duncan laughs and gives my right hand a squeeze with his good hand. "Don't worry, just something a bunch of us did one night before an away game to waste some time. Not my normal thing for sure."

"You are anything but normal," I answer, but Duncan's face clouds. "What is it?"

"I didn't tell you about it before the surgery . . . but you know about my dad, right?"

"Of course. You told me how he wanted you to throw the game. Kinda cool that you actually caught the game, literally, instead." Tyler Paulson may have won the MVP award for his passing, but Duncan's performance hadn't been overlooked. "Why?"

"Well, I got a message from my stepmom. First time

I've ever spoken with her, in fact. Dad's markers were called in, and in order to cover it all, they're taking everything, including most of my stuff too. I'm pretty much wiped out."

I nod, considering. "What's left?"

"The apartment—that was pre-paid until the end of the school year—my personal stuff like my computer, my team swag . . . but that's it. Sorry, babe. I don't think we're taking any more motorcycle rides up to Mission Park for a while."

I lean over and kiss him, smiling at his worries. "I'm not with you because of your money. You could be dirt poor, with no job prospects, and I'd still love you because of who you are."

Duncan smiles and gives me an awkward, one-armed hug. "Well, lucky for you, I'm not quite dirt poor yet. I still have a thousand or so in a personal account. And with your help, I've got great employment prospects. So hang on for just a while, and we'll be on easy street."

"Easy street? Hmm, maybe. But first, we've gotta get that arm rehabbed. You know, I'm surprised that Coach Bainridge didn't stop by."

Duncan shakes his head. "Coach sent me a text right before the surgery. He's got a meeting with the University President and the AD, then he'll come by after that. He wants to talk about when Western is going to schedule its Pro Day for the scouts. I think he wants to give me as much time as I can to rehab the arm."

"Sounds like he cares about you."

"I know. Funny, huh? In June, I would have sworn he didn't give a damn about me. Then again, I didn't give a damn about him either. I guess things have changed."

189

I give Duncan a kiss, our lips playing with each other. When his hand comes up, cupping my breast through my t-shirt, I moan and chuckle at the same time, breaking the kiss to look him in the eyes. "Well, you haven't changed all that much."

* * *

Two days later, I get a phone call just as I'm helping Duncan change the wrapping on his sutures. We're in the bedroom, since I've put all the stuff for Duncan's care on the dresser that I've moved from my dorm room to the apartment. I pick up my phone, surprised when I see who it is. "Whoa. It's the Honor Board."

"Well, are you going to answer it?" Duncan asks, taking the rest of the bandage from me and wrapping it himself. He's wearing a team polo shirt and some shorts, since before changing out his bandage, we did his first rehab session, just passive movement that had me moving his arm for him. "Not pretty, but it'll do."

"Hello?" I say, answering the call. Duncan tucks the end of his bandage into the rest and attaches the clips. "This is Carrie Mittel."

"Miss Mittel, this is Dean Friar. How are you this evening?"

"Just fine, Dean. Happy New Year."

He hums in appreciation, and I can imagine him nodding on the other end of the line. "Why, thank you. And Happy New Year to you, too. In fact, I have some good news to start your new year. I just got done reading the report, and I'm ordering that all concerns involving you and the Honor Board are dismissed. We just got the rest of the computer

190

forensic report on your phone finished. I must apologize to you."

"What happened anyway?" I ask. While I talk, Duncan's moved behind me, massaging my shoulders. His hands are strong, and I groan slightly when he finds a tight little knot next to my neck and rubs it until it releases. It feels so good.

"Miss Mittel? Are you okay?"

"Yes," I reply, and I hear Duncan chuckle behind me. He knows what he's doing, and right now, I don't mind too much either. We haven't been able to be intimate since right before I left on Christmas break, which means that for over a week, the most we've been able to do is hug and frequently kiss. But his hands . . . oh God, his hands . . . "Just happy to have it over."

"Well, the forensics have shown that it was, in fact, Chelsea Brown who was behind it all. If you don't mind, when did she have access to your personal materials?" I have to think twice about what he just said, because Duncan's hands have moved from my neck and shoulders down my back, urging me to lie down. I roll over, onto my belly, and he straddles my hips, his cock already hard in his shorts and his fingers working in slow, wonderful circles up and down my spine.

"Probably the trainer's office, or maybe my dorm room. She knew where I lived. She stopped by every once in a while. We were . . . friends, or at least I thought so." Duncan's hands sweep outward, working my back muscles, and I lift my hips just a little, feeling his cock pushing against my shorts. So hard . . . so perfect. My breathing quickens, and I know the Dean can hear me near-panting.

At least, he sounds concerned as he continues. "Well,

191

in any case, I've notified the Athletic Department, and you are now eligible to resume your internship. Best of luck."

"Thank you, Dean. Good evening."

I hang up my phone and toss it to the side, growling and working around, rolling underneath Duncan until I'm on my back, his hips still straddling mine. "You are incorrigible!" I laugh reproachfully. "You hear me on the phone with the Dean of the Honor Board, and you pick that time to try to seduce me?"

"Well, you looked so good, I couldn't resist," Duncan says, leaning down and kissing me. Our tongues slide past each other, and warmth radiates out from between my legs as we continue to taste each other. "And what's this about trying to seduce you? I'd say I *have* seduced you."

"You can seduce me with a glance and a smile," I admit, wrapping my arms around him and pulling him down on top of me. "Especially since it's been so long."

"I've missed it too," Duncan says, tilting his head to nibble on my earlobe. How he does it, I don't know, but each touch of his tongue and nip of his teeth brings fresh waves of arousal through my body. "But . . . shit."

"Not into that," I tease, a common joke I've developed with him. I'm trying to get Duncan to not talk as much like a jock. He's far too smart for that much gutter language, so I always pretend that I'm not understanding what he's saying.

He chuckles, then sighs. "What I meant is . . . we're out of condoms. I remember checking yesterday, out of curiosity, but we never picked any up."

I push his head up and shake my head. "Not a problem, is it? I mean, I'm still on the pill, and we've been together long

192

enough that I trust you."

Duncan stops, then nods and kisses me tenderly. I can sense his feelings, the level of trust that I'm putting in him, but I know I trust him with more than that. The past two nights, I've dreamed of a family life with him, and they've all been great dreams.

We kiss again, and Duncan kisses his way down to my waistband, even over my t-shirt. He pauses at my waist and shifts back onto his knees. "I'd normally do this myself, but do you think you can give me a hand?"

I chuckle and nod, pushing my shorts and panties down and off, feeling so sexy as his eyes drink me in.

Duncan slides back on the bed, bringing his head between my legs. His breath tickles over my slick skin, and I lean back, closing my eyes because it feels so good. Every inch of my skin is hypersensitive, singing in pleasure even from the non-touch of his breath.

When his tongue strokes my outer lips for the first time, it feels so amazing. I twitch as wave after wave of sensation washes through my body, my toes curling when Duncan brings his lips to mine and kisses my pussy like he's kissing my mouth, his tongue slipping inside and working back and forth. "Oh, God."

He continues to lick and taste my deepest inner flesh. I grind up into his mouth, nearly screaming when my clit rubs against the firmness of his nose, and he pulls back just enough to bring his tongue up to my tender button, new meanings of the word heaven opening up as he wraps his tongue around my clit, sucking and drawing it between his lips.

I feel my climax rushing on me, and Duncan's not

stopping, his tongue flicking back and forth faster and faster on my clit, circling around the edges before dragging the whole of his tongue over the top, then starting the maddening licks again.

"I'm going to come," I warn him, and he brings his good right arm up and places his hand on my stomach, holding me firmly while his tongue never ceases, never stops the amazing sensations. I clench, paused, trembling on the edge, and with a final lick, he pushes me over the edge. I'm coming, crying out his name softly as the amazing feelings wash through me, tears in my eyes as I've missed this for so long. At least, going a week and some change without it feels like an eternity, with Duncan bringing me higher again. "Duncan . . . stop . . . I can't take any more."

He sits up, his face shiny with my juices. "That was delicious."

I gasp, recovering my breath. "I'd reciprocate, but I want you a different way right now."

Duncan grins and nods, pushing his shorts down. He pulls his shirt off, and I'm again caught breathless as his muscular body is exposed to me. Six months, hundreds of times seeing it, but it doesn't matter. I love this man, and his body is another way he is perfect for me. "I need you on your back."

"Why?" Duncan asks but still complies. I wait until he's lying comfortably before rolling to my side and wrapping my fingers around the thick, veiny shaft of his cock.

"Because I don't want you using that arm," I admonish him. I get to my knees and pull my t-shirt off, my breasts free from a bra since we're staying home tonight. "Instead, I was thinking this."

I swing my leg over, and I reach down, taking his cock and aligning it with my entrance. "As long as we can, okay?"

"Okay," Duncan replies, resting his hands on my hips as I guide him inside me. Duncan's fingers clench on my hips as I sink down onto him, and I'm moaning too, even though I came just a few minutes ago. "Carrie . . . you're so tight."

"Ten days without you." I chuckle in reply, lifting myself up and sinking down again. Duncan's cock thrills me, hard and perfect, my pussy wrapping around it and clinging to it. It feels so good. Duncan adds another level of pleasure to my ride when he cups my breasts with his hands, my nipples between his fingers, stiff and electric.

I shift back and forth, lifting and riding him, relishing the sensations of being on top of my man, his cock filling me over and over, my clit rubbing each time I grind down on him. It feels good, so good and natural. He's warm and thick . . . my hips move faster and faster as I open my eyes to look Duncan in the eyes. The gray orbs sparkle with glitters of amber and red, his pupils widening as we move together. I'm on the edge again, Duncan filling me so much, and when I nod, he nods too, his cock growing even thicker inside me before, with a deep groan that starts in his chest and runs all the way down his body, he explodes, triggering another orgasm that sends me away into delirium. I collapse on top of him, laying my head on his chest. Duncan holds me, his hands warm on my back, and I let my eyes close, safe and warm.

* * *

"Hey, Carrie! God, it's good to have you back!"

I laugh as I take my bag off my shoulder and see Alicia

hopping from foot to foot while I get my gear ready. "Come on, Chicha. It's not that bad."

I see Alicia's hopping stop, and I tilt my head in confusion. Alicia catches my expression, and she chuckles before getting up on the training table. "Sorry, I remember that you're with Duncan now, but sometimes, I still forget. He's the only other person to call me Chicha. What would it take for you to not be your man's personal rehab specialist and work just for me and the girl's basketball team?"

I laugh and shake my head. "Sorry, but you don't swing enough weight to do that. I'll be happy to wrap your ankles for practice and home games, but Duncan's my main focus right now. Coach Taylor's even letting me do it as part of my internship, a project in supposed 'professional athlete draft preparation'. I hear Tyler and a few of the other guys who are going to try for the combine are going to join in."

"Sounds sweet. I'd love to make grades by hanging out with a bunch of hot jocks and my man at the same time. Next thing you're going to say is that you get to get all sexy fit with them too."

I blush, then nod. "Well, they do need to have someone show them what to do."

Alicia shakes her head as I finish up her ankle. "You're the luckiest woman I know."

I finish up wrapping both of Alicia's ankles and help her off the table. "Have a good practice. See you after for the ice and mobility work."

After Alicia leaves, I hear my phone ring, and I pull it out. Since Dean Friar told me that it had been cloned, I've become a bit obsessed about keeping it next to me, wanting to

196

prevent another incident. I'd thought of changing my number and getting a new phone, but I never did.

Still, I'm surprised when I see that it is, in fact, Chelsea on the other end of the call. I'm tempted to reject it and block the number, but I have too many questions that I need answered, and I hit the green button. "Hello, Chelsea."

"Hello to you too, Carrie. I am glad to see there are no hard feelings between us."

"There are plenty of hard feelings, but I figure there's a reason behind your call. Actually, there has to be at least some sort of reason behind everything you did to me. I'd like to know why."

There's a bit of a laugh on the other side, and for the first time, I seriously worry about Chelsea's sanity. There's something not right in that laugh. "I didn't start with hard feelings for you. Actually, I liked you. You were just in the way."

"In the way of what?" I ask, flabbergasted. "You were a senior, you had the internship too, and you were rocking along. If anything, I looked up to you!"

"Your mistake," and I hear real venom in her voice. "You were so smart, weren't you? Just two years after you start school, and Coach T's got you working with teams and players. You were working with *Duncan*."

"Wait . . . all this, all the lies, the bullshit, the hell you put me through, was about Duncan?"

Holy shit. I mean, I understand being angry at a guy who dumped you, but to take it to such extreme levels?

Chelsea didn't seem to grasp that simple fact. "It started as just against Duncan, but as I saw you climbing up to

197

being Coach T's favorite, it became about you, too. I wanted to hurt Duncan and eliminate you from being in my way. Unfortunately, I didn't count on Duncan being quite so . . . loyal. You were so cocky. After the first time you fucked him, I could see it in your eyes. Hell, everyone did. You were floating and walking bowlegged at the same time. Worst of all is that I could see it already. You were falling in love with him, even after I warned you about him."

"Yeah, you did. Doesn't matter, though. I've had the Hart Attack, and I love it," I dig back, tired of her bullshit. If she wants to get rude with me, I'm not going to hold back on her. This bitch nearly ruined my life. "In fact, I might just have it again tonight."

"That's good," Chelsea teases back, nearly laughing. "After my little gift, that'd be smart."

Ice runs through my veins, and my throat closes in horror. "What did you do, you crazy bitch?"

"I just paid a visit to your dorm room when you weren't around. At the same time I flashed and hacked your phone, I did a little switcheroo. Those birth control pills I found in your room . . . well, since then, you've been taking sugar pills."

My fingers go numb. Is she fucking joking? "You really are an evil, psycho bitch, you know that?"

"I know. Just think, you might even have Duncan's baby in your belly right now. I wonder how well he's going to react when you drop that little bomb on him. Or maybe you'll just . . . hmmm, nah, you're not the type to do that."

Chelsea hangs up, and I look at my phone before dropping it and crushing it under my foot.

I think about what Chelsea said—about how long I've been taking sugar pills thinking they were my birth control. How is Duncan going to react, especially if I *am* pregnant? Then again, she could just be fucking with me.

Chapter 21
Duncan

It sucks sitting in the Pavilion, watching the Pro Combine with Carrie and Coach Thibs and Coach Taylor. Not that I don't enjoy the company. I do. But watching the other tight ends go through their drills and stations, I want to be out there. My hands are constantly wringing, and my feet twitch as I watch them do their drills, wishing I could be taking part. But not yet.

"Oh, come on, they invited *that* guy?" I ask as the tight end from Northern Virginia runs the 40-yard dash. "He's a blowhard with weak hands, and he can't read blocks!"

"Tell us how you really feel," Carrie teases me, smiling a little bit. The past few weeks have been awesome, although Carrie's been looking a little tense. I can understand. I've been feeling tense too. While I'm sitting here trying to focus just on rehab, there are two other members of the Western Bulldogs who got invites to the Combine. Tyler already had his workout with the other quarterbacks, while tomorrow, Joe Manfredi gets a chance with the defensive backs. Today, though—today is the tight ends, and I'm watching my competition on the screen. "I mean, don't hold back at all."

"He is holding back," Coach Taylor jokes. "At least, based off that stream of curse words that would make a sailor blush that he let go the other day."

"Hey, I missed the weight," I weakly justify. "I got pissed. Besides, considering what you do in the weight room,

I'm the Pope."

"Still, I didn't know there were so many different ways to use the word 'fuck' in a single sentence without repeating yourself," Coach Thibs jokes. "You might want to work on that before you do the sit down interview portion of the Pro Day."

"Speaking of which, thanks for delaying it as much as you guys did," I say. One week before the draft, and I'm having to do a Pro Day. I could skip that too, but it'd hurt my draft position. The pro teams know about my elbow. There was no way to hide it after the first injury, and certainly not after my surgery. I have to show them that not only am I changed as a person, but full-strength as a player. I need the Pro Day. "Are Tyler and the other guys upset about it?"

Coach Thibs shakes his head. "Nah. Only Tyler and Joe have a legit shot at the League. The rest of the guys, they might get some indoor contracts or overseas, if they're willing to deal with the cultural stuff. So for them, they're figuring on not getting drafted anyway. But having a little more time to be polished and strong for a Pro Day might get them an invite to a training camp. So they're cool with it. How about you?"

"I—I'm good. My elbow's feeling as good as I assume it's going to be for a while, and I'm getting stronger still."

In reality, I'm not good. I'm nervous as hell, but I don't need to tell Coach Thibs that. Instead, I finish watching the review of the tight ends who did the Combine, a whole day's worth of stuff condensed to a single two-hour special. The best part, at least to me, was the analyst review at the end. "So with fifteen tight ends displaying their skills at this year's combine, there is still a sense of incompleteness with the absence of what many scouts are saying is potentially the best tight end available

201

this year, Western's Duncan Hart."

"That's true, Tony," the other analyst says, a former player whom I remember watching growing up. "If it wasn't for an early season reputation for being a hothead, a half-game suspension after being tossed from the Clement game, and of course, the elbow injury that forced him out of the crucial minutes of Western's loss in their last home game, Hart was in line for quite a few awards. With on-field numbers like he put up, it's hard to argue that he could potentially be a top ten pick, something that hasn't happened for tight ends in over a decade. While reports from Western say that Hart is currently rehabbing from elbow surgery, his second in a year on his left arm, he will participate in a Pro Day for the scouts at Western."

"Hart's a good player, and in the latter half of the season, he showed a lot more maturity to go with that amazing talent," the first analyst objected, "but I don't agree with the hype of him being a top ten pick. I'm not saying he's not a great tight end, but with the current needs of the teams in the top ten, they'd be better to spend the money and the picks on the bigger issues like quarterbacks, the big linemen, and linebackers. I wouldn't be all that surprised if Hart falls all the way to the second round, and maybe the third if his Pro Day isn't as successful as he's hoping."

"That ain't going to happen," Carrie says next to me, her inner fire showing. "I'll kick your ass if it does."

"Yes, Ma'am!" I retort with a mock salute, which earns a smile from everyone. "Speaking of kicking my ass, shouldn't we get to work? I mean, watching this is nice and all, but I need to get my work done too."

Carrie gives me a kiss, and we leave the coaches' office,

going down to the weight room. If there has been anything that has been good about my rehab, it's been the opportunity to work with Carrie again on a daily basis, both in rehabbing my arm and in getting everything else ready to go. Except for the skill work that I've been working with Coach Thibs on, Carrie's been my main trainer, spending two to three hours a day with me. And like over the summer, she goes rep for rep with me.

We get changed and set up the safety squat bar, a device I hate with a passion but with my elbow screwed up, I have to use. "This thing always knocks me off balance," I gripe as I set up for the first warm-up set. "Why'd they make it this way anyway?"

"Precisely to knock you off balance," Carrie replies with a laugh. "If you get off balance, you have to keep your form tight. You can't just bounce and momentum your way out of the hole."

"No shit," I grunt as I start the reps. It's not too bad at first. The bar's only sixty pounds, but as we add plates, it gets harder and harder. I have to keep my stomach tight and my hips under control, or else, I start to fall backward. We work side by side in adjacent squat racks, and after I leave, my legs feel like they're about to catch on fire.

"What's next?"

"Kettlebell swings. We're going to up the weight, thirty-five pounds this time. Just remember to keep the hand palm downward, and it'll be fine on the elbow."

I nod and wait while Carrie goes through her final set, gritting her teeth and grunting the last few reps, and it's amazingly sexy, especially with her ass stretching her shorts tight each time she goes down. Watching Carrie work, motivation to push harder is easy to find.

We get through the rest of the workout, including the five minutes of hell at the end that Carrie deceptively calls 'high-intensity intervals'. I call them five minutes of hell, but I know that in terms of creating football-based endurance, there isn't much better. As the moon rises behind the hills in the east, I'm wiped, but still, the little worm that's been twisting in my guts since seeing the special on the Combine won't let go. We go back to the apartment, and Carrie breaks out the massage oil, a nightly treat that both of us enjoy since I always return the favor, which usually leads to the bed.

"You're tense tonight," Carrie says as she rubs the eucalyptus-laced oil into my back. "What's wrong, babe?"

I chuckle, thinking about how the first time I ever called Carrie that, I nearly killed our relationship. Now, we use it, but only when we're having fun with each other, trying to get the other person to answer a difficult question. "Sorry. Just having a hard time letting go today."

"I noticed. It showed in the sprints and jumps at the end there. Even with the squats we did, you were off."

I nod and lay my head down on the pillow. Maybe it's not a professional massage table, but having the woman you love rub soothing oil into your back should be done on a bed, not a table anyway. "Yeah, I know. I guess I'm just worried. All that talk I did, I'm still worried that I'm going to screw up come Pro Day. We've only got a few weeks."

"And your plan is put together by the best of the best in the country, and you're right on schedule," Carrie replies, her thumbs working magic on my spine as they work in alternating outward circles. "What's *really* bothering you?"

I sigh, the tenseness inside mixing with the outer muscular relaxation in an unpleasant blend. I know what Carrie's doing. She's trying to massage my mind as much as she is my body, and it's coming out. Months together, and I'm still shocked at the strange mix of biology, exercise science, psychology, and just in general bad assedness Carrie's picked up in her studies so far. "This is the first time I'm really operating without a net?"

"You mean your Dad's money?"

I nod. Carrie's insight is clear. "Yeah. My entire life, I could go all out, knowing that if I fu— I screwed up, I'd have a bail out. In some ways, I'm surprised I didn't screw up more often, just in order to get his attention. But now . . . now, there's no safety net, not even his money. I'm going to have to back myself, and it's a new feeling."

I chuckle and open an eye to look up at Carrie, whose eyes are so full of understanding, I feel something move in my chest. "I guess you do understand. You've been backing yourself your entire time here. How have you done it?"

"By being scared almost all the time," Carrie says, leaning down and kissing my cheek. "But by doing it anyway. I was scared about loving you. I was scared that I was opening myself to a whole realm of heartbreak. I was scared when I told you no outside the stadium. But I did it anyway."

"You did," I whisper, smiling. "And that worked out well, hasn't it?"

"Because you got over being scared of yourself," Carrie reassures me. "You backed yourself then, and I'm backing you now. Now relax, and let me get your muscles as loose as they need to be before we get ready for bed."

"Hmm, I like getting ready for bed with you. Too bad we're going to have to restrain ourselves for a few days around the Pro Day."

"Oh, I'll still be here for you," Carrie reassures me as her fingers find the tired muscles of my hamstrings and begin to knead them gently. "Maybe we can't be as frisky as normal, but I'm here for you."

I relax, letting go at least for the moment, knowing that Carrie is here for me. Her hands never tire, and when she has me turn over, I pull her to me, ignoring the rest of the massage. "I didn't do anything for my chest or arms today. I think we can skip that," I say softly as I kiss her. "How about we work up an appetite before dinner?"

* * *

There are a lot of scouts in attendance, which I guess helps some with my nervousness. After all, if they didn't think I was worth the time, they wouldn't still be sticking around, right?

Tyler's getting ready to run his three-cone drill again, after we've done our forty-yard dashes. Tyler ran a better time at the Combine, but he still has a decent 4.9-second time today, decent enough for a quarterback. His big test would come later as he goes through his throwing drills.

My forty was a personal best, 4.67, a very good time for a tight end, and I'm up next for the three-cone drill, something the scouts look at more for a tight end than the straight forty.

Tyler finishes his drill and goes off to warm up for the throwing drill while I square myself on the first cone. The lateral shuffle is important, and I explode as fast as I can, my feet remembering without me even thinking about the hundreds, if not thousands, of reps that Carrie and I had done

206

since my surgery. With my arm limited, we'd spent a lot of time running.

"Six point seven five seconds!" Coach Thibs, who's acting as the timekeeper, calls out as I cross the final cone. It's all laser timed. Western doesn't want there to be any doubt about the validity of our times, and I'm happy. That's a good running back time, let alone a tight end.

I grab my water bottle and go to the side, where Carrie is smiling and has a towel for me. "Nice. Time for the heavy stuff, then you've got routes. You're nailing it."

"Yeah, but the hard stuff's next."

Carrie pats my chest and shakes her head. "Don't worry about it. Remember, I'll be there the whole time. In fact, I talked Coach T into letting me be your spotter for the bench test."

"I hope you wore your panties then. I don't want to be distracted," I tease, and she slaps my chest harder, blushing. We go into the concourse of the stadium, where the bench is set up for the convenience of the scouts. I go over and do a few reps to warm up, getting the motion down, and roll up, ready to go.

"Okay, you can lift off. Time starts when the bar descends for the first time," Coach Taylor, who's scoring and running this event, says. Carrie gets onto the spotter's platform and helps me set the bar up in my hands, giving me a confident nod as we get the bar into position. I'm locked, and I start.

I've worked the bench a lot over the past few weeks, and I focus on making each rep perfect, lifting and lowering the 225 pounds exactly to form. The burn starts right about rep twelve, the fire spreading up my triceps from my elbows to my shoulders, and then across my chest. I'm trying to use my back even to help squeeze the bar and pin my elbows, trying to keep it as tight as possible, and forget about the count. Carrie's looking into my eyes, her brown gaze letting me set aside the pain for a moment, and I squeeze out three more before the bar pauses, and she catches it, guiding it into the safety catches.

"Thirty-two," Coach Taylor says. "Better than anyone at the Combine!"

I'm gasping for air, but glad. I have fifteen minutes, then the one non-standard event for our Pro Day. At the urging of Coach Taylor, I'm going to do a deadlift demonstration, putting my left arm in the greatest strain I could place it in, just so everyone sees that my elbow is of no concern. The bar is set up, and I see that seven teams have their scouts watching.

The idea is grueling, and straight out of Coach Taylor's strongman days. Starting with 315 pounds, I lift the bar once, then on command, set it down, where Carrie and Coach T put a twenty-five-pound plate on each side. I lift again, set it down, and the process repeats itself.

I work my way up to 465, and I can hear the scouts whispering to themselves. I'm getting into the heavy territory, where a lot of tight ends fail. I'm tall, with long legs. I'm not built for this like Coach T is. It doesn't matter.

Finally, at 615, I have to hitch the bar up, and I set it down, the demonstration finished. My lower back and hands feel like someone just coated them in napalm and set them on fire, but I'm happy with the looks in the scouts' faces.

"Damn good job, son," one of the scouts says as he leaves. "Hope you saved something to run routes though."

Tyler's also nervous, but we've got five receivers and me running for him. He's got plenty of options, and I've got plenty of rest in between reps. The cuts are sharp, my extension is good, and by the end of our demonstration, including Tyler hitting me with a very nice forty-yard-long heave, I'm happy. We nailed it.

The first thing I do after the last toss is grab Carrie in a hug, lifting her up and swinging her around. She's been just as nervous as I have. I've seen it in her face. She even threw up this morning because she was so nervous, something I'd never expect her to do, but now, she's just as happy as I am. "You did it, Duncan! You were amazing!"

"No. *We* did it," I tell her, setting her down. "I could've never done it without you."

Before Carrie can say anything, a man coughs politely behind us. "Excuse me, Duncan?"

I turn to see a man in his forties, maybe about two inches shorter than me, one of the scouts from the Pro Day. He's wearing a Jacksonville Wildcats jacket, and I remember him from the deadlift demonstration. He was the one who asked if I still had something left to run routes with. "Yes, how can I help you, sir? I hope I did well enough for the Wildcats to feel I didn't waste your time."

"Waste our time?" the scout asks with a laugh. "That was one of the most impressive Pro Day performances I've seen in eighteen years of doing this gig. By the way, I'm Scott Browning, head of scouting for the Jacksonville Wildcats."

"It's a pleasure, Mr. Browning. This is my girlfriend and trainer, Carrie Mittel."

Carrie shakes hands with Browning, who beams. "You

209

helped him prepare for this? You must be good."

"Thank you, Coach Taylor," Carrie says demurely. "He's the one who taught me so much."

"Duncan, I wanted to come by and congratulate you on a hell of a workout, and I was wondering . . . what would you say to playing in Jacksonville next year?"

I stop, blinking. "The Wildcats? Really?"

Browning nods. "Really. We got ourselves a hell of a deal a while back in a trade with Seattle. You may remember it. We got Troy Wood, and the way it fell out, the Hawks' first round draft pick in this draft. On the bad side, we had to give up our best wide receiver and a right tackle. Still, it was enough to get us to the Wild Card round of the playoffs, and this year, the coaches are telling me to look for offensive talent. I was thinking, if you're still on the board, that is, on using that number nine draft pick we've got to pick you. What do you say?"

I look at Carrie, who nods.

I laugh and look back to Browning. "I'd say if you do, I'll be happy to sign with the 'Cats."

"Great. Now, that's not formal. I still need to talk to the GM and coaches, but I swing a little weight around there. If you can, keep your schedules clear, and the team will probably want to fly you down to Florida for some interviews, see how you mesh with everyone. Say, Spring Break time?"

I nod, then hold up a finger. "One request, Mr. Browning. Think you can make it two tickets? Carrie trained me, and she should get a chance to go too."

Browning smiles while Carrie looks at me in happy surprise. "I think we can arrange that. I'll be in touch, Duncan.

210

Great work today."

I've been to the campus health clinic before. I mean, almost every girl has. Even after Duncan and I first made love, I still came down here, just to get checked. Duncan knew about that. He did it himself, too, and we both had a laugh over exchanging our test results after they came back. Call it the reality of sex in the twenty-first century.

But now I'm nervous. When my period was late, I hoped that it was because of all the extra workouts I've been doing. I've always been a bit irregular when I work out hard. But for the week since Duncan's Pro Day, I've been relaxing, catching up on my school work, and ramping down my workouts.

At least, my weight room ones. Duncan and I have made love every night the past week, and my body aches pleasantly with everything we've done.

Today, though, I can't wait any longer. I need the peace of mind, or at least an answer. Duncan's in class for the morning, and I've got a kinesiology class in an hour, so this is the perfect time to come get checked out.

The volunteer nurse who takes my information looks bored, like she's done this all before, and most likely, she has. I mean, Western's got about thirty thousand students between all the different programs, more than my entire hometown, and that's a lot of people in the middle of their sexual blossoming.

"Let's just check. You're not worried about an STD test, correct?"

"Yes," I answer. "We've been monogamous for around six months, and we've both been tested in that time."

The nurse shrugs and checks a box on her form. "Okay. Have you taken a pregnancy test before? It's not hard, but if you want help, we can provide it."

"No, I'll be fine. If I need help, I'll ring."

The nurse shrugs and hands over the white cardboard box, then points. "Bathroom's down the hall on the left. You can work up a little pee, right?"

"Yeah, thanks."

I go down to the bathroom and lock the door behind me, opening the box. Dropping my jeans, I pee on the little tip, then cap it and wait, looking at my new phone's clock to make sure of the minutes. When the :41 quickly changes to :42, then :43, I turn the test over, my fingers going numb as I see the little plus sign in the indicator window.

"Well."

I don't know what to say. I'm alone in a locked bathroom, a pregnancy test in front of me, my boyfriend's finishing up his management classes for the day before going to the Pavilion for a school-hosted Draft Party, and I'm . . . pregnant.

Should I start to panic now?

Why? Because you're a college girl who got pregnant? That doesn't make you all that special. I bet at least a hundred girls got

212

pregnant at Western last year. Maybe more, with the amount of sex that goes on around here, I think to myself.

I chuckle. What do I do?

Go to class, then go to the party. Later on, maybe you can talk. You have time.

I barely pay attention in class, and when I get to the Draft Party, I see Duncan, Tyler, Joe, and a few of the other guys already there. There's a cameraman from the Football Network, along with a guy from the League, who's there to present 'draft day jerseys' for anyone who gets drafted.

Looking at his table, I notice that there is only one copy of each team's jersey, and they aren't personalized. "What's the deal?"

"Oh, I have the name plates for the three projected prospects. I pin them on in the minute or so it takes to get the call and make the formal announcement. The players get their real draft jersey afterward. I'll sew the name plate on after the day's over."

"What if two guys get drafted by the same team?"

The League rep smiles and points to a box under the table. "I've got another copy of each jersey, so that's no big deal. Besides, this is all for Hart, really. Paulson and Manfredi aren't expected to be picked until tomorrow."

"Hey, you made it!" I hear behind me, and I turn to see Duncan coming over. He's relaxed and smiling, finally able to take a day off after the stress of the past few months. He swallows me in a hug, kissing the top of my head as I let my worries go for a few minutes. "How was class?"

I smile and give Duncan a quick kiss. "I barely paid attention. My mind was somewhere else," I say honestly. "How

213

about you?"

Duncan shakes his head, and we turn, looking around the room where the party is taking place. We're using the athlete lounge, a luxurious room that's shared by all the different teams, although in theory, it's supposed to be only used by athletes in season at the time. I've never been in here before, and I'll be honest, I'm a bit jealous. If the difference between the student athletic center and Coach Taylor's weight room is a measuring stick, the difference between the general student union and this lounge is astronomical. Seriously, what sort of student lounge has leather sofas? And . . . three PlayStations? When do they ever study?

"Chill, Carrie, you're going hormonal," I admonish myself, and Duncan looks over, confused.

"What's that?"

"Nothing, just feeling a bit of jealousy. I didn't know how nice this room was before. Come on, let's grab a seat and watch. So you're really not nervous?"

Duncan shakes his head again. "Nah. You guys got me as ready for the draft as I could have ever dreamed of. Especially you. So whatever happens today, I'm ready for it. And if Jacksonville doesn't bite, someone will. I *know* it."

We take a seat, and Joe Manfredi comes over with a bowl of popcorn. "Hey, Carrie. How are you doing?"

"Good, Joe. You?"

"I won't get nervous until tonight, maybe tomorrow. This first round, I'm just chillin' until your man here gets the call. Draft analysts are saying J-ville. Nice deal, wish I got to go there."

"We'll see," Duncan says, and the draft starts. It's as

214

boring as it is nerve-racking, the first round. With up to fifteen minutes between picks, there's a lot of waiting around, but at the same time, nervousness fills me each time the League commissioner comes up to the front of the draft room on the television and makes any announcements.

The first player taken is a left tackle from Alabama, not unexpected, considering the state of the first couple of teams. Next are a couple of quarterbacks, linebackers, and an offensive tackle to round out the top six.

"You'll be hitting the board soon," Coach Thibs says, patting Duncan on the shoulder. He's actually relaxed. His talk earlier wasn't any sort of false confidence, and he's been talking with everyone about what he thinks about each pick as they come around. Pick number seven . . . eight . . .

"Jacksonville's up next," Coach Bainridge says, who joined us almost as if by magic. I hadn't even seen him come in, but then again, I've spent the past ten minutes chewing my fingernails and barely breathing, Duncan's arm around me and a bemused look on his face as he sees my nervousness.

Suddenly, two phones ring almost simultaneously, one by the League's shirt guy, and another on the conference call phone that's been set up on the table in front of our sofa. Everyone in the room stops, except for Coach Taylor, who hits the mute button on the TV before turning his eyes along with everyone else to Duncan.

"Well? Are you going to answer it?"

Duncan grins and nods, reaching out and hitting the pickup button. "Hello?"

"Hello. Is this Duncan Hart?"

"Yes, who's calling?"

I can't help it. I laugh at Duncan's casualness. He sounds like a little kid answering his home phone, not someone who's about to be drafted to a multimillion-dollar contract. Duncan gives me a smile and takes my hand, kissing the knuckles before going back to the phone.

"Hi, Duncan, I'm Gerry Lippincourt, General Manager of the Jacksonville Wildcats. Are you watching the draft?"

"Yes I am, sir. You guys are on the clock. Hope you use your pick wisely."

"We plan on it. I wanted to give you a heads up, and a last-minute chance to voice your opinion. We'd like to select you with our choice, if that's okay with you?"

"I'd be honored, sir."

"Do you have an agent, Duncan?"

"No, but if you have any paperwork you want to send over, fax it to the football team here at Western. I'll find an agent soon enough."

"Okay. We'll send over some documents in a minute. In the meantime, let's do the announcement."

The phone hangs up, and we watch as a Jacksonville representative walks up to the stage, handing a slip of paper to the Commissioner. He reads it, smiles, and turns to the microphones again. "And with the ninth pick, Jacksonville selects . . . Duncan Hart, of Western University."

* * *

Two days later, Duncan and I are in Jacksonville, where a member of the team's front office picks us up from the airport. Technically, Duncan has to still sign his contract, but he's already told everyone he's happy with Jacksonville's initial offer, and he's not going to worry about negotiations. "An

216

extra half-million on the signing bonus isn't worth worrying about," he told me as we got on the plane. "I'd rather just focus on being a good player."

We get to Wildcats Stadium, although it's got some corporate sponsor name on it that makes no sense, and get out to go into the Wildcats offices. Duncan meets with the owner, the general manager, and the head coach, a rather laid-back, excited guy who sounds as much like a California surfer dude as a football coach.

"Duncan, we know there's a lot to wrap your head around, so since this visit's a couple of days, we were thinking that you'd like to meet some of your teammates. How about dinner with one of the ones who lives here in Jacksonville?" the coach says. "You and I can have our get together tomorrow, and you can meet your new offensive coordinator."

Duncan looks at me, and I nod. I'm feeling a bit of jet lag, and I don't know if the churning in my stomach is morning sickness or just the hectic pace of the day so far combined with the time zone change. "I'd like that. A little normalcy, you know?"

Duncan nods and takes my hand, his fingers giving me the strength I need. I still haven't told him, after the craziness of the past few days, and I don't know when I am going to find the time. I need to do it soon, that's for sure. Duncan deserves to know the truth.

"You know, Coach, that sounds great. Who have you got in mind?"

"The man who's responsible for us getting the number nine pick," the coach says, grinning. "In fact, I think you two know each other already."

A player comes out, and while he's a bit shorter than Duncan, about six-two, he's just as big, but perhaps a bit thicker through the chest and back, with blond hair and blue eyes. He's ripped, and I wonder how this Nordic-looking Superman knows my Duncan.

"Well, we've run into each other a time or two," the man says, extending his hand. "Four years ago, Western versus Clement? It's nice to meet you again, Troy Wood."

It makes sense now. The guy who got traded to the Wildcats along with the draft pick that Jacksonville used for Duncan. Duncan, on his part, is beaming. "Yeah, I remember that beating. Glad to be working with you instead of against you."

"At least until next year's Western-Clement game, right?" Troy says with a laugh. "Come on, I'd like to show you my home. My wife is excited—she's spent the past two days trying to figure out how to entertain you. When we heard you were bringing a lady with you, well, she and my daughter are ecstatic. You must be Carrie Mittel. Sorry for the slow greeting. Our scout told me some of the stories he heard about what you did to help Duncan rehab that elbow. If even half of them are true, I think some of the team's going to be coming to you for help this summer."

"I've still got a year of school left," I counter, but his kind words help me feel good. "So Troy, you've got a daughter?"

"A daughter and a son, actually. You can meet them both at the house. Come on, and I hope you don't mind riding in a regular car. I heard you like motorcycles, Duncan?"

"I did. I guess I do, but I was thinking I should give

218

that up," Duncan says. "It's a lot better for taking Carrie out on dates."

Troy nods and holds the door open like a gentleman for us both. "And better for your career."

* * *

For a superstar linebacker, Troy Wood's house is remarkably understated, even if it is bigger than what I'd grown up in. A four-bedroom house, it's been done tastefully if rather . . . normally, I guess is the best way to put it. If you upgraded the size of my parents' house, you'd have Troy Wood's.

Whitney Wood, on the other hand, is anything but normal, with long brown hair and a great smile that immediately puts me at ease. "It's good to meet you," she says while the guys go off wandering into the back yard. Troy's taken his daughter, Laurie, with him, and she's already been hanging on Duncan, begging him for a horsey ride. Duncan sweeps Laurie off her feet and deposits the nearly seven-year-old on his shoulders, much to the girl's delight, while Whitney and I have a seat on the screened in porch. On the floor between us is Travis, Whitney and Troy's infant son.

"Thanks. It's great that you two are being so kind."

"Trust me, it's going to be nice having some more players our age around. Most of the young guys, the rookies and such, they're on the wild side. But your Duncan, he's shown a change of heart recently. Troy appreciates that."

"I bet. But Whitney, before you get any ideas, Duncan and I . . . we're not married, or even engaged. We've just been dating for a few months."

"And in those few months, he went from a major player to a decent guy. Trust me, I did my research. It pays, in my line of work."

"What is that, by the way? I'm still getting my head wrapped around Duncan being a Wildcat."

"I'm an art dealer, actually," Whitney says with a touch of pride. It explains so much. Her touch around the house is now evident, as perhaps the one extravagance the house has is an amazing selection of artwork, something in nearly every room. "I guess you'll hear the story eventually, but Troy and I . . . well, it's a long story, but we only got married about a year ago now. After his first half-season with Jacksonville."

"Really? The way he and Laurie get along, I thought you'd been married since she was born."

Whitney sits back and sips at her iced tea, which she'd brought out for both of us. "No, I actually got pregnant with Laurie back in high school. Troy was my first, and I had Laurie in Europe. Troy and I didn't see each other until Laurie was five, and he didn't know Laurie was his daughter for a while after that. Remind me some time, and I'll tell you the whole tale."

I nod, distracted as I think about my own current condition. Whitney notices and clears her throat. "You okay, Carrie? My best friend is a psychologist, and being in imports and exports, you tend to get a handle on people. You've been looking, well, I guess the best way to say it is preoccupied since you came in."

"Yeah, I guess I am," I answer, looking down at baby Travis. "He's cute. How old is he?"

"Two months," Whitney replies, watching as he kicks in his little chair and beams up at us. "We tried to get pregnant on our honeymoon, but it didn't actually happen until just before training camp. I still feel bad for the team. I swear, Troy was distracted in the playoffs because I had a pretty tough third trimester. Travis is like his father, huge and active. My belly looked like an alien movie."

I laugh. "Well, you are pretty petite. Getting yourself back into shape, though, I see."

"Mmm, can't be too strict though. Travis needs the milk, and Troy . . . well, he likes it too!"

Whitney's laughter causes me to smile, but my mind is still whirling. I feel tears well up in my eyes, and one escapes, trickling down my cheek. Whitney stops laughing and slides next to me, rubbing my back. "Hey, I'm sorry. I know it was a horrible joke."

I shake my head and wipe the tear away. "No, it was fine. Just . . . stuff's on my mind. Can I ask you some personal questions?"

"Sure. I'm hoping that we can become friends. I'm not trying to say a lot of the players' wives and girlfriends and I don't get along, but I spent five years in Italy after growing up in a small town in the Seattle area. Just different backgrounds is all."

"Well, do you ever . . . I don't know, have any regrets about the way it happened between you and Troy? I mean, if Laurie's six, you must have had her back in high school. That had to be tough."

"It was. And yes, I do have one regret about it all."

"What's that?"

"I regret the five years that Troy didn't know he had a daughter. Oh, I guess I had my justification for it at the time. Troy was also in high school, I didn't want to hurt his football career, yada yada. I wasn't even sure I was going to tell him until I did. I didn't want him to think I was gold digging on him. But I forgot something in all my excuses. I forgot about Troy and who he is. He was such a player before we met. I called him a manwhore, in fact, at first, and we joke about it still. But when he and I clicked . . . it was magic. He changed and matured before my very eyes. Then I got pregnant and forgot about all that. I just went off my fears, and it took me five years to rectify that mistake. So yeah, I do regret that. Watching Laurie and him play on that swing set outside that Troy built for her . . . that's my only regret."

I wipe at my eyes and think with Whitney staying right next to me. She doesn't ask any questions. I think she's pretty sure what's going on, because as we see the guys come back, stopping outside to let Laurie play on the swings, she pats my back again. "Tell him. Don't make the same mistake I did. Besides, I saw how he looks at you. He loves you, Carrie. That man is head over heels in love with you. Have faith in that, and you'll be fine."

Duncan, Troy and Laurie finish playing outside, coming back inside with Laurie leading the way. "Mama," she says, and I can pick out now the lilt to her accent. It's Italian, "Duncan can skip a rock five times across the pond!"

"Really?" Whitney asks, giving Duncan a smile. "Tell me you're not trying out for quarterback now too."

Duncan laughs and comes over, sitting down next to me. "Nah. Just a lucky find of a good stone, and the pond's as flat as ice. So did you two have a good chat?"

"We did," Whitney says. "Carrie's quite a catch. I wouldn't let go of her if I were you."

"I'm not," Duncan says, taking my hand again. "Not if I have anything to say about it."

Chapter 23
Duncan

It feels weird, after spending the past three months slowly watching my bank account dwindle as my money ran out, to see five figures on the screen as I take money out at the ATM. The Wildcats, understanding my predicament, gave me an advance on my signing bonus, the team President cutting me a personal check before Carrie and I left Jacksonville. I'm good to go while the paperwork winds its way through the lawyers, which are a lot more numerous than I thought there would be.

I take out two hundred bucks and tuck the cash into my wallet, then get my card. I tuck everything into my jacket and head toward campus, pulling my backpack up over my shoulder. While my contract is signed, I still have a college degree to finish up, and the Wildcats have been really understanding about that. They're trusting me to continue working with Carrie and Coach Taylor in working with my elbow and staying in playing shape, and three weeks after graduation, I'm to report to Jacksonville to do my first rookie camp.

Actually, that's the only concern I've had this whole time since being drafted. Classes are going okay. I'll get my degree, but the move to Jacksonville seems to be causing stress between Carrie and me. I don't understand why either, because I'm more dedicated to her than ever. Each time I turned around with the Wildcats, I was asking someone on the team advice on how to help Carrie adjust. The team even said they'd be willing to work with Western, if Carrie wants to do her last year as a split student. She can do the fall semester in Jacksonville, interning with the Wildcats and doing studies via distance learning, and then we can go back in the spring semester in order to let her wrap up her brick and mortar classes that she can't do in Jacksonville. The most we'd have to be apart is a month, and only if the Wildcats go deep in the playoffs.

So things should be great, but for some reason, they're not. Last night, for the first time since we moved in together, she was offish, not wanting to even cuddle on the couch. I chalked it up at the time to stress. I mean, we've both got reports and finals coming up pretty soon, but still, it's on my mind.

Walking by the Pavilion, I see Tyler Paulson. He didn't get drafted, but afterward, he got an invite to sign a contract with Toronto of the Canadian League. "Hey, Tyler. How's it going?"

"Not bad," Tyler says, waving. "Just got off the phone with the guys up in Toronto. They're sending down some stuff to help me find an apartment. No way am I moving up there full time. That city is stupid levels of expensive."

"What, you don't like T-dot girls?" I tease, and Tyler laughs.

"I hate that fucking nickname, and I haven't even

224

moved there yet. As for the honeys, oh, that city is crazy hot, but I can do that still being a part-timer. Remember, we're now famous professional athletes!"

"Yeah well, you can enjoy that particular side for the both of us. I'm off the market."

Tyler slows, and I stop. We're next to the big statue that's outside the stadium, put up back in the seventies after the basketball team won the national title two years in a row. Tyler turns to me, a half-smile on his face. "That serious, huh?"

I nod and reach into my jacket pocket. I pull out the little black case and show Tyler the diamond ring inside. "What do you think?"

"I think that you got it too small," Tyler says after he gasps, "but I'm touched. Of course I'll be your quarterback for life, Duncan! I didn't know you thought of me that way, but—"

"Oh shut up, asshole." I laugh. "Seriously, what do you think?"

Tyler looks at the ring for a second, and his smile widens. "I think it's great, man. Question, though, and don't get pissed, I'm just asking. Is this because of the distance? J-ville's a long way from Cali, you know."

"No. At least, not all of it," I reply. "I mean, I want to be with her forever, you know what I'm saying?"

"I had two girlfriends last month while prepping for the Pro Day. I have no idea what the fuck you're talking about," Tyler jokes, then grows serious. "But it's cool if you do. I'm just not there yet, man, but when I do, I hope it's with as good a girl as Carrie. When are you going to ask?"

I shake my head, shrugging. "I don't know. I mean, I was thinking of doing it last night, but she was a bit off, just

225

not her normal self. I guess I'm looking for the right time to ask, that's all. I just picked up the ring yesterday from the jewelers. It took me nearly two hours just to pick it out online and put the order in."

"How many game checks is it costing you?" Tyler asks, and I shrug again.

"It could cost me my entire signing bonus, and I'll count it as worth it."

"Careful, you're going to end up broke on the side of the road before you know it."

I laugh and punch Tyler in his left shoulder. "Hardly. Actually, I got some good advice and the name of a good investment banker from one of my new teammates. I figure if he's good enough to handle Troy Wood's money, he can handle mine too."

"You got to hang out with Troy Wood? I hate that guy! He picked me off twice that Western-Clement game we played him!" Tyler rebukes me with a laugh. "Don't tell me you're buddy-buddy with the guy?"

"He's a good dude. Had me over to his house to meet his wife and two kids. He let me really bend his ear, just find out what it's like as a pro. Anyway, one of the big things he advised me to do, and it makes sense after what happened to my dad, is to just live below my salary. I'm not saying the man's a tight ass, but he and his wife drive used cars, and their only real splurge is his house, which even then isn't even one year's worth of his contract. He's put away huge amounts of his income, some saved, a lot invested, and he's got a guy who's beaten the market by ten percent each of the past three years. I'm going to be giving him a call soon."

Tyler nods and chews his lip in thought. "I see. You got the man's number?"

"Yeah, back at my place. I'll email it to you. But I'm going to do the right thing for Carrie. I love her, and yeah, I want to marry her."

Tyler shakes his head in disbelief and smiles. "All right, then. It's a good ring. I'll even be nice for you and not tell her you showed me a ring. How's that?"

"Thanks. I'll see you later. I've got lunch with Carrie in about twenty, and I don't want to be late."

I head off and get to the restaurant just before Carrie and I agreed to meet up. She had a lab this morning, and I want to give her a chance to relax after a stressful morning before we start our afternoon classes. It's been kind of nice this final semester of college to actually have classes that start late and end late, with no need to duck out early to make practice.

I see Carrie walking up, and I stand up, reaching out for a hug. "Hey, how was class?"

"Terrible," Carrie grumps, dropping into her seat. "I'm totally screwing up this damn thing. I'm maybe going to get a B if I'm lucky and pull something out of my ass for the final."

"It happens to everyone. Don't sweat it. This hasn't been an easy semester for us."

"Yeah, well, I'm not the one without any classes starting earlier than ten four days out of five," Carrie complains, then stops. "I . . . I'm sorry, Duncan. That was uncalled-for."

I shake my head, refusing to get upset. How can I, when I have a ring in my pocket? "It's nothing, Carrie. You're right. I picked this semester to be a bit lazy. I'm going to finish my degree, but the fact is that despite my admiration of learning, my main degree was the one I just got signed to do. And you helped me with it. So yeah, I'm chilling out a bit, and no, it's not fair to you that you've been doing double-duty as my trainer and trying to keep up your own studies. You're amazing that way."

Carrie stops, and suddenly, she breaks down crying. I go to reach for her, and she pushes my hands away, wiping at her eyes. "No, no . . . it's nothing. Seriously, it's nothing. Let's just have lunch."

"Carrie, it's not nothing," I say, setting aside my water glass. "You've been disturbed ever since Draft Day, really, but it's kicked into high gear since we got back from Jacksonville. What's going on?"

"Just . . . hormonal," Carrie says before wiping at her eyes. "I'm okay. I'm afraid, Duncan. I still have a year of school, and you're going to be in Jacksonville . . ."

"We can handle that," I urge her, reaching across and taking a hand. "We talked about this with the team, remember? You can do your internship with their staff, and then finish out your degree in the offseason. That's not so bad, is it?"

"I know, but there are so many challenges."

"Carrie," I interrupt her, fear taking over. "Don't say that you're having second thoughts . . . about us?"

Carrie stops, her mouth dropping open. "You . . . you think that I'm . . . Duncan, I'm not having second thoughts at all!"

"Then, what is it? Because I'm worried, Carrie. You've been pensive, moody, like you said, hormonal—"

"Duncan, I'm pregnant!"

Every person in the restaurant stops at Carrie's yell, and

heads turn on a swivel to look in our direction. I'm left in a daze again, blinking stupidly at Carrie as it all falls into place. The nervousness, the mood swings, the sudden desire for insane amounts of ramen . . . all of it. "You're pregnant? You're pregnant."

"Please, Duncan, I'm not trying to gold dig on you," Carrie starts, before I cut her off with a hug and a kiss. She resists me at first, before she realizes that I'm happy, and she melts into my arms, her lips softening and her hands coming to wrap around my neck while I lift her carefully into the air. When I set her down, I can see that she's crying. "You're not upset?"

I laugh and reach into my pocket, pulling out the box inside. "How about this for an answer?"

I get down on one knee, and I can hear the intake of breath from at least half a dozen people around us, and someone on the phone saying, "Oh my God, he just got down. I think he's going to propose."

"Duncan, how . . . why . . ." Carrie starts, but I cut her off by opening the box.

"Carrie Mittel, I want to be with you for the rest of my life. Will you marry me?"

Carrie nods, fresh tears streaming down her face, and I take her hand, sliding the platinum and diamond ring onto her finger. When it's done, the whole restaurant breaks into applause, along with a few cheers as well. Carrie looks at the ring one more time, still trying to find her voice, when someone interjects. "Hey, my sister-in-law wants to know if you say yes! Make it official!"

"Yes . . . yes!" Carrie cries out, finding her voice,

229

smothering my face in kisses. "Oh God, yes!"

We hold each other, just letting our fears go, when Carrie chuckles. "This is a hell of a way to start lunch."

"Let's get some, shall we? Then we can get to class afterward."

Carrie nods and sits down, looking at her ring finger where her new ring sparkles. "I was so stupid, worrying about you. I'm sorry."

"Don't be. No regrets, Carrie. I've racked my head for days looking for the perfect moment to ask, when all the time, I should have just done it. I didn't have the ring then, but I would have asked you on Draft Day if I had the guts." I pick up the menu, then set it down, looking across the table at her. "So you've known a while?"

"Since Draft Day," Carrie says, looking down, ashamed. "I . . . I should have told you earlier."

She lifts her head, and when she sees my smile, she returns it, perking up. "Right, no regrets. I'm just glad I did say something."

"I think fate brought us together this way, you know?" I reply, opening the menu to decide what to order. "I mean, I seriously didn't know about the baby. Actually, you know when I first started thinking about asking you?"

"Mission Park?" Carrie asks, and I jerk my head up, surprised. "Me too. You did go down to a knee there. Since then, you know, in those idle moments or when I've let my daydreams go a bit, I've seen it."

"Me too, although my fantasies are a bit more . . . well . . ."

Carrie laughs and gives me a look that sends warm

230

tingles throughout my body. "Trust me. Me too."

* * *

"You really want to? It won't hurt you or anything?"

Carrie laughs and kisses me tenderly. We've decided to stay in to celebrate our engagement, relishing an evening without the stress of everyone else knowing.

"Duncan, you're an expert in football and a genius when it comes to pleasuring my body, but you don't know much about pregnancy, do you?"

"Well, I know there's a stork, and he'll come flying by somewhere around New Year's if my math is right, and then he drops the baby down a chimney, and viola! Am I close?"

Carrie rolls her eyes and chuckles. We're naked, but so far, we haven't done much more than just lay together on the sofa, and I'm enjoying the feeling of having her in my arms. "Not quite. Actually, after finding out about the baby, I did a lot of my own research online. I need to do some health-related stuff, but I can schedule that with the on-campus clinic before finals. Then over the summer, well, I guess you'll have to contact the Wildcats about adding me to your health insurance. Do they cover family?"

"I don't know. I'm sure. We'll find out, though. But it's really okay?"

"Barring complications, some of the sources I read said that we could have sex up until the eighth month . . . if you don't mind my swollen belly."

"I won't mind. Every day, you get more beautiful to me. You could have triplets in there, and that won't do anything but make you more beautiful."

"Triplets? Oh, hell no!" Carrie laughs, leaning back

231

against my chest. "Giving birth to triplets during the playoffs? Whitney told me how distracted Troy was during the playoffs. I'd hate to imagine what you'd be like. They'd have to attach Velcro to your helmet to catch the ball!"

We lie back, taking our time. We have all night, and there's no rush, and as our hands join, I can feel the warmth spreading through my body. I lean in, and kiss the curve of Carrie's neck, tasting the soft spiciness of her skin, and cup her left breast with my hand. "Carrie?"

"Yes?"

"Join me for a shower?"

Carrie nods and turns her head, kissing me softly. "You'd better hurry, because another part of me wants to just turn over and make love to you on the couch right now."

I shift out to the side, and before Carrie can get up, I scoop her up in my arms, carrying her toward the bathroom. Carrie smiles and puts her head against my shoulder. "You know, you're the only man who's ever made me feel petite and fragile."

I set Carrie down on her feet while I turn on the shower and the bathtub at the same time. The Vista has nice baths, and I have enjoyed the fact that my own apartment has a built-in massaging jet bathtub. "Come, let me wash your hair while the bath fills," I tell Carrie, guiding her into the shower stall. "You're giving me such an amazing gift, and I want to serve you tonight."

Carrie smiles her angelic smile and strokes my face. "You can serve me by being the strong, wonderful man you are. You don't know how good you make me feel."

Running my fingers through Carrie's beautiful hair is

232

sensual, erotic as I gently massage the lather into her pale golden locks, the scent of the herbal shampoo she'd gotten as a Christmas gift filling the shower stall as I rinse her off. She reaches back, her eyes closed but still finding my cock, which is hard and aching after being so close for so long. Her fingers are wet and slippery, sweet torture as she strokes me slowly, smiling as I tremble, running my hands through her hair again to rub in the conditioner. "You say you like me strong . . . yet you're doing a good job teasing me while I serve."

"Mmm, maybe I like you serving and being strong at the same time," Carrie replies. "Just like I promise to serve you."

I somehow keep control of myself as the conditioner soaks in, and I rinse it out, Carrie not letting go of my cock the entire time. We leave the shower and walk the few steps to the bath, Carrie letting me go in first before she follows, nestling between my legs. Leaning back into me, she lets her head rest on my chest, tilting her head up and back so that we can kiss. "Thank you," she whispers after our kiss. "For everything."

I reach over and take the soap in my hands. Working up a lather, I set it aside and wash her, starting with her shoulders and collarbones before working my fingers over her breasts, slipping and sliding over the smooth, beautiful skin. How a woman can have such strength as Carrie does but still have silky smooth skin is magical, in my opinion. The deep groan from her chest when I cup both of her nipples is electric, and my cock twitches under the water. "You didn't want to help me wash up at all."

"We can wash later," I promise, my hands moving in circles. I find Carrie's nipples again and lightly pinch them

233

between my thumbs and forefingers, relishing the gasp that escapes from her lips. Every inch of Carrie is beautiful to me, but her breasts are out of this world, sensitive, perfect in shape and texture, heavy and soft. "Right now, I'm making love with my soon to be wife."

"Say it again," she whispers, her eyes closed in the haze of sensation washing over her. "Call me that again."

"My wife," I whisper in her ear. Carrie trembles, her body on the edge of coming, and I pause, kissing her. "I'm giving you a choice. You can come now, or wait for me."

With a deep, calming breath, Carrie nods. "Take me to bed . . . my husband."

Once again, I carry her through the apartment, wrapped in a towel to lay her on our bed. Setting her down, I gently unwrap the cotton from around her, smiling at her little pose. "Beautiful."

Carrie spreads her legs, urging me between them, and I line myself up, pausing. "What is it?"

I smile and tease the tip of my cock between her lips, rubbing it up and down, over her clit before nestling it at her entrance again. "It just . . . has a lot of meaning now, more than ever before."

"I know," Carrie answers, reaching down and taking my hand. "Sexy, isn't it?"

I push in, my cock sinking into her. Our fingers interlock, palms together as I finish sliding all the way inside her. We stay that way for a moment, the beauty of the meaning not lost on either of us before I pull back and slip inside again.

Carrie takes it all and gives it back, giving herself to me while demanding everything from me. We let the speed and pace be dictated only by our own desires, our eyes locked on each other even as our hands never part. When I lean down to kiss her, pushing our hands over her head so that I can still keep our loving grip, her lips are amazingly soft and loving. My hips speed up, faster and faster. I give myself to her, the only sounds in the bedroom the thunder of our hearts, the gasp of air in our lungs, and the sharp slapping sound of my hips driving my cock over and over again deep into her. We are both pushing, reaching that peak which only Carrie has ever brought me to, an intensity that captures my heart, body and soul in one instant.

"Duncan," Carrie gasps, her voice failing her. She's so close . . . only a few more seconds.

"Carrie!" I cry, my cock erupting. Coming with Carrie is something I'll never be able to fully explain, except that it moves my soul, and I'm groaning as I give myself fully to this woman, the woman I want to spend the rest of my life with.

Afterward, Carrie lays on top of me, her head on my chest, her right hand lazily tracing my stomach muscles. "I've missed that."

"Never again . . . well, except for months eight and nine," I hum, rubbing her shoulder.

"Oh, the things I'll sacrifice to become a mother and wife," she mock laments, reaching down and taking my now soft cock in her hand. "It's going to be such a hard life."

"Keep that up, and it will be." I sigh happily as she pumps me slowly. It hasn't been long enough for me to be ready again, barely ten minutes, but it still feels wonderful.

"Actually, I just had a thought," Carrie says, her hand pausing. "We've got some people to tell about this and some decisions to make."

"Oh, our friends might be a bit surprised, but I doubt any will be all that shocked. And for school, where we'll live in Jacksonville and how—"

"Actually, I meant my parents." Carrie laughs lightly. "Don't you think we should tell them?"

I stick out my lower lips, nodding thoughtfully. "Good point. Okay, let's fly them down and break the news to them, and we can discuss the other stuff when my mind isn't somewhere else."

"Oh, you mean here?" Carrie asks as she shifts down, licking her lips before kissing the tip of my now rapidly-swelling cock.

Chapter 24
Carrie

I'm nervous pulling up to the airport with Duncan in his new car. Well, not new. He followed Troy Wood's advice and bought a slightly used car, a two-year-old Volvo XC90, a choice that still makes me laugh. It's not that it isn't a great choice, it's just that I'm sure somewhere inside Duncan is the motorcycle-riding thrill-seeker, but he's holding off until we're settled in more.

"Hey, it's going to be okay," Duncan says, taking my hand as I stand in the short-term parking lot. "Come on, if this Volvo doesn't convince them that I'm a changed man who is worthy of their daughter's hand, I'm not sure what will. Unfortunately, I can't remove the tatts easily."

"What are you talking about? You *added* to your ink," I remind him, touching his chest. It had been a spur of the moment decision, but we both sported ink now, Duncan wearing 'Carrie' over his heart while I now have 'Duncan' inscribed on the inside of my left wrist. I'd wanted it over my heart as well, but Duncan asked that I not put ink on, what he called, the most perfect breasts ever created. "I still feel weird not wearing my ring to keep this surprise. Just make sure you keep your shirt on until after we tell my folks, okay?"

"That shouldn't be a problem. I doubt your Dad wants to see me shirtless anyway," Duncan teases back, taking my hand and kissing the fingertips before holding it. "It'll be okay."

I nod, and we walk into the baggage terminal. Mom and Dad's flight is supposed to land in just a few minutes, so we're definitely early. I take a seat on one of the benches, Duncan taking the seat next to me.

"I know it's going to be okay, I just . . . my parents, you know?" I say, taking a seat. "I'd like to keep things good between us. I'm not blaming you for your relationship with your parents. Your dad is a certifiable bastard, but it'd be nice if our baby has at least one set of good grandparents."

"I agree," Duncan says without any rancor about me calling his dad a bastard. Actually, nobody has seen or heard from Winston Hart in months, and there have even been questions raised. The police, in fact, called Duncan yesterday, but he told them everything he knew, and that since then, he hadn't seen his father at all. I suspect that if anyone does find Winston Hart, it'll most likely be in Nevada. There's a lot of empty space in Nevada, a lot of desert where men can just . . . disappear. Still, part of me, a kinder part, hopes he's safe somewhere.

"Delta Flight 7231, bags arriving at Carousel 12," a public address system says, and we stand up to make our way over.

"That's them," I say, waiting. The airport is huge, so big that even the baggage area needs multiple entrances and exits, and it's still another five minutes before I see Mom and Dad come down the escalator from the upper floor of the airport. "Mom! Dad!"

They wave, Dad with their carry-on over his shoulder, and I'm relieved to see that they look good. Dad's not looking as stressed out as before, and Mom, if anything, looks younger.

"Honey!" Mom calls, greeting me. She gives me a hug over the security barrier while Dad gets their bag, a single roller that they're sharing. "Oh, it was so nice to get your invitation. A surprise, but a welcome one."

"I'm just glad Dad was able to make his schedule fit," I say as Mom lets go. "It's so awesome that you can come down."

"Well, when you get such a mysterious invitation, how can you say no? Big news, a paid four days in a five-star hotel, and Duncan's graduating soon? By the way, it's good to see you, Duncan. You're looking very handsome today."

"And you, Mrs. Mittel, are as lovely as your daughter," Duncan replies, giving Mom a hug and kiss on the cheek. "I'm glad you're staying in a hotel, because if you go anywhere near campus, you're going to have college guys all over you, and your husband is going to be very jealous."

Mom actually blushes and smiles, playfully pushing Duncan away. "You're incorrigible, Duncan. And do I need to tell you again? Call me Cora."

"Carrie tells me that all the time. But I'll try to remember, Cora."

Dad comes over, and Duncan offers his hand, which Dad takes, if not with a lot of enthusiasm, at least he isn't chilly. After all, in his point of view, Duncan and I have been dating for eight months now, so he's at least somewhat accepting of Duncan being part of my life. "Duncan, congrats on getting drafted."

"Thank you, Mr. Mittel. I'm glad you guys get to be here for a visit. It means a lot to me."

We go out to the Volvo, which surprises Dad. "Where'd you get this?"

"Uh, there have been a lot of changes since the Sunshine Bowl," I say. "I didn't tell you, but Duncan lost his bike."

"What happened? Did you get in an accident?" Mom asks, and Duncan shakes his head.

"No, Cora, it was repossessed," Duncan answers without any shame. "Most of my lifestyle prior to the Sunshine Bowl was funded by my father. He got himself into a lot of financial troubles, and when the banks came to collect, I ended up with not a lot left. I'm just lucky that my apartment and school were pre-paid."

"Well, that is news," Dad says, a new tone creeping into his voice. Is it grudging respect? "You must have learned a lot."

"I have," Duncan says as he starts up and pulls out. He pays the machine, and we drive toward the Westin Downtown, where Mom and Dad are staying. "I learned a lot about how everyone else lives. It's given me some more appreciation of the contract that the Wildcats offered me."

"It's an impressive one, I'll say," Dad says, not sure how to broach the subject. I mean, how do you talk to a man twenty-four years your junior who just signed a contract with a multimillion-dollar signing bonus, and another ten million dollars in guaranteed money over the next four years? "It even made the news."

"Thanks. I really didn't want to haggle over it, and their first offer was good enough. And I've gotten in touch with the right financial people. Things are looking good there. Speaking of that, how's the trucking business going, Mr. Mittel?"

"Good, but the back's acting up," Dad answers with a grumble. "I really need to drop a few pounds, get a decent health program going."

"Well, if I can make a recommendation, your daughter's a miracle worker on that. I don't know about lower backs, but her work with elbows is world-class."

I blush even though I've heard it before, but Dad looks pleased. We continue to exchange small talk until we get to the hotel, and Duncan parks, all of us going inside. In the lobby, Duncan stops, taking my hand. I clear my throat, exchanging a look with him. It's time. "Uh, Mom, Dad?"

"Yes, sweetie?" Mom says, turning around. Dad, who's gone on a few steps ahead with his wheeling bag, also stops, raising an eyebrow. I think he's expecting what's coming next, even if he might have his reservations about it.

"Before you check in, Duncan and I have something to tell you," I say. I elbow Duncan, who's actually blushing and

240

trying not to grin as realization dawns on Mom's face. "Duncan?"

"Well, you guys know that Carrie and I have been dating for quite a few months now, and a week ago, I asked Carrie to marry me," Duncan says, reaching into his shirt pocket and taking out my ring, where we'd stashed it temporarily for safekeeping. I slip it on, while Dad comes up next to Mom, taking her hand, both of them lost with the reality of what's happening in front of them. "I'm happy to say she said yes."

"You . . . you two are engaged," Dad says, then he swallows something in his throat and sets his bag up on his wheels before coming forward, giving me a hug before offering another handshake to Duncan. "Congratulations, Duncan."

"Thank you, sir," Duncan says while Mom hugs me. "I know you've got your concerns, and with what Whitney's told me, I can't say I wouldn't have the same. I hope that you can set them aside in time for the wedding."

Dad swallows again, looking a bit lost. "I guess . . . I'm still shocked. I'm a little old-fashioned, Duncan, and I was hoping that Carrie would have approached me to talk about this, maybe even gotten my blessing before accepting your proposal."

"I understand," Duncan says. "I know it's a lot to swallow, so how about we talk about it at dinner? I've got a class this afternoon, last one of the week before I take the weekend off, and Carrie's gotten us reservations at some place called Tres Amigos. Apparently, you have a thing for Mexican food?"

Dad nods, while Mom stands there, still speechless in

241

shock. "Okay. Cora, let's get checked in and washed up. Carrie, are you going with Duncan, or can you stay with us for the afternoon?"

"I cleared it with Coach Taylor. I'm taking the whole weekend off from interning," I say. "With basketball over, and the only big sports left being baseball and track, the load on the trainers is light for a while. Actually, I'd like to talk with you guys about that, too."

"Oh good, you're not dropping out of school!" Mom says, her first words since our announcement. "I don't know why, but that just kept running around and around in my head."

I give Duncan a kiss, and he says his farewells, going out to the car. He actually does have a class, and we thought my parents might need some time to adjust. Dad finishes check-in, and we take our key up to the suite that Duncan rented for the whole stay. It's nice, and while not a penthouse, it's a good room. Dad sets their bag on the bed, while Mom finds the chair by the window and I arrange myself comfortably on the bed. I'm not showing yet, but I am feeling my body start to change, and it feels wonderful. I feel more complete than ever, powerful, and especially sexy when I see the desire in Duncan's eyes. "Thanks for not making a scene in the lobby, Dad. I could read it in your eyes."

"Carrie, it's not that I'm not happy for you. It's obvious that you love Duncan very much, and after this many months, I guess my initial worries about your being a fling for him have to be set aside. But, what about school? What about your future? I mean, if Duncan blows out his knee or pops that elbow again, you're not going to be living a rich life."

"Dad, Duncan's already taken the advice of one of the other players, and he has gotten in touch with a good investment banker. He's putting aside a good chunk of his signing bonus into savings and investments. He could never play a down of pro ball, and we'll be fine. Besides, he's got his degree, and I'll have mine too. We're going to be fine."

"But honey, I don't want to . . . what's it you college kids say, *throw shade?*" Mom asks, and I laugh.

"Don't try it, Mom. Just be you. And I can read your mind. Duncan's going to be away from home for half the games, there are football groupies, and all that, right? Don't worry, that was part of what we wanted to talk to you about. I discussed it all with Coach Taylor right after Duncan got drafted, even before he proposed. I'm going to move to Jacksonville with Duncan and do an internship with the Wildcats. I can also do a class online during the summer and the fall terms, so that after the season, I come back here, and I can wrap up my degree on time with one semester back at Western. If things go right, I'll even be in line for a position with the Wildcats myself next season. You guys can see me walk in May next year, just like we all planned."

"You two have planned out a lot of this already," Mom says. "I'm surprised."

"We've been talking about this since football season, when we realized that we were looking at this being long-term. So some of these plans have been around a while. It was just his proposal that kind of came up suddenly, although Duncan told me he wanted to ask me for weeks prior to when he did."

"What about the wedding?" Dad asks. "I mean, honeymoons, ceremonies, all that."

243

I shake my head. "We're going to do it in two stages. After Duncan graduates, we're going to go to Vegas, and yeah, I know that sounds trite, but it's what we want. We're going to get married there, and then Duncan and I are going to go to Jacksonville to get settled in. He hasn't specifically picked out which house we're getting yet, but we're going to go down, pick something out, and then get to work. Duncan wants to get to the playoffs his rookie year, and I agree with him. Too many rookies with first-round picks show up thinking they don't have to put in the work. If he's learned anything since he and I started his rehab the first time, it's that he knows how to buckle down and work. We'll do our honeymoon later on— we'll find the time."

"Well, if you say so. Let's save the rest of this until dinner, why don't we? Tell us about your trip to Jacksonville. I know it's kind of related, but in your emails, you sounded like you had a ton of fun."

"I did. You two will love it when you visit. In fact, I think I made a new friend, a woman named Whitney."

* * *

Tres Amigos is a nice restaurant, and even Dad relaxes as the appetizers come to the table. "To Duncan and Carrie," Dad says, raising his bottle of Dos Equis for a toast. The rest of us, who aren't drinking for various reasons, lift our glasses. Mom doesn't like alcohol, Duncan's driving, and well, I'm pregnant, although Mom and Dad still don't know. "Duncan, I hope you realize how lucky you are."

"Trust me, I know," Duncan says. "Carrie is precious, and I'm a lucky man to be starting a family with her."

Mom, who sips at her iced tea, hums. "A family? That

would be nice some day. I've sometimes thought about little grandchildren running around that I can dote on."

"Actually Mom, it's going to be sooner than you think," I say. "We didn't want to throw everything at you at once. We wanted to save this for a time when you could absorb it, and maybe celebrate, but I'm . . . well, we're going to have a baby."

Dad drops his bottle of Dos Equis, which explodes on the tile floor of the restaurant. The waiter rushes over with a towel and offers to get him a new drink, but he waves him off. "Tea, please. I—I think I've had enough alcohol."

The waiter leaves, and Dad turns to Duncan, his eyes burning with intensity. "One question. Did you know about this *before* you asked Carrie to marry you?"

Duncan and I exchange looks, and he chuckles. "In a remarkable coincidence, Mr. Mittel, I bought the ring and was taking Carrie to dinner to propose when she told me."

Dad considers it, then nods. "Vince. Duncan, my name is Vince."

Dad stands up and comes around the table next to me. I stand, and moments later, we're hugging, before Mom and Duncan join us for a group hug. I'm in the middle of the three people whom I love the most in the world, and it's the best feeling in the world.

Epilogue
Duncan

245

"Happy anniversary, bro."

"Thanks," I say, clinking glasses of tea with Troy. "Thanks for having me and Carrie over for the barbecue."

Troy laughs as we sit on the back porch of his house. The late spring sun is low in the horizon, and we're both relaxing after a good day of off-season conditioning. The humidity is tough on me. Carrie and I have only been back in Jacksonville a week since her graduation, and after the California dryness, it takes a while. "Duncan, you live two blocks away. You, me and Carrie carpooled to work half the time last season. I think having you over the day after your first wedding anniversary is hardly out of the question."

"Still," I say, leaning back. "It was nice of you and Whit to cut your time in Silver Lake Falls short in order to come back here."

"Well, after Patricia's news, this summer's going to be pretty hectic. I thought you and I might just get our heads in the right zone before everything goes nuts. I mean, we've already had Carrie's graduation and your anniversary. Then what, you two go off on your honeymoon, and Cory and Patricia's wedding—all of this before training camp, by the way."

I smile and nod, sipping the tea. It's good, and Troy insists on the best quality. He doesn't knock me for the occasional beer, but since he's dry as a bone, I don't drink at all around him. It just isn't right to treat your friend that way. "Yeah, that's gotta be a brain buster, your new father-in-law being your high school teammate. We'll all be busy, though. But you stayed in good shape up there in Washington. At least, Carrie said so."

246

"Your wife is a taskmaster in the weight room." Troy laughs. "It's weird to be intimidated by a woman who's pushing you to work harder when she just had a baby six months ago. By the way, Whit's a bit jealous at how quickly Carrie bounced back to her pre-baby weight."

I snort. "Oh, like she has anything to worry about. I see the way you look at her. You need to be careful, or else you're going to be having child number three soon enough."

"That'd be nice," Troy says, and he means it, I can tell. "One kid for each bedroom . . . it'd be nice. Kind of completes the house."

"It would, wouldn't it?"

We sit for a few more minutes, thinking our own thoughts. Carrie and Whitney are out. Whitney's got a line on some new artist she wants to work with, and Carrie's taking our daughter, Cammy, in for a checkup, giving Troy and I some guy time before we start the grill. Even Laurie and Travis are gone, off with their mother for a little while.

"So are you looking forward to next season?"

"Aren't you?" Troy asks with a grin. "We made the conference championship this year. I want to get back at Denver for that last-minute field goal. I missed the block by— man, I saw the tape a hundred times. I missed tipping that ball by less than an inch."

"I know. I keep going over that missed catch I had that led to the final punt. You know, the Pro Bowl and taking third in Rookie of the Year were nice, but I'd have liked that conference champion's ring, and of course, the Super Bowl."

"It sounds strange to say it, but I think it'll happen," Troy says. "I mean, I know that every player says that, but with what we've got going here, the chances are good."

We hear two cars pull up out front, and Troy and I quickly finish our teas and get up, Troy opening up the grill and starting to scrub the grate while I go inside and get the steaks out of the fridge. The front door flies open, and Laurie comes tearing in, her little brother trying to keep up, but his soon to be two-year-old legs can't keep up with his sister, and Travis lags behind. "Hi, Duncan!" Laurie calls out as she streaks past, looking for her target. "Daddy!"

Troy puts down his grill brush and sweeps his daughter up and into a hug. She might be eight, but missing those five years, she still loves getting hugs and playing with her father, and Troy's a good one. Travis comes by, his little toddler legs working hard, and Troy sets Laurie down long enough to give his son a hug before going back to his work while they go off to play in the back yard.

The front door closes, and Whitney and Carrie come in, Cammy on Carrie's back in her sling and something between them. "What in the world did you get?"

"It's a landscape," Whitney says matter-of-factly, patting the huge brown paper-wrapped package. "The artist had it available, and I bought it for you guys."

"Whitney, you didn't need to," I say honestly. "I mean, you've got a great eye, and that piece in our living room is great, but . . . that thing's huge!"

"Oh, we'll find room for it after we get back from the Bahamas," Carrie says, coming over and giving me a kiss. "How are you doing?"

"I could use a rub-down," I tease, kissing her lips. "Even Troy was whining about what you put us through."

"Hey, thank Coach T. He helped me on the design. But we'll see what we can do, especially if you return the favor."

Carrie turns, and I see that Cammy's fallen asleep on her mother's back, a content little smile on her face. I kiss my daughter's mostly still-bald head, and whisper in her ear, "Daddy loves you, my angel."

"So how was her doctor's appointment?"

"We're both doing fine," Carrie says, exchanging looks with Whitney, who chuckles and nods. "In fact, Whitney and I have some news for both of you. Troy?"

Troy, who's started the gas grill, closes the lid and comes to the door while Laurie and Travis play outside in their play area. "Yes, Carrie?"

Whitney looks at Carrie again, and I can see they've been planning something, sharing a secret. "Well, we wanted to tell you together. The visit to Dr. Lee's—we kind of both asked her to check us out as well."

"Is everything okay?" Troy asks, and Whitney nods. She goes over and puts her arms around Troy's neck, standing on her tiptoes to give him a kiss.

"It's perfect. Actually, Troy, our summer just got a bit busier. Congratulations, Daddy. You have a third child on the way."

"No fu— no way!" I say, grinning. "You dog! Weren't we just talking about that?"

"Oh, don't celebrate too early," Carrie says, pulling me into a kiss. "Because Whitney's not the only one pregnant again."

Carrie's words hit my mind, and our kiss deepens, my heart swelling at her news. Troy coughs politely, and I realize

249

that I'm cupping my wife's breast in the middle of his kitchen. "Sorry. Got carried away."

"Well, it's not like there's a problem with that." Whitney laughs. "Carrie and I both admitted we were feeling a bit strange while we were out, and so on a whim, we asked Dr. Lee to give us the tests."

I look at Troy, and he's just as happy as I am. "You know what this means, right, EC?"

EC is my personal nickname for Troy, since he keeps going on and on about *emotional content*. He's even got a t-shirt that he wears under his shoulder pads with that printed on it.

Troy looks back and nods. "Damn right. We're going to have to go all the way this year. Super Bowl champs."

I take Carrie's hand and kiss her knuckles. "With the right team around us, how can we fail?"

If you enjoyed this book, please take a moment to leave a review. If you haven't read it already, make sure to pick up Blitzed, Book 1 in this sports romance series. You'll get to see Troy and Whitney's journey... it was certainly a roller coaster!

Thank you for reading!

Made in the USA
Lexington, KY
09 September 2016